The Last Days of Johnny North

The Last Days of Johnny North

stories

David Swann

ELASTIC
PRESS

ISBN number: 0-9548812-5-7

Printed by MRT Services, Bristol, England

Cover Design by Rachel Dorling
Cover layout by Dean Harkness
Typeset by Marie O'Regan

Published by:
Elastic Press
85 Gertrude Road
Norwich
UK

elasticpress@elasticpress.com
www.elasticpress.com

To Geoff & Jennie Swann
and
Piet & Truus Vermond

– goeie mensen

"Suddenly I realize
That if I stepped out of my body I would break
Into blossom."

– James Wright, 'A Blessing'
(*'Above the River'*, Bloodaxe Books)

"Outside a book a dog is a man's best friend.
Inside a dog it's too dark to read."
– Groucho Marx

Acknowledgments

I am grateful to the magazines, journals, competitions, and small presses that have published my work over the last decade. 'High Tide' appeared in *Watch Fire*, ed. Chris Kenworthy (Darius, 1995). 'Badly Good' was published in *Northern Stories*, Vol. 6, ed. David Dabydeen and A.L. Kennedy (Arc, 1995). Earlier versions of 'A Harbour in the Hills' (then called 'In Pieces') and 'A Polder, a Place to Live' were awarded prizes by Michael Dobbs and Lynne Reid Banks in *The Bridport Prize* international short story competitions in 1996 and 2000. 'The Last Days of Johnny North' was awarded third place in *The Bridport Prize* by Rose Tremain in 2003. 'Speedbone Sauna Blues' was originally published in *Northern Stories*, Vol. 7, ed. Mark Illis & Jane Rogers (Arc, 1996). 'The Spike' appeared in *Arc Short Stories*, Vol. 9, ed. Sarah Dunant & Tibor Fischer (1998). 'In That Brilliant Village' was awarded first prize by Jane Gardam in *Connections* magazine's national short story competition in 2002. 'The news at 10' and 'Voodoo Address Book' appeared in *Staple*, 58 (2003). An early version of 'News at 10' won first prize in *Stamford Writers'* 1996 Open Story Competition, judged by Nigel Colborn. 'Birds' has been accepted for publication by *Liar Republic*. A very short version of 'The Privilege of Rain' was published in *Nottingham Poetry International*. The full version appeared in *Staple*, 55/6 (2002). 'In the Path of the Comet' appeared in the Alt-Gen edition of *Staple*, 62 (2005). 'The Maker's Name' was awarded third prize by Robert Holdstock in the *Library of Avalon* Short Story Competition (1997) and 'In the Country of Daft Pink Things' won the same prize in the same competition in 2003. An early version of 'The Radioactive Lowry', then called 'More Like Rock', won second prize in the *Northern New Writers' Award* (1996), judged by Patrick Wright & Eileen Upton. 'Another Bloody Cowboy' was awarded third prize by Margaret Drabble in *The Wells Festival of Literature Short Story Competition* (2001) and performed live on tour with *Words Allowed* at Portsmouth Arts Centre in 2002. 'The Collector of Small Town Secrets' won first prize at the *Wells Festival of Literature* national competition in 2003, judged by Sarah Harrison.

Formative versions of 'Lucifer Brings Light' and 'The Only Fruit' (then called 'The Mask') were commended in competitions run by *Northern Stories* and *Wells Festival of Literature*. 'The Boggart Hole' and 'The Coming Attractions' were placed on the final long-list of 50 for 2005's Bridport Prize. 'Except in Song' was shortlisted for the 2005 Wells Festival of Literature Short Story Competition. Material in this book has also appeared in *Zembla* (2005), *Staple* (2002), *Texts'Bones* (2003-4), *Beyond the Wall* (1998) and *Dreaming Beasts* (2005). Others are to feature in the U.S. chapbook *Subtraction*, co-authored with Chris Aggs (Spitfire Press, 2005).

I wish to acknowledge moral and financial support from the Arts Council of England, Lancaster University, University College Chichester, Elastic Press, and HMP Nottingham. Individuals and organisations deserving of further gratitude are listed at the back of this book.

Table of contents

The Boggart Hole

A few months after her operation, Lucy was taken to recover at a relative's farm, where the doctors hoped she'd gain respite from Manchester's fumes and traffic.

The journey took Lucy's family through a chain of villages surrounded by fields and shining rivers. The fields were watched over by a long isolated hill that resembled a dog lying down to eat. Her mother said it was Pendle, where they'd burned the witches.

To Lucy's precocious 13-year-old eyes, the landscape looked unfinished, as if awaiting factories and houses.

"How come it's full of turds?" she asked.

Since the operation, her parents had played it calm. Now the hypnotising effect of the journey had made them even quieter.

Lucy sighed. She studied her face in the rear-view mirror. Illness and growth-spurts had stretched it, but her eyes, for all their weariness, remained clear and blue.

"Why don't they sweep up the turds?" she persisted.

Her parents' softly-softly policy had the virtue of allowing her to swear like a trooper.

Swear like a bastard.

"Any more of that, we'll wash your mouth out with soap," replied her dad at length, feigning nonchalance.

"If you can find any," said Lucy, twisting her hair. It was the colour of asphalt.

Her mood wasn't improved by the lingering sense that she'd left something important behind in Manchester.

She went over the list: CDs, lipstick, chewing gum...

"Well," said her mum, "if there's no soap, you can wash in the dew. Like in the olden days..."

"When public burnings were also popular."

Her parents held their peace. The operation had been touch-and-go; Lucy needed rest and stability.

She stared into the mirror, looking her illness in the eye. Her parents should face it too. Any trace of rosy cheeks or russet tresses had gone. Her slender body was the colour of a city on a map. The scar that wove under her breast and out past her shoulder-blade was its main 'A'-road, straight and red.

Fields continued, relentless. Two hours out of Manchester, the last stumpy chimney had passed them by. No neon signs, no dirty canals.

Lucy longed to hear the lifeless smack of some cheap football off a garage door.

"That cow's been pissing for ages," she remarked in a dull voice.

*

The first thing she heard when they arrived was the whine of a chain-saw. Then a motorbike. Then someone screaming at errant sheep-dogs.

Lucy's parents breathed it in, seemingly oblivious.

"Fresh air," they smiled.

Whenever her parents smelled turds, they did that: smiled and said *fresh air*. They should probably move to a sewage farm. Live the dream.

Across the fields, Pendle was still visible. It was hard not to think of burning women.

"How come they set them on fire, anyway?" she scowled.

"Hmmm?"

"The witches..."

Her mum unfastened a gate. "The milk. They'd meddled with the milk. Or turned into cats, or something..."

Lucy stared at puddles.

"Into *cats*?"

Her Dad offered Lucy a pair of boots. They had turned-down flaps. The flaps looked like ears turned inside out.

"I wish I was a cat," said Lucy.

*

Lucy was used to weird houses. Her friend Terri's house smelled of Spam. Nicola's had a massive inflatable Santa in the garden. And Amanda's carpet was threaded with labrador hairs even though her family didn't have a labrador.

But Uncle Tom's farmhouse was something else. It resembled a massive child, shy of its own size. The walls were bulbous with rain, but its windows were tiny, as if the house – already lost in a field – was about to burst into tears.

Then the weirdest thing about the child-house: it had side-burns. Misshapen clumps of ivy that drooped from the gables.

"Like in the adverts," her Mum swooned.

Off-hand, Lucy couldn't recall any adverts featuring massive panicking kids with side-burns. But she held her peace. A child's illness was bad for its parents.

Instead, she devoted her energies to ignoring the local teenager leaning into a hedge, staring at her long bare legs.

"Yo," said the boy, "what's happening?"

"Nothing," said Lucy, out of parental earshot. "That's the whole problem."

The hip-hop villager shrugged. Lucy decided he was probably called Tarquin, probably prone to boasting about *the shit going down in this hamlet*. He had on a hooded top, pressed flat by an iron. His trainers looked like bulldozer wheels. They were splattered with cow shit.

"Charming, man," said the teenager.

"Woman, to you. Or have you burned them all?"

The hip-hop villager twisted a loony-finger at his temple, turned away. "Intensity," he muttered as he sloped off.

*

Uncle Tom showed them round. As far as Lucy could understand, his job was to take great care of animals that he then sent away to be killed.

Uncle Thomas's vocabulary consisted mainly of the words *thrutch*, *flurr*, *glanders*, and *callafudge*. She feigned interest whenever he plodded to another portion of land to explain its peat content.

Plodding proved to be the best way of getting about since the farm suffered from particularly heavy gravity and had been neatly designed to fit the exact dimensions of an underlying morass.

"You'll be glad of them boots soon," said her Dad.

Lucy lagged behind. It seemed important that she was shown how to operate a muck-spreader.

She shouted, "I think it's been spread, Uncle Thomas. I don't think this muck could be any more *spread*."

The cows stared at her, like animals.

"Think you're hard, eh?" she asked them quietly.

Ahead, her parents waited. Distantly, the chain-saw was still buzzing, the same farmer screaming at his dog...

Uncle Thomas stood poised to explain foot-rot: "You twiddle in the slots of the hoof with a pen-knife. Any dope can do it."

Lucy's parents turned away, but Lucy watched. The sheep kicked, then calmed. It had either lost fear or gained trust, depending on how you looked at it.

Uncle Tom worked slowly and patiently, whistling tunelessly under his breath.

Lucy studied her nails. They were flecked with white spots. A calcium deficit, the doctors said.

We've got claws too, she thought. People, sheep, lobsters... we were all the same once...

"Penny for your thoughts, lass," said her Dad, hesitant in the face of their imminent parting.

"I was thinking," Lucy replied, "how we used to be lobsters, Dad."

He hummed quietly, studying his watch. Didn't answer.

"You'll ring every day," Lucy's Mum reminded her.

"And we'll come each fortnight," put in her Dad.

"Until you're better..."

Lucy considered weirding them out with more claw-talk, but decided better of it. They hugged in the morass, like bog-people in the Seamus poems at school.

That was when she remembered what she'd left in Manchester. "My books!" she cried. "My books are still under the bed!"

Her parents broke the tearful clinch, promising to bring the books in a fortnight. Meanwhile, Thomas said she'd borrow reading-matter from Bryan.

"Although he can be possessive when he puts his mind to it..."

"Reading-matter?" said Lucy. "Do you mean books, Uncle Tom?"

"Aye, happen there'll be some books in wi' it, lass..."

Lucy stared down the ploughed field of his face. It was hedged with wiry hair. His eyes were blue pools.

"And never thee fret," he assured her parents. "If this lass suffers a tumble, I'll catch her. Count on that."

At the top of the hill, on the threshold of the last gate, her mum and dad stopped to wave. Or maybe to signal that they were sinking.

It had come to this: the final punishment for falling sick. Lucy bit her lip. At least she wasn't in hospital. Surrounded by charts. Bullied by rules.

"Now then," said the farmer: "a poorly lass like thee – I reckon it'll be bed-time soon."

"But it's seven o'clock, Uncle Thomas."

"That's midnight to a cow."

"I'm not a cow."

"The cows are though, lass."

"That one over there isn't. It's just pretending to be a cow."

15

Her uncle scratched his head.

"Its eyes, Uncle Tom. Can't you tell by its eyes?"

The farmer leaned forward on his stick.

"Its eyes are sort of looking out from inside it."

Uncle Tom nodded thoughtfully. "I knew there were summat odd about yon customer."

"It's doleful," said Lucy.

Her uncle nodded. "Aye. There are some rum lads out theer."

Distantly, the angry farmer was still screaming.

"Not least yonder character..."

Lucy weighed up the distant voice. "Is he still mad at his dog?"

"He's mad, lass. That's for sure."

"His voice is high-pitched. Like a fox."

"A fox, eh?"

"When they scream at night."

"Aye? And how's a city-girl know about foxes?"

"We hear them in back-alleys. Under the bin-holes. Because you lot drove them there. You farmers. And they stick to each other when they mate. So there's a noise like murdered babies. Which sounds like that bloke on the next farm."

"Frank the Fox, eh?" said Thomas, studying the inside of his cap as if his neighbour's new nickname was printed there. "Aye, well, I wouldn't know about that. Nor about bin-holes. But I'll tell thee this: leave yon creature in his lair, lass."

"In case he screams at me too?"

Her uncle nodded. "Aye, lass. In case he screams at thee too."

*

Lucy was shown other chores, explained by words such as provender and *bieldy*. It was like talking to a badger. A medieval badger.

After the final instruction, she bent at the knee as if in need of the toilet, trying to work out what was expected of her.

Of course, she *did* need the toilet. She'd needed it for ages. It was these fields, the lack of cover. You were yourself, and you were also your bones and skin. You were your body, but you had to fight

16

your body. It had a mind of its own. Your body could beat you with one hand tied behind its back.

"Can you say it again, please, Uncle Thomas?"

The farmer said it again, this time in English. She was to go to the beck and fetch her cousin before his food grew cold.

She was directed into the valley where the mud had first calved. The chain-saw prickled in her ears as she squelched nearer.

*

Lucy's first sight of her cousin was unpromising.

Bryan was slathered on his knees in the beck's shallows, far down between steep, crumbling mudstone cliffs. There was an expression of deadly intent on his milky teenage face. Clenched in his hands was the chain-saw, its cord ripped, the petrol fuming.

He looked up from the shallows, face splattered with blood, the beck running red around his knees. Before him lay a dismembered cow.

Lucy's weakened heart leapt in its cage. Her cousin threw a cow leg onto a pile made of other cow legs.

*

After that, things worsened for a while.

Despite Uncle Tom's apology, Lucy remained wary of Bryan. It seemed to Lucy, watching him dismember fallen trees and beasts, that her cousin was struggling to tame more than the land.

Even worse than Bryan's noise was the silence that pounded when the farmers finally turned off their machines. Then the sky was dark and clear, and stars stretched through it like lines of nerves.

On Lucy's first night, the stars seemed to fizz as she gazed through the attic window, disturbed from shallow sleep by the conviction that someone had been calling her name, yet waking to hear only hooves clattering on the farm-track.

Finally, she calmed herself by rhyming the distant beck with the flow of her own blood. But before she slept again, the hospital surged up and she remembered Suzie, the crazy girl in the next bed, who had secretly hoarded dry-skin and corns harvested from her own feet.

"Rank!" Lucy protested.

Suzie opened a box whose lid was lined with tiny pebbles, painted red.

"My skin-box," she declared. Her smile was full of secrets. "If I never come out of hospital, they'll look in this box. See me. Smell me. I won't all be dead."

The box merged with other memories – doctors' faces, a line of stitches, the voice calling her back to her body as she awoke from the operation.

But calling me back from where? she'd wondered afterwards.

"Lucy... Luc-eeee..."

She sat up, hearing her uncle's voice. Dawn had struggled into the attic. She was being summoned to learn the lore of troughs and eggs, twine and geese...

*

After that – afternoons. Tracts of time as endless as the farm's open spaces, with no-one to talk to except Cecil, a bloated teenager from the neighbouring farm who was good with knots and had a burgundy-coloured head.

Cecil was Lucy's special friend. He came each morning, apparently to demonstrate his dexterity with string and to teach Lucy superstitions. Sometimes he followed her for hours, droning about invisible creatures known as Skykers, who screamed from the dark cloughs. He said he'd tell her about The Written Stone and Jenny Green Teeth too...

"... except you'd be ignorant of such matters, coming from That Manchester."

Lucy wondered which Manchester Cecil meant. Evidently there were two of them.

One morning, Lucy managed to slip Cecil's clutches, only to see him peeping through chinks in a wall. Then Frank's screams flushed him out. Apparently Frank the Fox didn't like his younger brother touching the stones.

"I reckon yon lad's sweet on thee," her uncle remarked after Cecil's seventh consecutive dawn visit.

"He's got a funny way of showing it."

"Folks round here tend to show things a bit different."

"Like his brother. Like The Fox."

Her uncle scratched his head.

"Does he scream *all* the time, Uncle Thomas?"

"Most of it, lass."

"Always at his dog?"

"Sometimes at the sheep too."

"And Cecil. He screams at Cecil."

"Aye," said her uncle, his voice quiet.

Frank's flushing of Cecil from the wall – that had been the closest Lucy had yet strayed to The Fox. After hearing his mighty screams, she'd expected some fabulous creature, possibly the size of a bison. But, in the seconds before he'd vanished into the tractor's dark booth, Cecil's brother had turned out to be disappointingly small, with a meagre nose and slits for eyes.

"I think he's frustrated," said Lucy.

"Aye, well. Blame the horse that clopped him when he were little."

"Did it clop Cecil too?"

Tom tried not to laugh. "It'd take more than a dented head to explain yon Cecil."

"But does Frank ever scream at *you*, Uncle Thomas?"

The farmer turned serious. "Listen to me, Lucy: forget Frank. Got it? Put him out of your mind."

"How come?"

"Because he's not all there, lass."

"Where did the rest of him go?"

The farmer laughed despite himself. "Many have asked the same question."

"What sort of clop was it, Uncle Thomas?"

"The same clop you'll get if you keep asking daft questions."

Lucy stared into the field. She imagined pieces of Frank still out there, lying where they'd fallen, in the grass.

*

As for Lucy's cousin, she'd have liked a horse to clop *him*.

Bryan's favourite topic was the stupidity of townies, but he sometimes took time to rage about the trespass laws too.

Last thing at night, Bryan checked the fences, plugging gaps. Afterwards, he lay awake listening for the loosening of distant gates.

"They use hikers to case the joint," he told Lucy, chewing heads off a pan of mushrooms. It was dawn. His hands were already covered in oil. "They team up together."

"Like Al Quaeida, eh?"

"I've no time now for your twaddle, Lucy."

"Me neither. But it's either this or a conversation about twine with Cecil."

Bryan snorted. He wiped his hands with a cloth. "If my dad asks after me, I'll be up near yon Written Stone, mending my..."

"Mending your 'bike," yawned Lucy. "As usual."

Bryan spent half his time lecturing townies about fumes and noise and the other half revving 'bikes until they caught fire. It was what all the farm boys did – all of them except Cecil, who had other fish to fry.

"Where the hell *is* this Written Stone, anyway?" she moaned.

The chop-bone of her cousin's nose pulled tight and yellow. "What's it to you where it is?"

"In case your dad sends me to interrupt again when you're murdering things."

Bryan shook his head. "How often have I to say? That bullock were already dead. It fell off yon cliff."

"And you couldn't squeeze a tractor in..."

"... so there were nowt else for it..."

"You unfortunately had to hack it into pieces with a chain-saw."

Bryan looked at her. "That beast were rotting into the water-

20

supply. But I shouldn't expect a townie to know owt about *that*."

"No, we just loll around, reading books. Well, *used to...*"

Her hopes for Bryan's reading-matter hadn't been great. Nevertheless, the greasy pile had proved as much of a puzzle as his porn-stash.

Why anyone needed more than *one* publication full of identical pictures, Lucy couldn't guess. Maybe it was the parts. The unique internal workings of all those shiny goods.

"By the way, ta for *Treasure Island*," she grunted. "Especially the pages you didn't splash with cow-guts."

Bryan got up, bullock-hoofed. "It's my heart they should be fussing over," he grunted. "My heart, wi' the strain of putting up with *thee*."

Lucy leaned back and listened to the clock's thud. Soon Cecil would arrive. Soon they'd be trudging through the mud, discussing twine.

No wonder the cows were throwing themselves off cliffs...

Through the farmhouse window, she made out an early-morning walker against the skyline.

"Help! I'm a prisoner!" she yelled.

The hiker plodded on, pretending to check a map, probably radioing instructions to Tora-Bora.

Almost six more weeks. Forty days and nights before she was rounded up, before they dug her out of the mud...

*

It wasn't just increased gravity; they'd also slowed down the speed of light.

By the eighth day, Lucy was so desperate for variety, she'd started calling on Cecil.

Cecil and Frank shared a cottage with their superstitious old mother, a wild-haired nomad who slept on a straw-mat that she carried to whichever room took her fancy.

"Frank out again?" Lucy asked at the door, a white portal secured by black studs, stoutly bearing its horseshoe.

The mother beat out her mat. "The beast is in the fields," she said.

"Cecil?"

"At trough within."

Lucy followed the thin finger, noticing faint hieroglyphics etched into the lintel. Bundling back curtains, she found Cecil crunching porridge at the table.

The room smelled of ham and sawdust.

"Fancy a trudge, Cecil?"

Cecil turned his moon-face to her. He wasn't bad looking, if you ignored the blank eyes and his table manners. Also, his ears and some other parts of his face.

"I've mastered the Bolland Loop," he announced.

"Good."

"It was devised in the 16th Century by local monks. Our Frank says it's an admirable achievement."

"Is that what he said, Cecil?"

"In those exact words."

Lucy frowned slightly.

On the way back through the curtains, the old woman called: "And think on: stay away from your brother. He's in an evil temper today."

Boy, thought Lucy.

*

Smells of shite wafted over the fields. Gulls had chained their line to a distant tractor.

Eight days on the farm. The same old stuff.

"Don't you wish you lived on a *street,* Cecil?"

Cecil puffed his cheeks, wrestling a knot. Lucy sighed. Further off, the errant sheepdog was trying to kill lambs, Cecil's brother screaming.

Cecil didn't reply. Lucy wasn't even sure she'd asked.

"Cecil, have you noticed: townies want peace, but bumpkins are after noise?"

Her friend was flushed from trying to walk while making knots. The backs of his ears were waxy and cracked.

"This one's got a bigger loop," he explained. "But the trick with this one is to tie it back on itself."

Lucy said, "At least you smell nice. Of apples and trees. That's more than can be said for the rest of them."

"Except my brother."

"Your brother?"

"Frank," said Cecil. "He's a ladies' man. He puts that stuff on."

"What stuff?"

Her neighbour studied the parsnips of his fingers, threatening to vanish into another reverie.

"Cecil, *what* stuff?"

He shrugged slowly, like a barn settling on its foundations. "Aftershave, he calls it. He reckons you dab it under your ears... But what about this one? The double-reef?"

Lucy fought down an urge to rip up Cecil's knot.

"A ladies' man? *Here*?"

"He reckons, if you dab it on, it makes the birds randy."

Lucy stroked her thigh. Thighs worked on some lads. That wanker in the hedge, for example. Tarquin, or whatever his name was. The woman-burner.

He'd slid his eyes over her skin.

But getting Cecil's attention was like rounding up sheep. Worse. Rounding up cats.

"I bet you can't guess it, Cecil – our nickname for Frank."

She relaxed the muscle in her leg. It trembled gently. Sunlight picked out blonde down on the calf. A week in the fields had tanned her skin, restored some of its health.

"It's wrong to call people by false names, Lucy."

She scowled. "Who's to say what Frank's really called? What *anything's* really called? Even this place..."

"Slaythwaite," said Cecil. "This place is Slaythwaite."

"Not Slaythwaite, you bullock. The Earth. We don't know what The Earth's really called. We couldn't even be bothered to think of a proper pretend name."

23

Frown-marks riddled the bridge of Cecil's nose. "You lot..."

"Which lot?"

"You townies."

Lucy was caught between a growl and a hoot. It came out as a yawn. "Like *you're* normal! Chopping up cows. Screaming in fox-voices. Going on about knots. Plus, superstitions. I mean – squiggles everywhere. Horseshoes on every..."

"Horseshoes ward off the sperrits," Cecil interrupted.

"Then the ones round here must be bust. Because they're obviously not working. Maybe the boggarts smashed them, eh?"

"You shouldn't make fun of boggarts either, Lucy."

"Why? Are they listening?"

"And watching. My mum's seen them in our shippon. They look like woolsacks."

Lucy began to laugh.

"Woolsacks with flaming eyes," said Cecil.

"Listen to me: boggarts are what daft, superstitious folk like your mum blame for things they can't face."

She hit her chest, harder than she'd meant to. A high thin twinge ran down her sternum.

"Bad things inside themselves," she said, a little quieter, feeling a sock slide into her boot.

Cecil's slow gaze dawdled on her leg.

"And here's what blokes have inside them," she hissed, stomping away through the mud: "pervs."

She looked back just once, to make sure Cecil was following.

*

Eventually, her neighbour's slow trudge brought him alongside Lucy again. He stared at her, as reproachful as a thrashed donkey.

"False naming's a sin, Lucy."

"And so's believing in boggarts, Terry."

"I'm not called Terry. I'm called..."

"Look," said Lucy, watching a line of smoke cross the horizon: "if it's monsters you want, come with me to That Manchester. I'll

24

show you monsters. Real ones. With two arms and one head. Monsters that look like people. Not wool-sacks. Not this peasant-shit."

Cecil looked at the mud.

"I mean," she said, in a softer voice, "you wouldn't want the doctors rooting about inside me again, would you?"

"No," said Cecil. "I wouldn't want that."

"So will you give me a rest and stop going on about boggarts?"

Cecil shook his head. He took her hand. "If I prove that boggarts are real, will you be my bird?"

Lucy had the sensation that something deep down inside her was pounding to get out.

His fingers were great white bulbs, damp and tuberous. Their grip was firm.

*

He led her across the high meadows, into the tallest grass, where the mud had yet to penetrate. Here and there, foundation stones lay at angles in the undergrowth, as if tossed by giants.

Further down the field, motorbikes had slithered trails into the ramshackle shed where Bryan patched together his creations.

Cecil rooted around in various places, folding back curtains of weeds and herbs, mumbling and sweating. Lucy's hand was still damp from where he'd held it. The only sound was the breeze in the grass.

Dreaming, she thought. I'm under the gas, and dreaming. Soon, the voice will call me back.

"Lucy," said Cecil. "Lucy!"

At his feet, he uncovered a stone slab. On the slab, carved in crude letters similar to the hieroglyphics above Cecil's door, was the following warning:

"LET IT BE KNOWN
THAT THE TENANT MARTIN CUNLIFFE
ENTOMBED A BOGGART IN A HOLE BENEATH THIS SLAB,
OCTOBER 9TH, THE YEAR OF OUR LORD 1795.
PEACE BE ON THIS PLACE AT LAST,
AND CURSED THE FELLOW WHO LIFTS THE STONE."

Shadows pooled over the field. Cecil let the grass fall again. It covered the stone.

"That's just its hole," Lucy muttered, solemn and afraid. "Dig it out. Prove there's something down there. Show me the boggart."

A breeze pulsed in the meadow. It stirred in her dress. The sunlight came and went, as subtle and fleeting as thoughts. The long sedges whirred.

"Dig out the boggart for me, Cecil."

Her neighbour turned away, as if glad to be distracted. The line of smoke on the horizon had resolved itself into a spluttering shape. It was Bryan, charging towards them on his latest fix-up.

When Bryan's passenger stepped down from the pillion, amid a storm of smoke, Lucy saw it was Tarquin, the hip-hop villager.

"If it isn't Marshall Mathers," she said. "What are you looking at?"

"Not much," he muttered.

But she felt his eyes slide over her skin.

Bryan said nothing. The 'bike rocked slowly under his weight. He rested a cigarette lighter on the handlebar and busied himself over its rough flint, conjuring sparks with the meat of his thumb. A jerry-can of petrol was pressed between his thighs.

The hip-hop villager waved an air rifle at Cecil. "Hey, dude, we're going to smoke out the rats. What do you say, man?"

"He's showing me the Written Stone," Lucy told the villager. "Isn't that right, Cecil?"

"I'll shoot rats now," her neighbour whispered.

Bryan gunned the engine. The 'bike swept away.

"Cecil," said Lucy,

Her friend stepped into the hail of mud and plodded down the 'bike's wet furrow, his face as pale and unreadable as a turnip.

Lucy watched until the three farm-lads were distant specks.

Presently, she pulled back the long grass and stretched out on The Written Stone, relishing its coolness on her back, watching a column of smoke rise from the dump.

The sun's rays were as strong as hospital lights. She closed her eyes and drifted towards sleep, her mind the only real place, her body just a box of skin lying in some far corner of a distant meadow.

She knew he was there without him saying a word.

Maybe it was the aftershave, cheap and strong... maybe some talent for danger brought on by her body's woes.

How long he watched her as she lay there on the boggart's grave, her back cool on the stone, the sun a weight forcing her eyes shut, she wasn't sure. But when she finally sat up, shivering under a passing cloud, The Fox had gone, leaving no trace.

It would be like this for a long time to come in her life: men's eyes on her body. And pleasure in that. But a feeling deep down that the pleasure didn't matter, that the men were wrong.

Lucy slid off the written stone, rearranging her dress, aware of its frailty, the smooth thin coolness of the cotton.

She ran for the farmhouse, and didn't stop until she was safe on the other side of the garden gate, breathing deep under its hairy eaves.

All the while, the *pop-pop-pop* of the farm-boys' air rifles echoed off the surrounding hills.

The Trees On Earth, The Trees In Space

All our neighbours looked like the snooker star Ray Reardon: black slicks of hair swept back from their foreheads with fierce brushes.

They were stoop-backed prowlers with watchful eyes. In the summer months of 1984 they swilled cars in the alley, later leaning on their back doors to smoke cigarettes and admire their handiwork.

When they spoke, which they rarely did, it was to say, in voices as flat as the Fylde, "Ey up, cocker."

We shunned them.

The moors were our place: treeless white places swept by wind, notched with trenches dug by long-dead soldiers.

Most days, we lay in the wavy-hair grass there and looked down over town, over the slate roofs and biscuit-coloured streets. There was a lot to talk about: school, and films, and the dryness of grass. And the thing that had happened to Mandy's dad. Words too – because he'd pressed books on her, and she'd read them.

For instance, *roof* and *roofs*, and why not *rooves*?

There were never any answers, and so what.

It was hot, had been hot for ages. Each morning we dragged open the curtains and the sun was still shining, as if it had been there all night.

"*The Day the Sun Shone All Night*," I said.

Mandy laughed from a deep place in the moor. It was our

game, inventing names for science-fiction films they hadn't made yet.

She twirled her long blonde hair. Not blonde – white. Whiter than the bleached grass. We made up a nickname for her – Village Of The Damned, after a film in which telepathic albino kids came from a cold star to destroy the Earth. You killed the aliens by tucking a bomb in your briefcase and thinking of brick walls.

Ka-booom!

"What am I thinking of now?" I said.

"Cake," said Mandy.

"Ha!" I said. "Your powers are on the wane. It was Ray Reardon, the snooker player Ray Reardon."

"The... break... goes... to... 27..." said Mandy in a slow robot voice.

"Say what you like about snooker," I told her, wondering how she could have known it was cake: "I bet you couldn't hit it in them tiny pockets."

"I don't want to hit it into tiny pockets. I want to go to Sweden again. Swim in a warm lake, forget all about snooker... forget these Ray Reardons!"

No-one knew when the Ray Reardons had first appeared. It had been a stealthy encroachment, individual Reardon by Reardon.

But, one day, we turned around to find they surrounded us.

"They've stuffed our real neighbours into bins," I said. "And *we're next, we're next*." Which was our catchphrase. We took it from a film in which aliens turned everybody into vegetable replicas and a bloke ran along the motorways, banging on cars, warning the drivers, *You're next! You're next!*

But everybody was too scared to wind down their windows, so they were all doomed.

"Lucky for us we got snooker players," I told Mandy. "It could have been lizards."

She sighed from the deep place in the grass, unstirred by wind. The sun was a mallet. It kept on bashing. Soon we'd be as flat as our shadows. "I wish it *had* been lizards," she said. "I wish them creeps in our back alley would clear off."

"Clear off where?"

"Back to the planet they came from."

"Their Own World Is Dying," I said, in a sad voice.

"It's the way they prowl," hissed Mandy. "And how they *lean*. Lean in their doorways, staring. Like they want to... want to..."

"Like they want to pot you," I said.

She looked at me for a long time, till the sun closed her face to a distant speck.

"Mandy – it's because they're redundant."

"It doesn't mean they have to be idle. And lie around watching snooker. And stare at people's legs."

"It's because they've shut the factories, Mandy."

"They ought to *do* something."

"They can't. Because of Thatcher," I said. "That cow, Thatcher."

Which is what you had to say after you'd said Thatcher.

Mandy shook her head.

"Their steady eyes," she said.

*

Then came talk of standpipes.

"Hottest summer since '76," sighed our mums, wiping foreheads, studying the sky.

"Because the sun has spun loose," I told my parents.

But we'd to be out from under the feet, out from under the feet right this minute.

"Your stupid fault," said Mandy. "Always coming out with *lines*."

We traipsed the alley's cobbles, clearing a path through the laundry, wet sheets hanging limp from black cables.

Here and there, in gaps between the washing, several Ray Reardons splashed their cars with water, dabbed red stuff over the hubs, rubbed wax into paintwork.

"Not be doing that much longer," I said.

Mandy kicked me on the shin, gestured towards the scariest Ray Reardon, the most silent. The possible Leader Of The Ray Reardons.

He rubbed his hubs with a moist cloth, scowling into the tiny cracks.

"Yep," I said, "the Earth is burning to a parched, blackened husk. Under the constantly beating sun..."

"Your big mouth," said Mandy, secretly giggling.

She had learned to read my mind and I had learned how to make her laugh. When they say we wasted the drought summer of 1984, they have absolutely no idea what they are talking about.

*

"It's like that book," said Mandy from the deep grass. "Exactly like Orwell's book."

"But what I don't get is, how come if it's *1984* it can be in the future?"

"Because he wrote it in 1948, you divv."

"Oh," I said.

"1984 *was* the future when he wrote it."

"But next year it'll be the past."

Mandy scratched her head.

"Like *Space 1999* and *2001 A Space Odyssey*. You'll be watching them in The Year 2004, and they'll not make any sen..."

"Look," said Mandy: "the point is, Trevor: it's like Orwell predicted. We're being constantly monitored. Except it's not the Government. It's a load of creepy redundant blokes. Don't you get it, Trevor? Can't you see?"

"Yes," I said.

I was watching blackflies crawl up the grass. Blackflies were invading. Because of the hot weather, because of Thatcher.

That cow, Thatcher.

"It's like them blackflies," I said.

Mandy frowned through the grass.

"Exactly like them blackflies," I said.

Mandy sank back into the hollow. "I don't know why I bother. You don't even read the books we talk about..."

"But I watch them," I said. "When they put them on telly. I watch them, Mandy."

"Unless there's snooker on," came her voice from the hollow.

"That's my Dad, though. Because he's got nowt else to do."

"Blame everyone. Get the rocks and flowers to say they did it," said Mandy.

"I don't know what you're talking about," I confessed.

"Because you don't read books. Because you're always on with your Dad's snooker."

"Because of Thatcher. That cow Th..."

Mandy sang the Hovis tune to me, sang it to me from out of the grass.

"There's no need for that," I said, when she'd finished.

"Well," said Mandy. "It's time you stopped blaming other people, and took responsibility for your actions. You're a man, aren't you?"

"Yes," I said, feeling my chin. My smooth and shiny chin.

"Then you should take a stand. Not just lie around watching snooker."

"But it's summer, Mandy. The snooker isn't even on."

"Exactly. So now they don't even watch it, let alone play it. They don't do anything at all." She flapped a hand, searched for words. "Real men," she said. "Real men *do* things. They drill for oil and drive trucks. They dig coal..."

"And root up trees to get it," I said. "They root up the trees to get the coal." I looked out over the hills, bare miles where there used to be forests. "It's like that film, Mandy. Like that film where they put the last forest into space. They put it in orbit because it wouldn't fit on earth anymore."

Mandy breathed out.

"But then the World Government decided it was costing too much."

"*What* World Government?" she said.

"This film was in the future. Like 1984."

"I thought you said 1984 wasn't in the future."

"It used to be."

Mandy wriggled impatiently in the grass. "What are you going *on* about, Trevor?"

"About this film. This film where they decided to switch off the orbiting forests. Because of cut-backs. Because they said there wasn't the cash."

Mandy looked at me.

"The trees on earth, the trees in space... they wanted to get rid of them all. There wouldn't be a tree left."

Sun fell on the grass between us, fell on the grass that covered the peat which had once been the roots of trees.

"Are you saying it's better they closed our dads' factory? Better that your dad's got no job? And that mine is... is..." She gathered herself. "Whose side are you on, Trevor?"

I shrugged.

Mandy was silent. The moorland grass hung limp. She lay back in a deep part of the trench, where I couldn't see her. She may as well have been under the ground.

"So what happened, anyway?" she said, at last.

"In the film? He went doo-lally."

"Who did?"

"Bruce Dern. The keeper of the forests. He killed the other astronauts and set off for outer space. He saved the trees."

Mandy's voice drifted through the grass. "See, that's what I'm saying. About real men. They stand up. At the vital moment, real men take a stand. Men like Winston Smith. At the vital moment, will you stand up and be counted, Trevor?"

"I will," I replied.

I stood up solemnly in the trench that had been dug by the long-dead soldiers. They dug them for practice, so they'd know what a war was like. Then they were killed. And that was what a war was like.

I sat back down again, inside the trench.

"I'm going to take a stand at the vital moment," I promised. "And stand up and be counted. But later on. When it's cooled down a bit."

33

*

Later on, though, we were still in the trench, talking about what kind of animals we'd be when we came back.

"A hawk," said Mandy.

"A hare," I said. "A mountain hare."

"Sky versus ground!" she squealed. "I'd swoop down and eat you."

"But you're a veggie."

"Not if I was a hawk."

"Typical. No principles."

Mandy laughed. "I'd eeet you and sheeet you out in my pellets."

"Dees-gusting."

"Jah," she said.

We went on like that, talking in Swedish voices, Swedish voices from Sweden, where Mandy's dad used to take them on holiday, to swim in warm lakes, in a fairer place.

We looked up at the sky. It was as flawless and perfect as toffee. Just one tap of a hammer would break it.

"You're thinking *I'll take a stand*," said Mandy.

"No, I'm thinking of cake stands."

Mandy giggled. Through the grass, she went on like that, giggling at my jokes, reading my mind.

*

When we came back we found the Ray Reardons massed in the alley, legions of them drooped over their back-steps, staring at wet cars, smoking.

"They look utterly defeated," said Mandy.

"Don't they realise they've won? That they conquered us?"

The Leader Of The Ray Reardons watched Mandy as we passed, watched the flapping of her summer dress, brief glimpses of skin.

Now I saw it. Now I knew their game.

"See," said Mandy, staring into his glazed billiard-ball eyes. "See what I said, Trevor."

"So It's True: They Have Come Here To Claim Our Women," I intoned.

She moved closer to my side. Close enough for me to smell the fields on her arms and neck, to maybe pick little white grasses from the shoulder straps of her dress.

The leader of the aliens went on staring after we'd passed, and his car gleamed, clean in the alley, where the washing hung, stiff and dried.

*

Later, I worked out that I must have been eating my tea when it happened.

The first we knew of it was his roar. After that a silence, brief and deafening. Then lots of voices – and his again, the loudest, the most frightening, the one like a bull in a shed.

When my mum went to the back step, he was there, face blazing into our yard – The Leader Of The Ray Reardons, his features knotted like sheets, angry words escaping down them, into the alley.

"Your son..." he raged. "Your bloody son..."

Mum made the shape of a star on our step.

"He did this," he foamed. "I have the evidence of my own eyes."

It was what had become of his car, I realised, as I edged forward. His beautiful car... covered in coal-slag, the workings of old mines daubed over shining chrome-work, sprinkled over his windscreen. And a single word – CAKE – traced by a slender finger through the dirt.

"The little bastard," said the man into my mother's face. "The wild little bastard..."

We locked the back-gate on him. We threw down the sneck and drew across the bolt while he shouted, as useless as a sacked worker outside a factory.

"Did you?" my mum asked.

I looked into her eyes, decided this was it. The vital moment.

"Yes," I said. "I covered his car in slag and coal. And I wrote CAKE in the dust. I did it because of the creepy way he looks at

Mandy. It was a stand I took – like the stand Mandy's dad took when they made him redundant."

"Yes, and look where that got him," said my mother. "In the ground from stress, the daft bugger."

"He was right, though."

"Right and dead," she said.

I looked at her.

"Trevor, you're 13, lad. You can't cover a fellah's car in coal. It doesn't matter what he did. You'll apologise. You'll clean his car every week. You'll make it up."

She gave me a cloth. She studied my face.

*

After that, I worked for the Leader Of The Ray Reardons. I was a sort of man-servant. He had me buffing up drainpipes and painting grates.

"See that sewer," he said, "I want you to lick it clean. Only joking. Grab this rag. Run it round those panes. Slower, though."

At least he'd learned how to talk again. That was my gift to him, I suppose. Mum said I'd brought him back to the world.

God knows where he'd been before.

Planet of the Apes, Mandy said.

When she came round to taunt me, I tried to ignore her, toiled with various brushes and spanners.

But it was hard. I kept thinking about the tops of her legs. It felt like I had new eyes. At nights, I lay in bed imagining I'd picked pieces of grass from her shoulder straps. Imagined a world where you could do that. Another life, on a new planet.

Plus, The Leader Of The Ray Reardons didn't like to see any slack, especially since the word had new connotations now.

The umpteenth time she pestered me, I said to her, "Mandy – can't you see he's *watching*?"

"Exactly," she hissed. "So throw down those rags."

"Take another stand?"

She flicked back her white hair, as white as coal is black. She

36

fixed me with her Village Of The Damned Eyes.

I tried to think of a brick wall, like in the film.

She said, "You're thinking *why did she empty coal slack over Ray Reardon's car?* You're thinking *Why did I lie for the stupid cow?*

"I was thinking about *CAKE*," I said.

Mandy laughed. "Do you know what *I'm* thinking?"

I looked into her eyes for a long time, but I didn't have a dead dad and I'd never read those hard books. There was nothing that would help me to read her mind.

"A flat green place," she said.

"A snooker table?" I asked.

She laughed, took the cloth from my hands, led me along the side of the shining car.

We walked past the Leader Of The Ray Reardons. He stared at Mandy's legs, his mouth open.

Then the last of the alley's damp white sheets closed behind us, and he was gone, and we were running – running from locked factories, and listless men, and politicians on telly droning, *No-one ever said it would be easy,* and the snooker's long sleep.

At a broken wall, where the streets ended and the ground swept upwards to brown peaks, I turned and looked back at my town.

"Where are we going, Mandy?"

"To the other side," she said.

She ran faster across the white moors, tracing tracks cut by soldiers and the wind.

She said the tracks led to Yorkshire and the North Sea and fairer lands beyond.

She said we'd find a flat green place, where people were happy and the trees crowded together.

"We're next," she called through the long white grass. "*We're next!*"

A Harbour In The Hills

Our house squints. When I look out through these tiny windows at the brown hills, I know we are a long way from anywhere. The wind is what joins us to the world. It blows all the time, bringing smoke from the towns and rain from America. Our house can stand it, it's a hard old thing. But it squints.

My name is Frances Corfe. I gather pails at the well and wrestle them across cobbles. I scoop peat from black heaps. I feed the stove. I bake, I am always baking. I fight dust. I lift bales and spread muck, hack at thistles and hoist provisions. I spend time looking out. The Pennine hills go on and on.

Some mornings, I look out and see a blue start. It brings a tired feeling. I've seen those mornings, I know their ways. By noontime, the clouds will have scuttled themselves on the hills. Like the day the aeroplane came: another daft blue start. I remember, I narrowed my eyes and looked up at the sky, the vividness of it, the endlessness. And somehow I knew that something would come out of it, but I didn't know what.

Arthur lumbered in. He took off his cap. "Seen summat interesting, lass?" he asked, and I shook my head. The way we were, the way we talked. I didn't turn round. I knew without looking that he was shrugging slowly, his big arms straight and hopeless by his side.

When he came to my side, I drew away. There wasn't room for the two of us in the small window. He said, "Allus looking up, lass.

Tha's allus looking up."

I glanced down, as if ashamed. I saw my body, its broad girth, the flour on the apron. They say I was beautiful once, but I can't remember. There was always work. There was no time for mirrors.

Straw was falling from my husband. I would sweep it over the slate floor, I would pick it out of the pegged rug. "Scarcely a wind," I said. "We're blessed today, owd lad."

"Aye. But a breeze is stirring now, right enough." He straightened his jacket, brushing away straw. He smelled of cattle and provender. He smelled of the moors.

Then it came. A small red aeroplane, dropping from the sky in glints and flashes.

Imagine it. Our only fuels were peat and water, and here was a 'plane, the first I'd ever seen, its wings moving like the arms of a child copying the machines it had seen in books.

A gust of wind put the 'plane in violent motion. Its frame shook. We crowded together in the window, listening to the dying splutters of its engine. I felt Arthur's lumpy hand move to me. The hairs on my neck rose to meet the pores in his fingers.

The aeroplane held its line and found the valley, but the pilot could not make its wheels bite. Each time the machine hit the ground, it bounced over tussocks and lifted again.

Ahead, was the dry-stone wall which divided the valley.

"Man alive," said my husband. His hand pressed harder on my neck, until it was a pain. We didn't move. We watched as the 'plane careered towards the wall.

The last time it fell, the craft took hold of a growling tussock. It skidded round in an arc and came to a halt facing the beck, only yards from the wall in the only flat spot for miles. There was never a stiller machine. I looked at its metal snout, thought of dogs and sheep and cows. Thought of falling.

"God be thanked," I said.

Arthur didn't speak. He hasn't been to church since we lost Robert in the accident. It's too far, he says, too far to walk. The same distance it always was, I tell him. But the space in him has shrunk.

Two figures began stirring in the 'plane. Tension left my husband's face, like ripples fading from a lake. The wind had got up. It trembled in the wings of the 'plane.

"Come on," said Arthur.

I gathered cheese and bread and a billy-can of squash and we hurried down the boggy slopes. I'm past my youth now, so I was breathing hard, but Arthur kept on. He had this look in his eye, as if the only thing in the world that mattered were these two far-off figures waving their hats and goggles, standing by their machine, turning to it occasionally to pat it and pet it.

We held out the basket of food. We didn't even know if they would speak English.

"A picnic, is it?" said the taller of the two. There was a line of sweat along his brow and greasy traces in his tangled hair. I guessed he was the pilot. Something in his bearing.

"Not harmed, is ta?" asked Arthur.

"Not us," laughed the man. His face looked suddenly daft, as if the scrape had released his younger self. "Sir, it would take more than an aeroplane crash to kill men of such mettle!"

His companion smiled vaguely. He had the embarrassed look of a person who would rather not be seen in a place.

"Alan Riddick," said the first man. He held out a long bony hand, and my husband took it. "Arthur Corfe," he said. For a big man, there's no life in his grip.

They stood there. I introduced myself. I learned that the co-pilot's name was Jeffrey Lake. He was a silent man. There wasn't much waft in him.

Riddick giggled. He slapped his quiet companion on the back. Lake's embarrassed smile flickered briefly. "Nearly lost it, eh, Lake? Nearly lost it, old boy," said the flyer. He doubled over, giggling. "Nearly lost it!"

Then we were all laughing.

"Shoosh," the pilot breathed. And even Lake was giggling now, even as Riddick hugged him, even as his face took on its harder cast once more.

"Man. What a scrape!" said Arthur.

"Scrape?" said Riddick, trying to find some breath. "Scrape, do you say, Mr Corfe? Next time I'll give you a ruddy scrape. We'll knock your chimney pot off!"

"In that owd bucket?" said Arthur.

Riddick laughed harder. Arthur looked at him, his smile wider than it had been for a long time. I thought of penned sheep breaking free. A relief it was, to laugh with strangers, a relief from the brown grass, the black peat and grey sky.

Sometimes when I watch my husband I feel that his moods are mine, as if I'm looking at my own face. Yet that was not the way I saw him then as he smiled, for I had found a still place in my mirth and I could see him, I could see my husband like a boot wiped clean and dubbed to a shine.

I could see things that I'd forgotten: the arch of his eyelashes, the generous, downy lobes, the crooked teeth which put daft angles in his grin. These vulnerable and feminine places in his big male body, like unexpected trees on a bare hill.

I wished that he would look at me, then. But he was talking to the pilot and he was pointing at the 'plane, and in their laughter they had made a bond, and I don't know why but I wanted to break it.

"I can see you're an admirer of beauty, Mr Corfe," said the pilot. His eyes moved from me to the fuselage.

Arthur didn't see it. He was staring at the 'plane. "Aye, lad," he said, "I like a decent engine, that's for sure."

"Then you'd have fancied this one in an uncommon way," said the pilot, his smile fading. I could not guess his age. "Until today, at least. Yes, sir. There was never a finer engine in the sky. Until today."

"What'll tha do?" Arthur asked.

"Oh," said Riddick, "fix it." He raised a droll eyebrow, and then winked at his companion. "Won't we, Lake?"

Lake nodded, almost imperceptibly. He looked down into the swamp grass. "We'll try," he said.

Riddick wiped a hand through his hair. "Mr Corfe," he said, "I have a business appointment in Southport this evening and I intend to be there. If this valley bottom was the Atlantic Ocean, I would find a way of taking off from it. Don't worry about us, my friend.

41

We came out of the blue and we will go back into it."

I met his gaze. I wondered why someone like him would want to flirt with a woman of the hills. With a woman at least a dozen years older. I tried to understand why a person so recently released from danger would wish immediately to seek it again. And then I looked away, into the blue, and thought about the plodding tread of my husband's feet.

Above, heavy clouds had begun to fill the hole that the flyers had squeezed through.

They say that a scrap of blue sky big enough to patch a ploughman's trouser at the knee is big enough to mend a day. But I smelled rain in that wind, in that brittle shade of blue.

"Now. About this picnic," said Riddick, sorting through the basket. "There's bread, there's cheese, there's... there's bread and cheese. Come on. Join us."

Lake moved to the 'plane. "It's just..." he said. He looked at me. His words faltered. "Excuse me, Mrs Corfe. But I appear to have lost my appetite."

"Damned engineers!" snorted Riddick. "Cool as a cucumber when the fire's roaring and nervous wrecks once they've doused it! What do you think, Mr and Mrs Corfe? Strange creatures, eh!"

My husband looked into his sandwich. "Strange? Nay, lad. I admire a lad as can tinker wi' a creation like that."

Riddick bit into his bread and went on speaking. It was impossible to understand a word he said. I believe that the crash was still going on inside him, that it would only end when his belly was full.

He and my husband swooped in their conversation. They talked about propellers and shafts, cranks and belts. Tanks, gauges, motors. There was never a man in the world who loved a machine more than a farmer. Work, that's the thing, it's all work. They say that a man in the town yearns for peace. Up here in the hills, we dream of noise. My husband would use machinery to suck meat from sheep if he could. We understand animals, but only because it's our job to kill them. Peace. A part of me had wanted that aeroplane to crash.

"Aerodynamics, Mr Corfe. That's the science for me," Riddick went on. "Fascinating stuff. You ought to get yourself a book or two on the subject. Who knows, you might get bitten by the flying bug yourself."

"I'm a bit past that, lad," said Arthur in his steady way, that way he has of distancing himself. There couldn't have been more than 15 years between Riddick and him. He was too young to talk that way.

"Nonsense, old chap," said Riddick with subtle force on the 'old'. He looked at me. "It's never too late to enjoy life, is it, Mrs Corfe?"

"He never said it wasn't," I told him.

A smile moved in a sudden pulse through him. He looked into the grass.

"Besides," said Arthur, as if no-one else had spoken while he was collecting his thoughts, "there's no place to get any such books."

"A public library, surely?" said Riddick.

"If you've got the legs for half a day's walking," said Arthur, the middle-aged man who wished himself old.

Riddick's eyes were a challenge. I said to him, "It's not the legs. It's the time. A long walk for books means one less meal on the table."

Riddick chewed his bread.

Then I knew why I was angry. Poor people are too generous to the rich. I hated him for flying over places where we could not afford to walk.

Arthur said, "Aye. But we get by. Somehow or other. Don't we, lass?"

The grass trembled around us. I matched my silence to Riddick's.

"Yet it must get lonely enough out here sometimes," the pilot said at length, as much to me as to my husband.

"Two's company enough," said Arthur.

"Then allow me to apologise, Mr Corfe, for disturbing the tranquillity of your haven."

Their talk put me in mind of the days when our crowd numbered three. I thought of Robert as he was then, asking thoughtful questions, eating bread too fast, wiping blond strands from his face. His hair would have been darker now, the line of his jaw harder. But he would still have squinted into the light, maybe still frowned when he lifted heavy buckets.

The valley's long grass vanished under snow. Time poured through me. I saw the valley in all its seasons, though all its changes. If no human being had ever lived, the wind would still blow, the drizzle still fall. I felt as if it was me who had fallen out of the sky, not Riddick.

Sweat gleamed yet in the pilot's hair. The first puckerings of age had found slack in the skin by his eyes. He was a man of ambition who had fallen from the sky. I felt pity for him.

"It's fixed," said Lake.

We turned to look.

"A loose connection," he said to Riddick.

The pilot wiped a crumb from his lip with a clean swipe and stood up with the confident gait of a man who does not expect to stay down long.

"Then what are we waiting for?" he said. "Let's thank these good people and be on our way. If I fail in clinching that contract this evening, there'll be hell to pay!"

He shook Arthur's hand vigorously. Arthur's hand was a dead fish in his grip. He looked past Riddick to the sky. It was strange, I respected him for that.

Riddick's hand came into mine more softly. He straightened his posture. He said, "Mrs Corfe, your food has restored us. One day I should like to thank you for the safe harbour that you granted us in these rugged hills." He turned to his engineer. "A pen, please, Lake."

Lake stared at him.

"C'mon, man. You're an engineer, for God's sake – you've got a pencil at least."

Lake's fingers moved to his pocket as if they belonged to another man. He passed a pen to Riddick.

"Now," said the pilot, laying a pad on the engine's hood, "if either of you are ever in my neck of the woods" – he looked at me as he wrote – "you must pay me a visit at this address. Tell the staff that you helped to rescue The Rose Of The Air. They'll know what you mean."

"No," I said.

He looked up.

"We don't get out much," I told him, trying to stay calm. I wanted to snatch the address from him and run home with it. I wanted to ram it down his throat.

He tore off a piece of paper and held it out. It fluttered between us.

"No?" he said.

I didn't look at him. The sun had gone. The sky had been too blue.

"Then perhaps your husband?"

Arthur was shaking hands with Lake, saying, "Tha's a good head on thi shoulders, lad. A good, strong head."

Lake's lips tightened. "Just doing my job, Mr Corfe," he replied. His eyes were hooded. They were trained on Riddick.

"Please," I said.

Riddick nodded. He shoved the paper into his pocket. "Think on, though," he said. "Your husband might enjoy a browse around my private library. And Cook's something special. The whole of the Wirral knows her famous roasts. Isn't that right, Lake?"

"Yes, sir," said Lake, his voice low. "That's right, sir."

I looked at Arthur, not the pilot. He was concentrating on the shiny red hood of the aeroplane.

"You are very kind," I said to Riddick.

"Onward and upwards then," said Riddick, pretending to sigh. "Work, work, work, you know!"

He bolted down a panel and clambered into the cockpit. The engine coughed. Lake wheeled the propeller and leapt back. Our valley filled with the engine's roar. The two men strapped on hoods and goggles, Riddick fiddling with the controls, adjusting loose strands of hair.

Lake didn't look back. Riddick shouted something that we couldn't hear. Their craft moved away onto a flat stretch of ground, clear of the beck. Then, as Riddick's thumb rose from the cockpit, the aeroplane picked up speed, wobbling away from us over the tussocks, holding its course.

As it rose into the sky, I tried to imagine what it would be like to be inside it, to be in the air beside Riddick. I fly in my dreams. My arms are my wings. I look down on the things below, and the heavy, dreaming men look up from the earth and cannot even force their dreaming selves to dream of flight.

Arthur watched the 'plane, hard. "That's some motor they've got theer," he said. "By heck, lass, that's some motor..."

We were there together in the long grass of the valley when we saw the aeroplane fall again. This time the craft didn't fight the wind with tilts and swerves. It fell like a sack of grain from a cliff.

It fell, and there was no harbour below them, only the bogs and rocks of the hills.

We scrambled for an hour through the cold grass before reaching the place where it had come down. By then, a small crowd of local folk had already gathered at the scene, several of them lingering by the wreckage, answering the questions of a solitary policeman. Others stood in a line behind an invisible cordon. The 'plane looked like it had been hit with hammers for a month.

When we heard the distant sirens of an ambulance, our neighbour Tom Cotten turned to us and said, "Bit late for that. Poor blighters never stood a chance."

I looked at the unrecognisable thing before us. Its metal was the colour of blood, there was no sun to make it shine. I didn't go closer. I've had my share of horrors.

"We knew them," I said.

Tom Cotten studied me. "Knew them?" he said, scratching the back of his head. "Nay, tha can't have known them, Frances lass. According to yon bobby, they were frae over Liverpool way. One of them were a right gent, they say. Owned a good portion of land on t' Wirral."

"How does he know that?" I asked. I felt dizzy. The ground wasn't solid under my feet.

"That's it, that's the funny thing," said Tom. He stretched, as if there wasn't enough room for him on the moor. "There's hardly a bone in their bodies as didn't get brokken. Yet they found a bit of paper. Not a mark on it. And there's his Lordship's address. Clear as day, as if he scribbled it theer on purpose." Tom's eyes scanned the wreckage. "Tha can never tell, can thi, lass?"

I shook my head, nodded it. I was watching Arthur. He had bent at the knee to study the laughable red remains of the cockpit. When he put out his hand to touch the wreckage, the policeman came towards him shaking his head.

They stood talking for a while, Arthur apologising for approaching the 'plane, his eyes still searching the wreckage as he spoke, the policeman taking notes in a pad.

I watched his hand move across the paper.

The world grew still, as if I was deep down inside myself, living to a different time-scale. I would not grow old. I would always be here, watching the shadows sweep and fade over these dog-shaped hills.

My son was ten when he died. He was dragged into a brand new threshing machine on Tom Cotten's farm. He was helping out. He leaned across too far and its moving parts pulled him in. I miss him.

Yesterday I was cleaning in the attic and I opened one of my husband's drawers. He is a tidy man in his own way but he thinks that if you cannot see it, it is not there. The drawer would barely budge, it was so stuffed with forgotten objects.

I took a sack and started to go through the drawer to remove the rubbish. I found a lighter that didn't work, half a pack of playing cards, two dominoes, three small batteries, eight foreign coins and twenty or so stale boiled sweets.

Underneath everything was a small piece of twisted red metal. I picked it out and held it in my hands. It was dull and smooth, slightly melted at the edges, a legacy of the crash. I put it back. I covered it with seventy-two cigarette cards, three novels, seven jigsaw pieces, two spanners, a hammer, two small screwdrivers and a watch-face separated from its bare working parts.

Except In Song

That was the summer I developed the power of E.S.P.

"Extra Sensory Perception," I explained in the Guest House, screwing up my eyes, concentrating on the shampoo bottle.

Mum rolled her eyes, bent to the sink. Evening sunlight struggled through salty windows, bloomed over the brown furniture.

I'd learned it off telly, off Kreskin. He was this geeky magician – black glasses, greasy hair – who moved objects By The Power Of Thought Alone. Who communicated without opening his mouth.

"G-n-n-n-n..."

I was going to spill that bottle.

Mum tutted. "It's the Chemist's for *you*, lad."

That broke the spell.

She pointed hair-curling tongs at me. "No wonder you're groaning. You've been guzzling toffee apples. You're constipated, Brian."

*

All this happened after they'd shut the mill gates for the last time.

The union said fight. But Dad was a swinger, not a clinger. The pay-off was a chance to use His Voice. He bought a shining white jacket with lapels like wings. He said, "You won't work in a factory, Brian. Trust me, cock."

His new group were The Nine-Stone Cowboys. And Not Just

48

Covers Merchants, either:

"These lads can play. Tongues are going to *wag...*"

So we'd wound up in a B&B on a windy Blackpool side-street, six blocks from the front, where the wallpaper clashed with the carpet and Mum twisted soap out of her hair while Dad prowled the room, and I concentrated, and our curtains stirred...

... and any second now, any second now...

But it must have been a warning to rest my Enormous Powers, because that bottle wouldn't budge. So I went back to my comic, The Incredible Hulk. Who was half-GP, half-monster. He locked himself in a Lead-Lined Vault Far Beneath The Earth, to protect the Earth from his fury.

Smells of wet sand and vinegar wafted in through the window. Downstairs, the landlady had been scalding the front step for ages. The scratchy noises of her brush seemed to match the smell of vinegar. It was good lying on the bed with my comic, listening to someone else work. It felt safe.

Mum was flicking through one of her glossies, humming *Killing Me Softly* while Dad paced the room in his new jacket. It was the first time he'd worn it.

Because tonight was the night.

At last, Mum couldn't bear it. "The state of us! Can't you practise, Wayne? Sing to stop you prowling? Get shut of these debut nerves?"

Dad tapped the skirting board with his cowboy boot. He stared at the wallpaper. It smelled of cooking fat. A warning had been taped on the wall above the cupboard. It covered up a yellowy patch that was exactly the same shape as France. The warning said:

NO NOISE AFTER MIDNIGHT.
NO LOUD MUSIC.
NO PETS.

White dog-hairs threaded the carpet.

Dad edged round the mysterious crusty patch between our beds. Mum called it The Cow Pat. We weren't to touch it with our bare

49

feet. He smoothed down the warning sign with fingers hardened by guitar-strings and cotton looms.

But the sticky tape had dried-out, it was no use.

"The Silent Treatment, ay?" said Mum, into the sink.

Dad's hands stiffened on the warnings. Coppery hairs glinted on his knuckles. He seemed far away, as though Blackpool's beach was between us.

Mum spotted him watching her. She tightened her hair to a point. "Wayne, is summat wrong?"

His lips moved without a sound.

She smiled. "Butterflies, eh, kid?"

The sun came through, a little stronger.

If I'd known then, I'd have used my Powers not to move things but to keep them still. I'd have locked everything inside that moment, made it as perfect as a song – taps gushing, suds trickling, the landlady scouring her step, and Mum twisting her hair while Dad watched, and she smiled, and sunlight sang over our faces.

*

On the pier, the old folk lay slathered in deck-chairs, mouths open, snoring.

"This lot'll not go hungry," said Mum.

"How come?"

"Cos they're catching flies, Dumbo! Eh, Wayne?"

But Dad had gone on ahead.

She frowned. "I thought a stroll might settle him before the concert..."

Then she saw the poster. "Look!" Her finger slid down it.

TONIGHT!
WAYNE SOLANO
AND THE NINE-STONE COWBOYS!

"Wayne," she said, "look, we're famous!"

In the photo, Dad's hair was piled as high as mash, with a

trench through it. His teeth were a solid white block. Someone had painted his face the colour of blood.

"Wayne!"

Dad stood further down the pier, arms over a curly cast-iron rail, staring at the listless brown sea.

Mum sighed. "Five hours without a word! Anybody'd think we lived in a monastery." She raised her voice: "This is your big night, you dope!"

"Mum..."

"It's not hard. You open your mouth, let the words out. A bit like singing – except you do it with your family, not complete strangers! *Talking*, they used to call it." She clattered down the pier. "Wait here, Brian."

"But..."

"Eat your rock, lad."

The planks bounced. She grabbed Dad's arm. They were out of earshot, I read her lips:

"Wayne – what do you mean?"

She tried to loosen Dad's grip on the rail. Muscles worked in her neck. Gulls squealed. I sucked on the rock.

Finally, she came back, breathing deep. "I'm going for a lie down," she said. "You're to stay with *him*."

"But, Mum..."

Her face flushed. "But Mum Nothing."

"The concert, though. Dad's concert..."

She fussed my collar flat, kissed my nose. "You look like you fell off a flitting, lad."

A smell of apples came from her hair. She turned quickly, then squeezed into a slot in the crowds.

*

The Silence stretched ahead.

Five hours... six hours...

In the seventh hour of his silence, it rained, and neon swam like oil through the gutters. Dad pulled me into a pub, The Tanner's Bag,

51

where I bubbled Coke with a straw and he looked into his jar.

Strangers' voices wafted through...

"I'd to shift that useless lump off the flaming beach. The tide were trying to get past him..."

The little man further down the bar flattened his hair with a narrow-toothed comb, cut tracks through the grease.

"As any sailor will tell you, Mr O'Leary – the drowned never rise again."

"Except in song, Mr Mulhendry. Except in song..."

The little man pulled out tram tickets, straightened them, pulled them out, put them back again. His eyes had circles underneath them, as if somebody had rested a glass on his face.

The pub smelled of ham, but no-one was eating. Smoke came out of their mouths.

I watched a singer set up his gear.

"He met his wife in t' tunnel of love, tha knows..."

"So I heard. Diggin' it, weren't she?"

The singer couldn't find an important lead for his microphone. His forehead was as lined as the beach after the tide went away.

"Dad," I said, "is this where you're singing, too?"

Dad studied his drink.

At last, the singer found his lead and plugged in. "Testing," he said. His loud voice made a few folk look up. "Two. One-two. Two. One-two..." Shrugging, he handed the microphone to a bloke with a red face and a bubble-perm. This was the warm-up man.

The warm-up man stood with his legs wide apart. His slacks didn't fit and his hair was the colour of an old Labrador, but he told a good one about a tapeworm and these cheese pies under the bedcovers. It was to do with the warm-up man's wife and a G.P.

"Get it?" I said to Dad: *"That bloody tapeworm!"*

Dad shuffled on his stool.

"Except it's not funny, is it, Dad? Because my mate, Jack – his Granddad had a tapeworm. A proper one, in his guts. Back in the olden days. And only a Mars Bar could get it out."

Dad smiled.

It was the E.S.P. I'd been sending him messages all night: *Dad,*

*g-n-n-n-n, this is your son, Brian. When will the concert start?
When will you be singing?*

When Dad smiled faintly, I told him more about the tapeworm
in the guts of Jack's Granddad in the olden days – how the chocolate
tempted it out, and they whacked it with a mallet.

And it stretched twice round the yard, twitching.

"They blamed The Worry, because Jack's Granddad were
redundant," I said. "The thing I don't get, though, Dad – why didn't
you get a tapeworm when they made you redu..."

Dad shuffled. "Think on – no swearing back at the hotel. Or
jokes either."

"Or Mum'll have my guts for garters."

"It's not *your* guts I'm worried about," he said.

Then the singer came on, and he took me from the pub.

*

Wind moaned through a grid; froth blew over the prom.

The Travelling Organ went by, lights flashing, pipes going, and
girls in police helmets with cold legs and whistles. And a drunk lying
on the tram tracks, singing, *Please Release Me, Let Me Go.* And
some bloke who wanted 67 pence off us.

When Dad gave it to him, the bloke screwed his face up at the
coins and said, "What do ye call this, then?"

"Sixty-seven pence," I told him.

"Ach. I meant sixty-seven pence *each.*"

It made Dad laugh.

Best of all, The Illuminations – purple and yellow puddles we
splashed through as we walked home, eating chips, and Dad quiet
again. And all the time I was sending messages at him with the E.S.P...

How long, Dad? G-n-n-n-n. How long till you sing?

*

In the doorway of the B&B, Dad stared down at me. It was the
quiet bit of town, cheaper, dark. No Illuminations.

"Brian lad... I've summat to tell you."

I looked up at him, into the sky. He shifted his weight to the other foot. His cowboy boots looked wet. We were both drenched. It had been a dog of a night.

"The singing," he said. "It's about the singing, Brian."

"What about the singing?"

"There isn't going to be any. We've split up, lad."

A wet feeling came to my temples. "You and Mu...?"

"The group," he said. "The group, lad. I had a call yesterday. Only I hadn't..." He wiped ketchup from my lips. Some of it went onto his lapel. "The truth is this, Brian: I didn't have the guts to tell you. I didn't have the guts to tell your Mum. I didn't have the guts."

I looked at his dark shape.

"So we'll be off in the morning, lad. And I want you to be good for your Mum. I don't want to hear any complaints about getting up early. Understand?"

"I've to be good for Mum," I repeated.

He touched my hair, then dug into his pocket for the key.

"What will you do, Dad?" I said. "Will you have to go and work in a factory again?"

He shook his head. "Ask Kreskin," was all that he said.

*

Later, after we'd skirted The Cow Pat and bumped into Mum's bed and woken her, and they'd argued, and everything had died down, I lay in bed staring across our room, listening to the rain.

Mum's hair trailed over the pillow, almost as far as Dad. But he'd moved away, to the edge of the bed. His lips were moving in his sleep, his eyelids flickering.

I concentrated on them both with All The Force At My Disposal. I knew that, just by looking at them, I could move them closer, make their bodies touch.

That's the power of E.S.P.

You don't even need to open your mouth.

The Last Days Of Johnny North

Misfortune had come upon them as thick as light.

When our neighbour Rose could no longer stand it, she awoke suddenly at 3 a.m. and broke her front window into pieces.

She used a sledgehammer.

Afterwards we marvelled at her ability to swing that fearful thing...

... "Such a tiny woman"...

... "Such a massive hammer"...

Now breezes from the hills sucked Rose's old brown curtains into the street and loosened the last pieces of glass.

We watched her boyfriend. His eyes were dull. He stared at the shards as if they were a trail of smashed thoughts that led to some vague idea of a hammer.

Eventually, he said *hasta la vista*, he was done with it all. He'd very likely flit as far as he could – to Australia: "Get to the bottom of this street, and me – I'm dust."

But he didn't go anywhere. He stood in their doorway for months, in his vest, staring into the street, smoking cigarettes.

"He can't bear it that she's gone," said Slatts.

"How can you tell?"

"By his eyes. And look, Michael – he taps the wood. That's a sign, too."

Rose's boyfriend bowed his weary head in the doorway. He was a droopy-moustached man, squashed-looking, and afflicted by facial warts. He looked like the singer Lemmy out of Motorhead. We never found out his name, we just called him Lemmy Out Of Motorhead.

"He's to tap the wood 27 times with his right hand and 28 times with his left."

"But what's it a sign of, Slatts?"

"That he can't stop chewing it over. That he'll have a bad do with his nerves."

"Like his woman," I said. "Like Rose."

Slatts bunched up his lips. "Like half the folk on our street..."

*

This is the way it happened to them: first, sad, then quiet. Then gone. Then they were THERE again, intense, wide-eyed. It was the start of the bad do.

The bad do came on them variously. Sometimes they saw UFOs over the moors, or accused you of chucking buckets of shite at their cars. Sometimes they stopped you in the street to give you information about atoms, or became convinced they were Spanish, or threw out all their windows and fled into the night.

One bloke put on his son's mask and crept up and down the street.

"What are you wearing that for?" our neighbours asked.

"I'm acting the goat," he replied.

"But it's a lamb mask," they said.

Another bloke, Peter Perfect, ended up patrolling the street with his hands behind his back, telling people his opinions of their fixtures and furnishings.

"If you think I'm living opposite THAT," he said to my mum, "then you are very much mistaken."

It was to do with the purple colour my Mum had suddenly decided to paint our front door.

When Peter Perfect left, he took the aerial off his roof, dug up the bulbs in his back yard, ordered the doormat to be packed.

Never lifted a finger to help the removals men, they said.

We missed him after he'd gone. It was quiet. And boring. You could do whatever you liked, which seemed pointless.

Later, he wrote to my mum from his new home. His note was written in blocks of blotched words, each as tiny as a flea, as hairy. "I am truly sorry," the note said. "I had temporarily lost touch with my faculties. They have now altered my medication, and my condition has mercifully abated. Please forgive me for any rash comments about the colour of your door."

MERCIFULLY ABATED. For months, I wrote the phrase on jotters and desks, and said it to myself when I was walking around or in bed, trying to sleep. It had a ring to it. You could imagine you were somebody else when you spoke it.

For those like Peter, the bad do happened slowly. They went mad over the years, indoors. They built land rovers in their front rooms. Acquired a series of small dogs, each the colour of their own hair. Hoarded wafers, to eat in wars. Wrote waves of letters to local 'papers about apostrophes. Pulled out their own teeth.

Slatts blamed the weather. "This drizzle," he said. "It makes people morbid."

He blamed our diet. "Pies, and that. Pasties," he said. "You can put anything in a pasty. Ask your Gran."

Slatts blamed the system. "They've got things just the way they want them."

He blamed the valley sides. "They breed closed minds, these valley sides. They keep out new ideas."

Mostly, though, he blamed his little brother. "This is Ash's fault, this is. If it weren't for that stick insect, none of this'd be happening."

Ashley Slater was the height of two big brothers, but the width of one little sister. He didn't grow; he stretched.

"It's not natural. He looks like a lamp post," said Slatts. "If he turns sideways, he disappears. The light shines through him. He's not a person, he's a gap."

"This is all because he's taller than you," I said.

"It is NOT because he's taller than me," Slatts growled. "I'm average height, I am. Ask anyone."

I eventually did. But first I had to find out about the pasties.

"Gran," I said, "what do they put in pasties?"

"Children who ask too many daft questions," she replied. She said childrrrrren, not children. It was to do with the valley she was born in, and her gums, which would never be right after The Bad Do.

"Only – Slatts said you'd know, Gran. Because of your job."

Gran sighed. She drove a white pie van with no brakes that she called The Gabriel Ratchets – her valley's name for unseen creatures that screamed at night.

The van growled its rrrrrrrrs too, and shook. It made her knuckles fair ache.

"I only deliver the stuff, I don't make it. How would I know what they put *in* the pasties, Michael?"

"But is it true they put in the front end of mice, Gran?"

"Not if they can get away with the back ends, kid."

I nodded. "Just as I thought," I said. "The hidden secret."

Gran studied me closely. "Have *you* been over-doing the pasties, Michael?"

"I rarely eat fatty food," I said.

She drove away, scowling at me, in her van with no brakes.

"Think on, Michael," she shouted. "Polish your life's star, son. Polish it till it shines."

Which was what she always shouted as she drove off.

The van's gears growled like slaughterhouse animals. BRYAN CLASSTY'S SUPERIOR PASTIES, it said on the side – although the owner's name wasn't really Bryan Classty. He'd changed it, for the rhyme... "...and for the conurbations of class," he told Gran.

Whatever that meant.

"See, he's another one," Slatts mused.

"Who is?"

"Classty, or whatever he's called. He's bound to go doo-lally."

"How can you tell?"

"By his eyes," said Slatts.

I laughed. The laugh sounded like The Gabriel Ratchets. Sounded like a van. Sounded like a slaughterhouse.

"You'd laugh if you saw me on fire, you would."

"Sorry, Slatts."

Slatts sniffed. "It's more than just his eyes. It's being a name-changer."

"What's one of them?"

"What do you think? Someone who changes his name. You donkey."

"Eee-aw," I said.

"Name changers have got unstable identities. It's obvious. Ask anyone."

"Alright," I said, "I will."

So I went down the street to ask The Guv'nor, this lad out of our class who said he'd *do* us if we failed from now on to call him The Guv'nor.

But halfway to The Guv'nor's house, I chickened out.

Besides, what would I say to his Mum: "Is the Guv'nor in, please"? It didn't sound right; you couldn't just change your name. It was your Christian name, given to you by Christ.

That's what Gran said.

Gran knew loads about God. Because of her Days of Doubt.

Then, big coincidence, who else but The Guv'nor sauntered by! His eyes were close-together. They had as much light in them as the beds of lakes.

"Unholy spawn of Satan," I muttered, this line from a video-nasty.

He gave me a sideways look, as if he was a tank that had to swing round to find targets.

I looked down the barrel of his eyes.

From now on, no way would I call him The Guv'nor. Even if he *did* me. I was going to call him 'Simon', because that was his God-given name.

"Stick that where the sun don't shine," I giggled. "Buster," I said. And I laughed even harder.

Then, though, a brilliant idea came to me. Today would be the day I called everybody Buster. Including Simon. Or The Guv'nor. Or whatever his name was.

"See how they like that!" I said, and I tripped off down the street, probably whistling.

*

That day, though, wherever I went, I strayed onto Gran's pie-round. I saw her van everywhere. It was as white as a goose, as much of a shock. It made *dying* noises.

"Have you nowt better to be doing wi' your summer holiday?" she asked.

"Yes, Buster," I said.

She let me in the van. It smelled of innards. The seats were scabbed with old leather. Belts flapped by the doors, as thin and limp as used bandages.

"I'd been courting a full year when I were your age," she said, clenching her teeth. She'd to do that, or they fell out when she was driving the van.

"Yes, Gran. But how are your knuckles? Is The Gabriel Ratchets fair hurting your knuckles today?"

"Shush with your moithering, lad."

She steered the van up the hill, over ruts and cobbles. "I've to do this bit slow, else the stock gets battered."

"Where are we off to, Gran?"

"Going to butter up Johnny North," she said, grimacing over the wheel.

She pulled up at the top of the hill and fed a pie to a rusty-coloured dog that she called The Last Of The Careful Eaters.

"That isn't its real name. Its real name's a riddle," she said.

She showed me the dog's name tag.

JIMMY RIDDLE, it said on the tag.

"This dog," she said, "has waited here for me, by this kerb, every day, in all weathers, at the same time, for each of the eleven months since I re-found my path. And every day it's had a pie off me."

The dog nibbled the pie out of Gran's hand, chewed each piece thoughtfully, as if it was an article in a magazine.

"But, Gran. It must cost you a fortune."

"Aye, lad. And look – it'll only eat my best stuff. The good stock, undamaged. Brought up proper, eh! It's a fair member, this

60

JIMMY RIDDLE. It is *that*. A fair member."

Which was Gran's way of saying... I don't know what. She called everyone a fair member – astronauts, ear specialists, grocers, dentists. Jimmy Stewart was a fair member. And Jackie Stewart. Anybody called Stewart – Andy Stewart, the Tudors and Stuarts, Ed 'Stewpot' Stuart (who might count as *two* fair members). Not to mention the neighbour who thought he was a security guard, but wasn't. And Rose with the sledgehammer. And the old woman who accused me of being her granddaughter.

"She's a fair member, that old lass," said Gran.

"But she thought I was a little girl."

"On account of her glaucoma."

"Will we see Johnny North soon?" I sighed.

"There isn't a sinner on this earth who won't see Johnny North soon, lad," she said, grinding the gears.

We went to shops, hundreds of shops, where we had to unload pies and say hello to rasping blokes with faces that had been opened to the winds.

"Damp," they said.

"Aye, it's damp," said Gran, swinging crates.

"Been far, lass?"

"As far as them top doings," she pointed.

The shopkeepers looked like they'd been buried alive, they looked like they'd been cooked in hot water. When they talked about the sky, they studied the stone floors of their back rooms. Their sideburns scared me, the threads and wires. Faces with fences, with KEEP OUT signs.

After each delivery, Gran gave me the gossip. She gave it me in mee-maw, lips stuck out to mime, dentures loose in her mouth. It was how they'd talked in the clanking mill, before they were laid off, when she was normal, before her bad do.

"That fellah," she said, "he's poorly-sick. He'll not live to see another Christmas. His niece is a cook for the Royals."...... "*Him*, he's as tight as a gnat's chuff – unpeels orange in his back pocket."...... "Don't look back. It makes that fella go queer if you look back."....... "As for *him* – he'll happen larn one day."

61

"Happen learn what, Gran?"

"The same thing you'll larn, lad." She bashed my knuckles. I was gripping the dashboard: "It's better to let go," she said, "than die from clinging."

She pressed pedals, crying, "Shooting pains! Ankles through to my hips!"

"This van's a death-trap," I groaned.

But by now she was burning with the thrill of lifting boxes and yanking gears and screaming at pedestrians to step away because of the lack of any controls.

"Aye!" she said. "A death-trap. And dusta know what, lad? There's no place on this earth I've ever felt so alive!"

It was to do with her Days of Doubt, she said.

"Daft as a Polly Dancer, I was, before I re-found my path and got the old Gabriel Ratchets!"

"But it hasn't got any brakes..."

We had crested the hill, and were plunging towards town. We may as well have been minor Biblical characters, disappearing into a whale.

"Is there a handbrake?" I said.

"Is there a handbrake," I demanded.

"Brakes? Leave tricks and brakes and sorcery to the likes of Johnny North!"

We hurtled over cobbles, fast, faster. The town opened its jaws.

"Faith," she shouted. "Faith's all tha needs!"

Everything bounced and rattled, and wanted to murder us. I gripped the seat belt, thought about words and meadows. Thought about the word 'meadow'. Thought: 'He died in a pie van'.

I imagined myself after the crash, standing by the kerb, dead. Only JIMMY RIDDLE would know I was there, because Dogs Can Sense Things.

"Hello," I would say to the dog. My ghost would say.

"Is the stock okay?" JIMMY RIDDLE would reply. "Have you damaged any of the stock, Michael?"

"I've lost *dentures* in this rattlesome thing," Gran was shouting, over the pounding cobbles. "But one thing they can't reach, or harm. Not all the sinners and evil creatures on this planet...

... Faith," she said.

The thing that may descend upon you after you get sad, then quiet. Then intense, and wide-eyed. After the bad do. After you've hurt yourself.

"It calms you down," she said, as we sailed into town.

"What does? What calms you down, Gran?"

But she couldn't hear me over the roar of the van, her emptied white van, which she had given the valley-name for wild swans that fly high in the night, for unseen howling dogs, and the lonely she-fox that screeches from dark cloughs.

"Man alive!" she said. "Hark at The Gabriel Ratchets! Hark at its holy racket!"

*

Afterwards, I sat on the kerb, trying to get calm, thinking about my teeth, about whether The Gabriel Ratchets had loosened my teeth.

"Maybe it's my turn," I said to Slatts.

"Turn for what?"

"Turn for a bad do," I said.

Slatts narrowed his eyes. "You're not really old enough."

"What about Trojan Treasure Boy?"

Slatts nodded reluctantly.

"Kept saying he'd found Trojan treasure on the moors. *He* had a bad do with his nerves."

"And he was only 13," said Slatts.

"A year younger than us. Happen I'm like him. Happen I'll start thinking I've seen stuff, too."

"Seeing what? Treasure?"

"Maybe I'll see... I don't know... evil sperrits."

Slatts looked at me. "You've been in that van again, haven't you?"

I nodded.

"And your Gran went on about sperrits, didn't she, Michael?"

"Sort of."

"And feeorin and Old Nick and Grimalkin..."

"Well, today it was Johnny North."

"No wonder you keep getting them weird teeth fears," said Slatts. "I'd get weird teeth fears if I were in your family."

I looked at my feet. "She says it was the best thing that ever happened to her."

"How do you mean?"

"The bad do. Says it brought her to her senses. That she'd to get out of her head so she could see herself again."

"Aye, well..."

"But this Johnny North. This stuff about buttering up Johnny North. What do you reckon that's all about, Slatts?"

Slatts shrugged.

"Went on and on about him. And faith. She said the key was faith."

"It is," said Slatts. "It *is* the key. Because your faith is where you keep your eyeth, your nothe, your lipth, and your tee..."

"Very funny. Extremely funny, Buster."

"Hilariouth," he said.

I scowled.

"Look," he said, "don't take it out on me. How often have I told you not to get in that van? You know what your Gran's been like ever since she. Ever since she..."

"... had the bad do, yes. But that happened because she was lying around the house, *thinking*. Because my Granddad had. Because he'd..."

"... passed on," said Slatts.

"Passed on," I said. "The thing is, though, she's getting better now. On account of her van. See – this delivery job, it's taken her out of herself. Got her through The Days of Doubt. She's even chucked out them crooked coins."

"What crooked coins?"

"Them crooked coins she stuffed in her pockets. She used to walk with her thumbs folded inside her fingers, too. To ward off the evil sperrits. Because she thought the sperrits were on her trail. But she doesn't even burn her nail clippings any more. She's like a new woman."

Slatts nodded. "Except she still goes on about sperrits and boggarts, and that."

"Not that often. Not like in her Days of Doubt."

Slatts grunted. "Ask me, Michael, she'd be better off with *no* superstitions."

"Well, I'm not asking you, am I! Slagging off an old woman! What harm has she ever done you?"

"Apart from the time she nearly ran me over, do you mean?"

"Apart from that time, yes."

Slatts spoke in a quiet voice. "When I had to jump out of the way to save my life, do you mean?"

"She didn't mean it," I said. "She was probably thinking of summat else."

"Evil sperrits that live in her mouth, do you mean?"

I stared at Slatts. "She's better now. She's re-found the pa..."

"Don't take this wrong, Michael. But old women ought to concentrate on the road. Especially if they're fagged-out, from lifting. They should be saving energy."

"That's just it," I told him. "Gran's only tired *before* work. *After* work, she says she can fight off tigers."

Slatts looked at me.

"The way she talks," I explained. "You know – like when she goes on about *misfortune as thick as light.*"

"Or *them who dreams of joy is heading for grief.*"

"Or *you may as well eat the devil as the broth he's boiled in.*"

We laughed. Slatts whacked me on the shoulder. I gave him a good one back.

"Brrrrrrrrrroth," we said.

We began poking each other in the ribs with sticks.

"Watch out, or I'll set Johnny North on you," said Slatts.

"Who the hell's *Johnny North*?" I asked eventually, still gasping.

Slatts started making grrrrrr noises. "The Grrrrrrinding gears of Gabrrrrriel Rrrrratchets," he said.

"Don't be tight, Slatts."

"Grrrrrrrrrrrrrrrrrrrrrrrrrrandma," he said.

"You're a sinner, you are. You'll burn in hell," I told him.

"Hell!" said Slatts. "Hell doesn't exist."

"Hell is the choices you make, Slatts."

Which was another of Gran's sayings.

Slatts stared at his stick. "Happen you're right," he said. "Happen you *are* having a bad do, Michael."

"It runs in our family," I said.

"Like noses in ours."

"Very funny, ha ha."

"Can't you take a joke, Michael?"

"No," I said. "I'm sick of jokes. Jokes always end up in punchlines. Like when you go on about lamp posts, and the punchline's to do with your Ashley."

Slatts stared at me.

I walked off down the street, swinging my arms. Then I stopped swinging my arms, because it looked weird to swing my arms for no reason. "Jokes make fun of them who can't help it," I shouted back at him. "Or who don't know any better. They're cruel, are jokes."

"What are you on about, Michael? Where the hell are you going?"

"To butter up Johnny North," I said.

"Well, steer clear of Lodge Street. Or the Atomic Man'll grab you."

"Thanks," I said.

"And don't forget to eat plenty of fresh fruit," he shouted. "And to change your underwear once a month, whether you need to or not!"

I twisted a finger against my temple, and went down Lodge Street, where the Atomic Man grabbed me.

It must have been my plan.

He said to me, "I'll tell you another thing. If a drop of water were magnified to the size of the world, right – then each atom in it would be the size of a cricket ball."

"Smart," I said. I shook his hand.

"It's rare to encounter such courtesy," he said, "in one so young," he added.

"Thanks," I said to The Atomic Man.

*

In town, I went to the bookshop. It was closing down, they had six books left – one by Desmond Bagley, one about low self-esteem and one about Tenerife. The other three were on Lancashire traditions.

"Cool," I said.

But the first one was all about slubbing-frames, and the second about broth and tea-cloths. When I turned the last book to 'J' for 'Johnny North', there was no 'J'. There was just 'L'.

LOST TEETH (Lancashire superstitions): the sufferer of a lost tooth must wrap the tooth in greaseproof paper, laced with vinegar. This must then be thrown into the core of a hot fire. Otherwise, the sufferer is doomed, after his death, to hunt the far reaches of hell, for all eternity, in search of his tooth.

I put the book down, fast. I left the shop, didn't look back.

"Misfortune has come upon me as thick as light," I said.

It was Gran's voice. What was Gran's voice doing in my head? Why was I talking out loud in someone else's voice?

I looked around to make sure that nobody had noticed.

The thing was, I thought maybe The Gabriel Ratchets had loosened one of my teeth, a pointed one at the front. I didn't have any proof, because I was too much of a coward to check. But the odds seemed likely.

The far reaches of hell, I thought.

How far was that?

*

At home, Mum asked me where I'd been.

"Nwre spcl," I said.

"What? Why are you talking like that, Michael?"

"No rsn," I said.

"What do I tell you, lad? Open your mouth and let the words come out."

"Ys," I said. "Opn my mth n lt th wrds cm ot."

"If it's your teeth again..."

"It's nt my tth," I said.

"Worrying yourself silly about... about *incisors*, of all things!" She wrung her hands on her pinny. "You know what the dentist said: there's nowt wrong with your teeth. Your teeth are fine, Michael." She turned to Dad, her face narrow and white. "He's got more of them daft ideas in his head..."

Dad looked at the lino.

Mum said, "Michael, it's clap-trap. Old wives' tales. You're a young lad – it's not the olden days anymore. We've got fluoride in the taps. Your teeth are fine."

"Ys," I said, "My tth r in gd cndtn."

She looked at me for a long time.

"But, mum," I said, recovering. "Who's Johnny North?"

"Johnny who?"

"Johnny North."

She shook her head. "This is your Grandmother's doing, isn't it? Filling your head with nonsense again."

"No, mum. She just said we'd to butter him up. Butter up Johnny North. But then we never even went to Johnny North's. We just went to loads of shops."

Mum looked at Dad. "Tell him he's not allowed in yon van. That it's not safe."

Dad said, "It's not safe in yon van. You're not allowed in yon van."

"But who's Johnny North?" I begged.

Mum said, "Johnny North isn't anybody. Johnny North is the wind. He used to blow witches into the sea – keep the hills free from mischief. But that was in your Gran's day. When people were superstitious."

"Before there was fluoride," said Dad. He searched the lino. "Michael, when your Gran pulled out her own tee... when she hurt herself... She was on her own. She'd got these ideas in her head..."

"But she's better now, isn't she?"

He stroked the arm of his chair.

"Except she still goes on about Johnny North. So maybe she isn't better, Dad. Maybe she's..."

"It's like this," he said: "Everybody needs comforting by something. In your Gran's day it was Johnny North. And these days it's something else. Do you get my drift, lad?"

I put my eyes where he'd put his, in the cracks between the lino. "You mean he's being blown away too..."

Dad said, "Aye. Everything gets blown away by summat else. Even the wind. Even Johnny North. One day, they'll probably call fluoride daft."

Mum frowned into her pinny pockets.

*

Later, after I'd brushed my teeth, I stood by the front window and opened my mouth, to check the reflection.

I breathed on the glass and wrote MERCIFULLY ABATED in the condensation.

Through the letters, I watched Lemmy Out Of Motorhead. He was standing in his usual place, the doorway, in his vest, tapping the wood. It was like Slatts said: he'd to tap it 27 times with his right hand, 28 with the left.

I thought of JIMMY RIDDLE by the roadside, putting his faith in what would come along. In the good ones, undamaged.

When I opened the window, the words vanished from the glass, and Gran's van rattled down the street, over the cobbles. It was her evening circuit of town. No pies, no reason... just the joy of not clinging.

"Polish your life's star!" she mee-mawed up to me. "Polish it till it shines, lad!"

I waved back.

For a long time after The Gabriel Ratchets had gone, its traces still lingered in my parents' bedroom, in stirrings of their curtains, and the thin trail of fumes that would drift away with me when I went to bed to think the good thoughts.

Not the bad thoughts, about the position of your tongue in your mouth.

I wiped the glass with my sleeve, almost ready.

Outside, as I turned to go, Lemmy was still smoking, still screwing his eyes into the falling sun.

And the last of that thick summer light gleamed over our purple door, on his facial warts, off the window that Rose had smashed to the roots, where he had leaned for weeks, and would lean weeks longer, waiting.

A Parliament Of Hares

Old Zeph swore he'd seen it once: a circle of hares sitting, as if in session, in the moonlight under the moor.

He'd been returning from a search for *straggs*, those mysterious young sheep who wander free from their flocks.

"Just a lad, I was then – as young and daft with loving as you two. But I know what I saw."

The old crofter's face retained its valley-tightness, but his eyes gleamed in the firelight. Beyond the timbers of his cottage, stars flashed like broken glass. Outside, our horses stirred on the cobbles.

The valley was to be dammed, our village flooded. They'd taken the slates from the roofs.

Soon it would be dawn – time to hitch the carts and trundle with their meagre loads down the track, into the new century.

When, at last, Zeph fell asleep, we crept into the fields he'd tended, searching for some miracle under the moor.

Mollie smiled. "Ma Tasker's fire is burning yet..."

"For a few hours longer."

"Aye."

I breathed in the smoke, watching the stirrings at Ma Tasker's window – two workers rousing themselves from sleep for the last time, both of them heavily-built and rough-faced, each of them billeted there by the Water Board after the old woman's refusal to leave.

In a few hours they would dowse the stubborn flame with her cow's milk.

The new towns are thirsty. They need your rain...

My lover and I lay one final time in grass that would never again be mown, watching light break over the rail-head.

Rubble filled the cars, pieces broken from barns and shippons.

"There will come a flood," Mollie whispered to the wide spaces of the valley.

Above her lovely head, the clouds passed in shoals.

A Polder, A Place To Live

Up against the lockers, under his fists. Every dinnertime, same as ever, the crowd of pasty faces.

"Do him, *do* him," chants Doyle.

Plug's pudgy fists, his faraway titters. And a sour locker smell, whiff of used gym kits and oranges, emptied Tupperware.

Drizzle. Always, through the leatherings, at the back of it – rain crawling over glass. Then a pause, and some waiting.

Plug looks at me, says, "Got you, eh, got you."

"Do him, *do* him," chants Doyle.

Plug's fists again: yellow bits of bones and skin. His hitting comes down – and the girls that watch, they've got pale legs, pleated skirts, green sweaters, stupid ties. Conscientious faraway fists: as if Plug's proud of his rubbish work, the worst kind of cowboy, a self-deceiver.

"Boring," says Doyle, squinty-eyed, bog-brush for hair. Had the squishes for the whole term, and still eating the same muck.

"Boring!" goes the chant, the bored chant. Some of Plug's watchers turn away, girls back inside their magazines, the quiet way they turn pages.

Rain, buildings, cooking. The whole world, there, going on.

In close now, Plug breathing the onion. Last night's meal, his life. Struggling to find the catch, as if he can open me, unroll me.

Fingers into the seams.

"Like that, eh?" he says, hands working the bones, searching out soft places.

I know every scratch on this floor, the soft tiles we slide over, our shoes studded with metal plates to make the scratches deeper. I know the place he'll hit me next. My body has the memory for it.

When they hit you, it's only the first hit that hurts. The joke's on him. On Plug.

His lips pop softly, it's disgusting. Our cheeks touch, and the locker comes open and a vest falls out, a white vest, grey and blue with old sweat. Plug looks down and stops hitting, there's no more hitting. His eye-corners water. He snuffles, puts a hand in his blazer pocket – as if it's all casual, this savagery, this need, the tears. I watch the wet eye, thinking: Wanker. Thinking: Try that again, go on.

The girls stare at me, the girls ignore me, their quiet page-turning – as if antelopes have seen another antelope felled.

Plug untwists his tie, the self-consciousness of the hand pushed down into the blazer pocket, all the fluff that's probably there. "You watch it, you," he says. The fight's gone out of him, he's useless, the feet on him, their pigeon-toes.

A bell goes and in comes Mr Vowel, the white slab of his face. He has never smiled in the thousand years since he was bolted together in a shed. One of those P.E. teachers who is forced by the system to pretend that he knows about Geography. There's a slide-set in his knobbly hands, it's about Dutch sluice-gates, how they keep the land dry – and nobody could give a toss, except maybe it would be interesting if Mr Vowel shut up.

"I did him," Plug whispers at them.

"Never," Doyle grunts.

"As per usual," says Plug. "Every fucking dinner."

But Doyle shakes his head and Plug knows he's one of those lads who's rubbish at saying fuck, so he quietens, preferring to admire his knuckles, as if they're made of teak, as if they shine.

I'm next to Big Mick, the quiet lad with the black narrow eyes. "Doug," he says, "why don't you fight him back? Why don't you?"

I slide back into the seat, this melted seat, they set a Bunsen-burner on it. And Big Mick's watching me, narrow-eyed, as if somewhere underneath there's the real Big Mick.

"Don't know," I tell him, the sentence hardly comes out, it's like a croak.

This is the Big Mick: taught himself kung-fu but never mentions it; got off with someone's wife in a chip shop but won't discuss it; bought a can of McEwan's lager on the school trip to Edinburgh and took it somewhere quiet, away from everyone. Big lad, into the music that you're into because your older cousin says it's great – but you're not into it really, and Big Mick is.

How must it sound to him, this throat-croak, these words that barely come out?

Big Mick refuses to say any more about it.

Mr Vowel drones on. He has so much face that there is barely room for eyes, they are tiny currants on a batter cake.

The opening of the sluice.

An equalisation of water levels.

Lights go off, the same old slide-set. God made the Earth, but the Dutch made Holland. Half their land would be under the sea if it were not for...

Off to the side, in the dark, I see Plug bawking again, the tears glimmering on his face. They came out from inside him. They're as fat and solid as warts.

When I nudge Big Mick to look too, he doesn't bother. He goes on staring at Vowel's slides, long mop of hair reaching nearly to his narrow eyes. The way those eyes can fix you, and that's enough. His pale face. He probably stays in probably shagging probably wanking probably whatever it is that Big Mick does when he stays in. He does whatever he likes – as if he knows most things are a waste of time, not even important enough to ignore.

But sometimes I look at the straight line of Big Mick's shoulders and he's clamping down, like I do when Plug's at me. Ready for it.

One who has nothing to lose is on the other side of me: Millett, a stick of a kid, who wears black jeans to school. No-one notices what Millett's wearing. The teachers never even look at him. Skinny tie, rolled-up sleeves, the bones on him. "Did you see it last night? It

75

was ace, did you see it?" His grey lips lack any moistness, his eyes bulge. He looks like he's fallen out of a nest.

The sluice gates are totally regulated, they are reliable in all weather conditions.

"That space ship they've got," Millett whispers. It's some telly programme he's on about, one that kids like him watch. I know. I watch it.

"The mother ship," says Millett, picking at his sleeves. He has sharp elbows and a thin nose. His hair will all fall out in one day when he's 23 years old. Whoosh. Gone.

"Warp thrust!" he hisses. "That ship! With the warp thrust!"

There is nowhere you can look, not at Millett, not Big Mick, not Plug, definitely not at Mr Vowel, his eyeless visage. He makes you think of tendons.

Doyle drops his guts, a waft of farty air. SBD: Silent But Deadly.

"Good arse," he says, satisfied with his work.

Everyone moves their chairs, holds their noses – everyone except Plug, who's as far off as I am when he beats me. It's almost as if we aren't mates, but we are. We were mates before we even came to secondary school, when it didn't matter that he had pigeon-toes and two arses, the weird potato shape of him.

*

I remember the first time I saw Plug, at the old school. We were nine-year-olds. He was new. He had brown eyes that watched – kind and scared, both at once.

"I was top scorer in my real school," he said. He stood in the dip of the yard, the place where all the water runs to. "I got 20 goals," he said.

"Which school?"

"In another town," he said. He flapped his hand towards the hills – a big blowy place, white grass and no trees. "My dad," he said, "he came to watch every match."

I wondered whether I should tell him that I never scored. I was

76

a right-back, which is virtually the goalkeeper, you never go near the other nets.

"We were top of the league," he said.

"Smart."

"What's your name?"

"Doug Roper," I told him.

"How many goals have you scored?"

"Eighteen."

The wind blew. I looked down at the bumps in the tarmac. His feet pointed inwards.

"That's two less than me," he said.

*

The lights come on. Suddenly everyone in the classroom is writing.

Millett won't let me be free. "That ship, the mothership – it can fly to the Edge of the Known Universe," he whispers. "It's got anti-grav and shift-throttle."

And: "Permanent water supply on the Planet of Mars."

"Millett," I beg him, "what are they all writing?"

And: "Sealed docking manoeuvre."

"With their pencils, Millett. What are they writing?"

This is what the pencils sound like: like a forest closing – trees folding in after you've gone through them, like they're whispering, like pencils, like Millett.

If I don't stop him, we will be hammered.

"Millett," I urge, "shut up, or Vow..."

"Roper!" Mr Vowel intones. "Have you something to say, Roper?"

"Sir, no, sir."

The class laughs. I try to growl at Millett, but his skeleton hand is at the corner of his mouth, skinny lips barely moving, going, "Reverse thrust system."

"Sir, Doug Roper is still talking, sir," says Doyle.

Mr Vowel stands up, no warning. The thick body that sends no warnings. He looks down on the class as if it's the massive sea.

"Silence," he orders. The thumb of his face comes to rest on Doyle. The only thing I can find to like about Vowel: he hates Doyle, has no time for him. "Read me your answer, Doyle."

Doyle stares at his own scribble, helpless. Vowel passes over. "Sandra," he commands, "tell this cretin what a polder is."

Sandra is one of the featureless waves. "Polders are reclaimed land in Holland," she reads carefully. "The sea is pumped out to create land for people to live on and for crops to be safely grown."

Vowel says, "See me later, Doyle." He has a colourless voice. There is no mercy in him. He won't bleat to us like the ones who beg forgiveness for their cruelty.

"... and they hurtled into another dimension," says Millett from behind his hand.

The lights go out again. Click. Another slide.

We move on through the afternoon, hearing the beating of rain behind the dark blinds.

There is a scenic quality to many of the villages that line the shores of the former Zuider Zee.

All the time, Plug looks down, staring at the desk, the desk he defaced last week – but only out of sight, underneath, which is typical. "Look," he told us, "look – I've *done* this desk!" He had to turn it over, and books fell off. In places where the teachers don't inspect, he'd scratched twat and bollocks, written BFC, though that's not his team. No team, two arses. That's just about typical. And it's all because of his feet and his dad. If it weren't for those things, he'd not kick my head in every dinnertime and I wouldn't be bothered about his lumpy two-arse shape, and we'd be proper best mates, not best mates that hate each other.

*

I saw what they did to Millett. It was after school on the green by the bus stop. He looked back, stumbled – and then he was lost. They fell on him, a big gang.

They booted the freckles off him.

When he got up out of the wet grass, clay smeared over him,

stringy bits of grass glimmering in his cuts, he just carried on walking, he didn't look back. It impressed me.

Doyle was there, of course he was. He must rent time on American spy satellites. "Ha! Skeletor!" he grinned. "Got it in the chops!" and Millett was pushed and shoved by Doyle because he had already been beaten to the ground by other boys, strangers.

These strangers, they were at another school. They wore stupid blazers, Millett didn't even know them.

Some kids know their targets before they see them. They lock on, like spaceships. They travel through walls. Before you know it, they're coming down on you, out of the sky. Millett stumbled once, and that cost him. It must have hurt; he hasn't got the skin, no padding.

The places that Millett walked into, the people he got battered by: they were strange to him. He was all at sea.

"Why do you never fight back?" Big Mick had asked me.

You just can't explain it.

*

On the first day I met Plug, we played penalties. He was quite good, but he tripped over his own feet. Then he missed a sitter that I'd have put away.

"The wind," he said.

"What wind?"

"It bent my shot. At my other school, it's not windy like this. I got 20 goals."

"You said."

"Don't you believe me? I'm a natural goal-scorer. If you're good at sport, it makes you popular." He looked at his watch. It was golden, and made silent ticks. "This watch," he said, "it cost a packet."

"Does it tell the right time?"

"Tell the right time, 'course it tells the right time!" He gave me a look, like he felt sorry for me, which was weird because I felt sorry for him.

"We can play for a bit longer if you like," I offered.

79

"Can't. My mates are waiting. We've synchronised our digital watches."

"Tomorrow, then?"

"Might do," said Plug. He kicked the ball to me. "I've got a good all-round game, my dad told me. He came to watch every game. Bang!" He pretended to kick. "In the old onion bag, that's what my dad calls it. A saying he's got."

"Is he a footballer, too, your dad?"

"He used to be," said Plug, and ran to meet his mates with the watches.

*

Who else has been terrorised?

Three teachers on the sick, including the maths bloke with the green eyes and small hands. Creeley. It was a stroke. He blinked when he first stood before us, and we saw the tiny crack, prised at it for weeks.

Weeks and more weeks.

He put a lot of Brylcream in his hair, you could imagine him staring into the mirror in the mornings before he came to school.

"Hallo, children," he said at first. Then he stopped saying it. Then he tried to turn back the tide.

"There will be changes," he said.

"A new regime," he said.

Rumours came down to us that the fifth formers had backed him into a curtain and pummelled him. It emboldened us.

Plug said that Creeley was a pervert. Creeley was a county badminton champion. He knew all the positions on the court. The only harm in him was his weakness. It terrified us.

He taught us about sub-sets, circles that cut through each other.

They tied an elastic band to a divider. Then they flicked a rubber at Creeley. We bust our guts laughing. It went right past his nose.

"How could you miss a target that size?" said Doyle, and he had a rolled-up cone over his nose.

Plug grabbed the cone and blew through it. "PERP!" he shouted. "PERP!"

"Pluggett," said Creeley.

"Sir, do you like my hooter, sir? It's a hooter. For hooting through, sir."

This was all because Creeley had a big nose.

"Give that to me," said Creeley. And he grabbed for the cone. "Give it to me, give it to me."

Plug held on.

Only Doyle was laughing by this stage. The rest of us were quiet, watching – even Millett, who usually preferred to study his pale blue arms, who usually kept his head down... while Plug and the teacher fought over the cone, tugging, tugging. As if it really were the teacher's nose.

Rain swarmed over the windows.

Films with fights in them are lies. The fists you hear in films, you'd think a tree had fallen over.

This is a real fight: shhh shhhhhh. Breath noises and soft things, concentration on faces, a rustling of polyester blazers, shirt-buttons over waxy desktops.

Creeley's silver cufflink catching and clicking on the edges.

Then the nose came away in Creeley's hand and there was a moment when he didn't know what to do with it, with his own nose, and nobody else did either.

He used to smile, but now he never did.

"Unfair!" he shouted, more shocking to us than if he had sworn.

He raised the nose to strike Plug, but Plug, who was crying, didn't flinch. He had made himself this scared in order to overcome his fear, and it was nearly the end for Mr Creeley – he wouldn't be telling us much more about circles that cut through each other, that divided sets, which we always pronounced as 'sex'.

Sir, can we talk about sex again today, sir?

Sir, sex, sir!

Sir, what is it about the subject of sex that fascinates you, sir?

So the door came open while he was ready to apply corporal punishment – using a version of his own nose – to the tearful face of

81

a second-former. And he was utterly without luck, it was the head mistress.

"Mr Creeley?" she said.

He looked back at her, along the line of his badminton shoulder. She had a tight little nose that no air could get up, glasses that pinched it still tighter shut. Her tiny nose, his hooter. It was an insult.

Miss Dray's glasses were solid black, they flared out to gigantic horns. "Can I talk to you please, Mr Creeley?" she said. Normally she shouted. This was serious, it was the same level tone she used to tell us about the dismantling of our Empire, the Gunboat Panther they sent to Agadir. Our empire was not like other empires.

"Yes, Miss Dray," he said in a low, beaten voice.

He was a small harmless guy with a thin neck. He was going to have a stroke. He put his hair back, fussed it to a quiff, I smelled the Brylcream. It made me sad, I hated him for that.

They were gone. No-one spoke, and then everyone did. The girls put hands over their mouths and gasped.

Plug's eyes gleamed.

Sandra, the tall one with thick legs and a ruddy face, nudged her friend Lynn, a girl I never noticed much. Lynn stared at the rainy glass and said, "Amazing!" in a dreamy voice, as if it was wonderful, but not good to look at.

Millett said, "That was like this programme I saw..."

Sparrowy twitters, a roar of unbroken voices.

"It was in outer space," said Millett, nudging me with the point of his elbow.

"Yes," I said.

He had big hooded watchful eyes that blinked too much. He was looking right at me, an orange-coloured boy with skeleton hands.

I watched Lynn, the dreamy one. I knew she was pretending to listen to Sandra, but loved all this and couldn't bear it, that she watched the rain because the rain's the usual old stuff, it makes you safe.

Only one person kept quiet: Big Mick, as mysterious as coal. His eyes had narrowed to slits, shoulders a solid line.

Gossip moved like water.

It was in the school hall.

They got him against some curtains...

They punched the shite out of him!
A scowl bit a hole in Doyle's face. He was little, creeping, sinister. "Shhhh!" he said. "Shhh, everyone. To Listen."

Then, as Doyle strained to eavesdrop on Creeley's ordeal, Miss Dray came back to us. She was a travelling cloud of vengeance, mighty as an empire. Her silence was louder than our noise. She didn't speak, she looked out from the enormous horns, taking in each face. Snipping, gathering.

Then she was gone again, and as the door swished shut, I saw Mr Creeley standing alone in the corridor. He was pretending to hum, like a bus might be coming. His eyes hadn't got anything to do with music, they were hurt eyes, like Plug's.

Even Doyle had shut up.

From the corridor came low tones, and I knew – by the dull red floor and the rain on the glass and the dented lockers – that our maths teacher, who had a kind voice, who wore clean shirts and had small careful hands and who knew exactly where to stand on the badminton court, that this harmless little man, who had somehow made us hate him, even though there was nothing wrong with him, would be going away for a long time.

And when he returned, just for one week, in many months' time, he would blink again at the wrong moment and we would finish the job, and a stroke would take him.

It would be Miss Dray who came back to us, and she would be terrifying.

*

The first time Plug beat me up in front of everyone at dinnertime, it was a mistake. I forgave him. "Don't worry about it," I said as we walked home.

"You were asking for it though," he said, and his eyes were wet, they were always wet, I was sick of how soft he was.

"You got me against the lockers," I said.

"You shouldn't have made me do it."

"I didn't mean to."

"The way you were looking at me," he said.

"What way?"

Plug wouldn't answer. He swung his bag over his shoulder. It was full of books.

"Is that homework?" I said.

Plug said, "Only puffs do homework."

"Oh, only I thought it was homework."

"Are you saying I'm a puff?"

Cars gleamed with rain. The sun had come out, there was a crack of blue sky. You can't trust it. Tricks and lies.

When we got to my house, Plug said, "I'll see you tomorrow."

He walked away, his stupid feet, his arses. The bag bulged. A watery shadow went with him, and faded.

Way down at the other end of the street he wasn't a big fat cushion of a boy with a ring of watchers any more. He was small and on his own, and it didn't matter how often he battered me, it wouldn't bring back his dad.

*

For the rest of our lives, we will be in this darkened room, behind the blinds, watching slides of dykes and canals taken in drizzly conditions in mainland Europe.

Eventually Mr Vowel will reach the section on Rotterdam and become almost emotional. He will quote facts at us about tonnages and shipments. He will repeatedly use the phrase *Europoort, a vast dock*. "From this vast dock, cargo is distributed to the world" – and just for a few seconds the cold lard of his voice will be slightly softer – "including faraway destinations such as Vancouver and Rio de Janeiro." And it might even occur to you that Mr Vowel lives in a house and has a wife and feeds his cat.

*

"Vowel's obsessed with Europoort," says Doyle. He kicks the pavement, spits. "Bloody nutter. See the way he went on at me?"

Plug and me don't say anything. It's battering it down. The walk home seems even longer when Doyle comes with us.

"I reckon he's got shares in Europoort," he says.

We keep our heads down. Cars and lorries chuck their dirty surf at our ankles.

"Stocks and shares and that," he mutters.

The rain has got us beaten, there aren't any dry places. Plug says, "You don't even know what them things are. Stocks and shares."

Doyle is wide in the eye. "I bloody do!" he rages. "My dad's got investments. I know what stocks and shares are."

Plug makes a sound with his lips. Doyle pushes him against the stained wall.

Plug looks down, there's spit and rain on Doyle's mouth. He gets in close at Plug's ear, hisses: "What would you know? You haven't even got a dad anymore!"

Plug looks back at him from the side of his eye.

*

Tomorrow, at dinnertime, when it's raining and the girls are quietly turning pages, Plug will come to my desk saying, "I know your type, Roper. You're one of them lads that never stands up for their mates."

I won't speak, and Big Mick will turn away. Then Doyle will be by Plug's side, going: "Do him *do* him" and Plug will ask, "Starting? Are you starting, Roper?" and I'll turn to the side, first punch to the kidney, the one that hurts.

"This is what you get for not standing up for your mates," Plug will tell me.

"Show him, Plug."

I will pull Plug to me, near, inside his onion breath, and the fist won't have room to work. This close, miles from his punches, I'll find the place that no-one else knows about, that even Millett's mothership can't reach.

"You're starting, I'm finishing," Plug will mutter, words off the telly. Another punch. "Do you like hospital food? Want to wake up in an ambulance? Pick your teeth up with a broken arm?"

I'll study Plug's ring of watchers, the only audience he ever gets – Sandra, excited, breathless, the one that knows about polders. Sandra pushing her dreaming friend as the second fists comes in, and Lynn nodding, looking through the punch to the window, where rain clings.

"Fight-FIGHT! Fight-FIGHT!"

Doyle will push Plug to beat me and Plug will need to do it because I saw Doyle beat him.

It won't be any use, I'll keep my eyes on the scratched floor, pretend no-one's watching. But I'll notice Millett and he'll be whistling, as if another bus is late. And my beating will remind him of what's waiting for him, the bullies he does not know, bullies with no gentleness in them, who have not even had their dads die.

*

It's late now, and cold. I lie in bed. Sometimes I wet it. I wake up when it's still dark and find the sheets warm. What you must do then is find a dry place and forget it. But the worst thing is, later, when the warmth has gone and the coldness of the piss wakes you, and it's still dark.

I turn again, to a dry place. No-one has seen any of this. I'm safe.

There's a big pump, working and working. A crowd of Netherlanders till it. The pump goes on with its work, the clackety-clack of its drainage.

Far off in the distance, a big ship is sailing away over the ocean. Everyone waves to it. The ship's hooter is a blessing.

I smile at the Netherlander working beside me, Big Mick. The pump goes clackety-clack in its drainage.

Soon the seabed will be a polder, and the polder will be a place to live.

The Collector of Small Town Secrets

At the local agricultural show, where it's obviously slashing down,
I'm reading a calming book after the incident with the bullock when
my fillings start tingling and I *know* before I've even turned round...
"The librarian," he greets me.
"Hello, Rod."
My rival from *The Belly Laugh* tuts. It sounds like a slate
smashing.
"This. A bullock did it," I explain.
He's got a tall girl in tow, about my age.
"Big one, was it, Kevin?" he asks, glancing round for scoops.

MARQUEE SLIGHTLY DISCOLOURED IN RAINFALL DRAMA

"Massive, Rod."
Rod the God looks down over the void of my career. "Books,"
he rumbles: "books won't save you, lad."
"Donna..." says the girl, offering her hand.
Rod mutters, "*The Telegraph*'s new cub."
"Trainee," she corrects him, in a whisper.
Rod doesn't react. He's working up to The Sex. Fathoms of
self-loathing to swim through – then he'll break the surface and come
at her gasping over his car's back seat.
We shake paws. When she smiles, it's unexpectedly tremendous,
it breaks tiny cracks in her make-up.

Rod yawns. "I'm mentoring her."

She aims a frown at my knee.

I can't help flinching. "It kicked me..."

Rod hitches his trousers by the buckle, like he's Nick Nolte. "A bullock in the bollocks, eh? Remind me: how long have you been in this game, son?"

"About eight mon..."

"Five months, and already on a Final Warning. Which means: one more incident and our friend Kevin will be as moribund as those *tomes* he lugs about."

"It's the same rules as Wrestling, except you can't submit," I explain, and am about to insist on eight months when Rod pokes his umbrella into my wound.

"First Principle: Confront. The. Pain. Of. The. Real. World."

"Ow."

"A reporter lives in the future, not the olden days. *Previously* is history, *now*'s old hat. All that matters is what's *poised to happen*. Is set to happen. Is on the brink of happening. Our readers crave threats. Warnings. They want news so new that it hasn't happened yet." His nostrils twitch. "Miss Mersea, exercise your clairvoyant faculty. Name that smell for me, please."

Donna's hand makes an awkward white brooch at her throat. "Its name is news," she tells him, as if rehearsing before a mirror.

He smiles malevolently. "The key principle, Kevin: The. Future. Has. Just. Happened. No need for sirens; the smoke's in your nostrils before the fire's started. Eh, lass?"

Donna coughs. "Like the `phone before it ri..."

"Not `phones. Sirens."

It feels as if Rod might start. Talking. In. Short. Sentences. Again. So I decide to step in and prevent that. "I wish you'd been around to sniff that bullock, Rod..."

He withers me with his powerful journalistic eyes. "Bullocks. Bullocks smell of shit. All I care about is the smell of news. And mark my words: the air by yon marquee is ripe."

"For kicking off?"

"Ripe," he says, striding away, little arms pumping.

Donna hesitates. "I... Are you...?"

I reach for my knee.

"Oh! Your injury... you ought to..."

"See a doctor?" I shrug, slightly American. "It's just a flesh wound."

"Farmhands," I add enigmatically.

Long pieces of rain stripe our faces. Donna studies the line of Rod's footprints. Their completely straight line. The marquee smells of trouble, even to me, even from here.

It's set to be at the centre of a storm.

"He... he *knows*," says Donna.

I nod, but turn to leave anyway. There's no point trying to scoop Rod the God. They call him the News Factory. Where Rod goes, news follows – just as it skulks into bushes when it spots me.

Besides, I don't like News.

News stinks.

I hobble away like Alan Ladd, willing my leg to take on increasingly American dimensions of pain. Around me, thin bitter trails of losers trickle into the mud: *"Not properly tethered! I were tethering goats before that judge were born!"*

When I turn, Donna has reached the end of Rod's footprints, is waving uncertainly, lifting the marquee's cape. She disappears under a sign that says: GUINEA PIGS: CONVENE AT 1.30 P.M.

Wet-haired stall-tenders fuss over surprised-looking cauliflowers, lost children dawdle in a caravan. I soak it all up, using various clairvoyant faculties, giving a wide berth to the larger animals and anything that looks like it might fall on me.

The world smells of imminent sirens.

*

En route to the office, I stop at Mr Death's to pick up The Cremations: blank accounts of how certain citizens got to be blowing around in the town's gutters.

"I'd appreciate a little more... prominence this week," says Mr Death.

"I'll have a word," I promise, beating it. Quick. Choply Choply (as Bill puts it). There are long shapes under covers in the back room.

*

The first word Bill says is, "And?"
I tell him about the bullock.
"But did anything *happen*, lad?"
"Yes. No. Well, except... these farmhands..."
Bill comes up close and breathes ham on me. He doesn't say anything. He just breathes ham on me.

*

So I'm on the trudge again, up the hill, to interview the HERO who PLUCKED a pensioner from an ICY CANAL.
THE HERO scratches his head. "Hero. I'm a grocer." He has dry hands, which he rasps as I work The Miracle Angle. "His number weren't up, that's all. It's a crowded country – tha just needs to shout. Some bugger'll have his ears peeled."
He is not just a HERO, he is a MODEST HERO.

*

Down the hill, my last call is on a scary-faced ex-mercenary called Billiards Eric, who runs the local snooker hall. He hands me lank slices of paper, barely looking up. My soft youth disgusts him. He never speaks, and smells of potato hash.
If I devote the next thirty years to grinding myself into pieces, Billiards Eric will respect me.
"You bastard," I mutter, and I actually think of going back in and punching him. Except most likely he'll be on the toilet. And I have small hands.
Through alleys dazed by clouds, I make my grey-jacketed way to the office, watching mothers in saris tug their giggling daughters

to town. Pink and lemon, pearl and silk.
They're trying to glow, trying to light this place...

*

Way back whenever, in the good old days, local newspaper journalists
wore tight black clips on the upper arm of one sleeve of their white
shirts and sun-visors on foreheads that glinted with a single bead of
perspiration.

Maybe they, like me, limped through persistent drizzle with the
results of poorly-attended contests for massive animals. But they held
the front page, and they were hard-pressed, and they did the right thing.

George Willard, for example. George Willard in *Winesburg,
Ohio* by the great American author, Sherwood Anderson.

George Willard.

*

Back at the office, I take a sign off the News Editor's desk that says
WIFE'S FISH. I have no idea why I do this. I hide it under old
domino results, sit down, bang my bad knee, and start writing.

"Any nearer, Kevin?" asks the News Editor.

"Coming up."

"Because you know we're behind..."

"Yes, Bill."

MASSIVE ANIMAL SKEWERS REPORTER – INTER-BRED FARMHANDS SENTENCED TO DEATH

I cross that one out, too.

In the distance, sirens whoop. I think about Rod. If things go
well in my career, I will become Rod.

When the sirens intensify Bill goes to the window and looks
out, hands on hips. "Call the fuzz, will you, Arthur," he urges the
Chief Reporter.

Arthur's hands crawl over a keyboard. He's as deaf as a post.

If I don't become Rod, I will become his counterpart on our newspaper. I will become Arthur. If I become Arthur, I will:

1.) Compensate for centuries of bachelorhood with a small fancy cake on Wednesdays.

3.) Say, "Eeee. What a bracing morning" every morning.

5.) Talk longingly about East Anglia at oddly inappropriate moments.

4.) Lose the ability to count.

6.) Spill lunch on my cardigan, and study this daily spillage, on every occasion, with surprise.

7.) Never have any sex for decades, and be proud of the fact.

Sex is what separates the rival Chief Reporters, Arthur and Rod. Arthur greatly disapproves of Rod's sexual antics. He told me. He said, "I greatly disapprove of Rod's sexual antics." In those exact words. Except he called him Rodney.

Rod tells me all about The Sex when we're in court, during quiet bits.

"In the newsroom, Kevin. Against the desk. The bloody desk."

"Erm, the magistrate is..."

"Gasping. For. It. And I gave it to her. Because that's the First Principle in this game, isn't it, Kevin?"

"Er... yes ..."

The sex. Eh? The bloody sex.

Rod knows I've never done it, The Sex. He can smell it with his nose: "And I'll tell you this, lad: no-one ever did it in a library. Or" – glancing at Arthur – "in a bloody cake shop."

I shut my eyes and see him mounting a cow in a cake shop. It makes my knee hurt, but I can't shift it, the thought of Rod mounting a cow in a cake shop.

"Kevin," the News Editor orders me, "open your eyes, Kevin."

*

After I've filed the story about the agricultural fair, Bill punishes me for nodding off.

All this is two hours before the early edition of *The Belly Laugh* arrives and I get the sack for walking away from a full-scale riot in a beer tent:

GOAT JUDGE CRIPPLED IN BOOZE BLAZE RAMPAGE
By Donna Mersea

But that's going to happen in a couple of hours, so I'm currently in the clear.

"Why me, Bill?"

"Because you're the cub, Kevin."

"I always do the loonies."

"It's broken better men than you, Kevin."

Hobbling downstairs, I imagine George Willard in my situation. He would soothe the loony. Encouraged, the loony would share a stunning moment of self-revelation. The loony would open himself to George Willard.

*

"Lights in the sky," says the hard-pressed man. He has wide eyes, and neat grey hair thrown back over one temple. "Hovering."

"Yes," I tell the loony, who I happen to recognise as Mr Charnock, the dad of an old school-friend, who isn't a loony, who's probably lonely. But how close those words are.

"And the creatures inside the craft waved."

I write the words *George Willard* on my pad.

Dust falls between us. Mr Charnock lowers his voice. "I won't be silenced." His eyes gleam. Tremors take his lips. He's reached the edge. Suddenly I know I can find a way to make him say it: "*Oh my God, Kevin, I'm so lonely, I'm crazy with it.*"

I am the collector of small-town secrets.

"What's *really* the matter, Mr Charnock?"

"Piss off with your cynicism," he replies.

He is Mr Charnock, the well-groomed dad of a school-friend, and he has mistaken his alienation for aliens. And he has stormed out.

*

The Last Days of Johnny North

Upstairs, Arthur, our deaf Chief Reporter, sidles to my, well, to my side.

"East Anglia, Kevin..." he says, through teary blue eyes. His breath smells of cakes from shops. Cinnamon and marzipan – sweet fillings squeezed onto cardigans. "Clarity of light. Immensity of sky."

From now on, I'm just going to come right out with it. "But what's *really* the matter, Arthur?"

"That's right, Kevin. Both the former and the latter."

*

At teatime I take my copy of *Winesburg, Ohio* somewhere quiet. To the old graveyard, which Rod calls Kevin's Office, where the book falls open at my favourite bit: *All day he had been making up his mind to go through with the adventure and now he was acting.*

This was because George Willard had received a letter in a feminine hand. The letter contained one sentence: *I'm yours if you want me.*

By coincidence, I also received a one-line message today. It was written in Billiards Eric's hand and it said: *Re. Errors in last week's snooker league table – no repetitions this week. Thanking you kindly.*

As usual, the presence of a book mysteriously draws Rod to my side. He screeches to a halt, opens the car window and croons: "Look, Donna – it's the Night Of The Living Dead. Ey, Kevin: heard about this lass? The siren of the sirens? Only gone and got her first scoop, eh!"

Donna calls softly from the dark car: "And yet what I will later recall of this day is your impressive disaffection from the world of journalism. I'm yours if you want me, Kevin."

Something like that, anyway.

Rod screeches away, shouting: "Excuse us, won't you? We've some mentoring to catch up with."

So now I'm left with an hour to explain to Bill how I came to limp away from the argument over the goat that provoked the punch which felled the judge who knocked over the heater that burned down the marquee that became my rival cub's first scoop:

"Gentlemen, it is as well that you are made familiar with my mission here. For, in truth, I am dedicated solely to the winkling of small-town epiphanies from the lonely and sad. That – rather than the tawdry gathering of news – is the reason I joined this great profession, and..."

While I'm rehearsing, I notice with my powerful journalistic eyes that a GHOUL has opened a tomb with a long yellow-handled crowbar so I climb awkwardly onto the monument, conjuring career-saving headlines: EAGLE-EYED CUB CHEATS SACK AFTER TOMB RAID SCOOP

At that moment, our News Editor races by the graveyard.

I wave the book at him. "Bill," I cry, "there's no need to sack me – a GHOUL has struck!"

Bill looks up the monument, surprised and fearful, his face red. "Fish," he gasps. "I forgot the wife's fucking fish!"

He pounds away, leaving me to wonder how someone with his breath can be scared of anyone... and why I hid the fish sign... and if Billiards Eric has killed people with his bare hands... and is Rod secretly sad because he can't get it up... and what's Arthur talking about when he talks about East Anglia... and... and...

My small-town secret is this: I know no-one's small-town secrets.

"What's the matter?" I shout as my bullock-skewered leg gives way, "what's *really* the matter?"

Poised in mid-fall, I've time to consider the ground as it rises to meet me, the weeds that will struggle in the hollow where I'll crack my head and later lie unseen, beyond the scope of even Rod's clairvoyance... where I'll spend the final moments of my employment, head resting on the book that broke my fall.

There in the graveyard where the small town secrets gather, in the shining grass.

Badly Good

We heard that lad's trousers from miles off. They used to fill up with air and make a flapping noise. He came down our street every Friday night in them: a bottle-green pair of bags with patch-pockets.

Bentley had counted the buttons on them. "It's a total of eighty," he told us.

"As if!" said Frazz. "You can't count that many buttons when somebody's walking past!"

Frazz had a funny laugh. It sounded like a horse. Everybody did 'Crazy Horses' when he laughed. It were the organ noise from that record, the one by The Osmonds. He'd moved up from Cheshire when his dad got a new job. He talked a bit funny but he were all right, unless you started making fun of the flatness in Cheshire. Or how there were only salt to eat down there.

"Them kecks," said Bentley, "have got between eighty and a hundred buttons. I know because I followed him."

"What, followed him, counting his buttons! Aye, right. *Yeah, bob*," said Frazz.

Yeah, bob were a way he had of saying the other person were a liar.

Bentley nodded and sniffed. "I didn't just follow him. I went out with him. So I had time to count them."

"Went out with him?" I said. "Into that club where he goes?"

Bentley sniffed. "I'm reporting the evidence of my own eyes."

Frazz shook his head. "Eyes, my arse. You never went in that

96

club with him. You've got to sign in to get in there."

"He *signed* me in," Bentley insisted. "He's a member. He uses false identities."

"False identities are sometimes a tactical necessity," said Wolsty. We all looked at Wolsty.

Wolsty kept his head down. Loads of spit had come onto his lips. He were like that coffee machine in the market hall. There were always froth on his face.

Bentley couldn't be stopped, not even by Wolsty. "It's like this. He sometimes writes down Brian. Then another night it might be Roger. He's got loads of names. There are blokes in that club who call him Bill."

"How come he's got all these names, Bentley?"

"I don't know. Ask him."

"You ask him. You're his best mate," said Frazz.

"I'm not his best mate. We just like the occasional pint together," said Bentley.

"O, yeah. Right, bob. Yeah, belm," said Frazz.

Right, bob and *yeah, belm* were two more ways we had of calling people liars. *Big belm* were another. You had to scratch the end of your chin when you said that. Loads of people got it wrong, though. They used to scratch their chins when they said, "Yeah, bob." But that wasn't it. It were up at Hollins where they used to do that.

Anyway, that night, Frazz decided he'd had enough of Bentley's porkers. He stopped the lad with the bags as he walked past and shouted: "Ey, is it true that you go for loads of pints with this lad here? With Bentley?"

The lad with the bags made a snorting noise. Wind was blowing through his perm. He had on a really ace pair of platform shoes. "I might go for a pint with him," he said. "I might, if he ever learns how to shave."

That was us then – laughing like Crazy Horses, Frazz most of all.

But Bentley just looked down at the flags on our street.

It were a bit crap, our street. It were built out of stone flags and cobbles. The cobbles were held together with tar. On hot days I used to put my fingers in the tar and roll it up into balls. It were hot quite a lot in them days, before it started chucking it down.

It used to amaze me, thinking how much tar there must be in our street. Bentley once reckoned he'd worked out the amount by rolling up one tiny little bit of tar and Doing A Mathematical Projection, but he wouldn't tell us the answer.

Later on, we held him down and threatened to hang his kecks up a tree, and he told us. It were over a million tons. But then he reckoned he'd just said that to stop us hanging his kecks up a tree. He said he'd written the real answer in his diary, a book that no-one was allowed to read until he was dead.

After the lads with the bags had gone, Wolsty started going on about his new obsession, the cadets and the army, as usual. I tried to change the subject but he got right twined. He started to frown and the spit came back onto his lips. And he blabbed on about the recruitment office in the town centre next to that place which burned down. There were a poster outside with a picture of a tank on it. "BE A MAN" or summat like that, it said. You could go in that office and talk about joining up, so Wolsty reckoned.

"They make you a cup of tea," he's aget.

I couldn't be bothered listening, though. The thing is, I'd have asked for coffee. It's what old women drink, is tea. I learned that from my Uncle Eddie. When he came to our house he always told my mum, "None of that bleeding tea. It's what old women drink, is tea."

But the day afterwards, I saw Wolsty sitting on the swings up at the park. And I realised why he'd been going on about the cadets – he'd had nearly all his hair chopped off! One pound thirty, it cost him! He'd have got a new head cheaper, my dad reckoned. Round our way, we all had hair that flounced out at the sides like it were covering up headphones. And yet there was Wolsty sitting on the swings, and he'd got these two greatbigmassive ears.

"Ey, Wolsty, you've got summat on t' side of your head," said Frazz, pointing at his ears. But Wolsty ignored him. It had got like he couldn't really look at you anymore when you talked to him.

"How come you've gone bald?" said Benny, this lad we used to knock around with. Benny weren't his real name. We called him that because he were thick, like that Benny on 'Crossroads'.

"I'm not bald."

"You are," said Benny. "You've gone right bald."

"At least I'm not called Benny."

"I'm not called Benny either," said Benny.

Wolsty scratched the end of his chin, sneaky-like. "If you ever go into the cadets," he said, "you'll need to go the barbers too, Benny."

"Barbers!" said Frazz.

"What do you call t' barbers then?" Wolsty asked him.

"Hairdressers!" said Frazz.

Wolsty said, "Call it whatever you like. But you'll need a short back and sides if you want to make a man of yourself."

Frazz did the Crazy Horses laugh and everybody went "Eeeeee-aah Eeeeeh-aah!" like on that Osmonds record.

From then on, though, Wolsty always used to be wearing camouflage, creeping about in undergrowth and stuff. One time I went to look at some pipes and he were inside one of them. On manoeuvres, he said. That's why he were crawling through the pipe. He had mud all over his face, and some of them green army kecks on. It were a funny place to find Wolsty, I reckon.

You wouldn't have caught me manoeuvring. I had more sense, my mum said. She wanted me to get some qualifications. "Aye, you'll not find many O' levels lying around in pipes," said my dad. He had a funny way of saying stuff, did my dad.

I told Wolsty what my dad said and he said, "Well, that's badly obvious." He were always saying *badly* in them days. I think he got it from them kids up Hollins. One time, Wolsty said the cadets were *badly good* and I said, "Big belm!" and scratched my chin and he said I'd got it wrong, that it should be *yeah, bob* when you scratched your chin. And the thing was, it was Wolsty who'd got it wrong! Just went to show what happened when you started going round with that lot from up Hollins.

If you ask me, he deserved some stick. He'd gone really boring. Whenever I used to talk about football, he'd say, "Actually that's kids' talk, that is, football." Funny thing was, he'd been a good defender. He kept kicking it off the line. Like, you thought you'd scored, but you hadn't, because Wolsty would have kicked it off the line.

Bentley, though, he said Frazz were tight for picking on Wolsty. "How would you like it?" he were aget. He were always going on about how we'd like it.

"Why don't you just go for a pint, Bentley?" said Frazz eventually.

"Yeah, for a jar with the lad in the bags," chipped in Jean Smindley.

"And you could take Wolsty with you. Because he's a man now. Aren't you, Field Marshall Wolstenholme?"

Jean Smindley blurted a laugh. She used to hang around with Frazz. She were only a girl, but her conker were a two hundred and twenty-er. It had been in vinegar for 16 years, she said. I didn't believe her, but Frazz got a monk on if you were tight to Jean, so I whispered it. "You never," I used to whisper. Under my breath, like. He could be dead hard, could Frazz. They reckoned he were once the cock of that flat place he came from. Cheshire, or whatever they called it.

Anyway, Craig Wolstenholme, that were Wolsty's other name, got right mad and he says to Frazz, "What do you know about Bentley going out for a pint? He might have adopted stealth procedures. In secret operations, discipline is the key."

That did it.

"Eee-aaaah," said Frazz.

"Eeeeee-aaaaaaah," said Jean.

And Frazz starts flicking Wolsty's ears – flicking them dead casual, a bit dopy-like. But Wolsty just sits there, taking it, not doing anything. Counting under his breath.

If I'd been Wolsty, I would have done something to stop Frazz flicking my ears. But when you think about it, if I'd been Wolsty, I'd never have joined the cadets. So my ears wouldn't have been sticking out in the first place.

It just goes to show.

Not long back, I asked Bentley how long Frazz went on flicking Wolsty's ears for. And Bentley said it depended if you counted it in seconds or minutes. "I know that, you knob," I said and he said,

"Then why did you ask?" and we started pushing each other. But he were too soft to start, and I had to go home because my mum had been shouting me in. She gets right mad if you don't come the third time. It used to be the second shout, but now it's the third.

Then, though, The Kraken Awoke.

That's what we called it when Mrs Doris came out. Mrs Doris was the neighbour from next-door-to-Wolsty's. They reckoned she had a seismograph in her house. She allus knew when summat were up.

That night, the seismograph must have picked up on Wolsty's ears being flicked. Because suddenly she were there on the street in front of us, shouting, "You lot! Belt up!"

It was scary when The Kraken Awoke. We all went very quiet and waited for her to go back to her Subterranean Lair, which she eventually did, leaving behind a faint whiff of pork chops.

And, meanwhile, Frazz – he were just pretending to flick Wolsty's ears and saying right quietly, "Wolsty! Wolsty! He hasn't got any wool on his ears!"

He said it so much, we all got the giggles, and then Frazz starts going, "Eee-eeeh-aaaah! Ee-eeee-aaaah!" right loud and I nearly had to go to the toilet because I were in hysterics and we were all going, "Ee-eeeeh-aah! Ee-eeeh-aaah!" and then Mrs Doris came out again and she were so mad it were unbelievable and she screamed, "Right. I'm bringing Craig's dad out to square you all up!"

We tonned it off down the street, even Wolsty. I don't know why he ran off, because Mrs Doris were going to fetch *his* dad. And Wolsty's dad should have been on his side when you think about it. But you can imagine what it were like in Wolsty's house. They used to have a plastic settee that got right sticky when you put the gas-fire on. It made a sort of trumping noise when you stood up.

You should have seen him though, Wolsty. He had this funny look in his eyes like he were doing an exam. And he's aget, "Perfect test conditions. I'm gonna run along them coyts." Coyts were what we called the walls in the back alleys.

I thought he might fall off, but he had good balance. It were to do with his eustachian tube, they said in Biology.

101

"Oy! Down off them coyts!" someone shouted, but Wolsty never turned round. I reckon he were a bit ignorant. I never said it to his face, though, because he were the second cock of our side of the block. Martin Pluverel were the first cock, but he never came out because of that infection.

After Wolsty had disappeared down the coyts, Bentley went in so I said to Frazz and Jean Smindley, "Are you coming to climb that greatbigmassive wall?" and Jean Smindley said, "No, we're going for a shag" but I don't reckon they were.

I went to climb it on my own, but they'd knocked it down. It were funny looking at all them bricks on the ground. "Oy! Stop looking at them bricks!" someone shouted, though, and I had to peg it again. You were always having to peg it off in them days.

The amazing thing were, though... the next day I came out of my house and Wolsty were sat on his door-step and Frazz were flicking his ears again, just like that, over and over, and Jean Smindley were pointing at the ears, going, "They're turned right red!" And they must have been there all night flicking Wolsty's ears, with Wolsty exercising Supreme Operational Discipline in the face of Enemy Provocation.

Or whatever he called it. The way he'd started talking.

You know, like, when your mum puts a tomato on the windowsill so that it goes red, well that's what Wolsty's ears were like. All red. Like a tomato on a window ledge. And Jean Smindley's saying, "You say tomato, I say potato" or summat daft like that. And it were amazing that it were happening again when you think that Wolsty used to be the second cock of our side of the block.

"Watch out, Frazz, or he'll do an illegal rabbit punch on you," said Jean Smindley. Illegal rabbit punching were Wolsty's hobby, or something. He reckoned he'd learned it from this cadet.

Then Martin Pluverel's little brother ran up the street, shouting, "Ey, you lot, there's a Dalek coming!" He were always on about Daleks.

"Piss off," laughed Frazz.

"Daleks!" said Jean Smindley.

"It's on Essex Street," shouted Little Pluverel.

"Eeeeee-aaaaaah! Eeeeee-aaaaaaah!"

"Scout's Honour," stuttered Little Pluverel, holding up his fingers and putting them on his chest. "These old women at a jumble sale on Steiner Street were exterminated."

"Big belm," shouted Jean Smindley, scratching her chin. I hadn't noticed it before but she had a massive chin. Happen it can grow from shagging. She didn't need to stick her chin out, didn't Jean Smindley.

Little Pluverel's cheeks were right red by now. He'd got to jumping up and down, holding his willy. "Scout's Honour. It's on Essex Street. I'm gonna tell me dad. Tell your dads."

"Eee-eeeh-aaah. Eeeee-eee-aaaaah."

Little Pluverel looked at them. His eyes were all wet and his cheeks had gone as red as Mrs Doris's when she chased us.

"EEEE-AAAAAH...."

Then I looked across and I saw that Wolsty were staring up at Little Pluverel from the step and his eyes were right wide. And Frazz and Jean Smindley didn't see it, but he started skryking. He did. We were looking up at Little Pluverel and then there were this wet all over his face. And I knew for definite that Wolsty were crying.

When he saw me looking, he covered his face right fast and legged it off down the street. He used to run everywhere in zig-zags in them days. He never ran straight. It were to get out of the way of snipers' bullets.

"Not down there," shouted Little Pluverel, "that's towards the Dalek!"

"Eee-eeee-aaaah. Eeee-eeee-aaaah."

Wolsty's zig-zagging made Frazz laugh even harder, and Jean Smindley, she were so tired from laughing that she couldn't even do the Crazy Horses noise.

Then I noticed Bentley, and he were watching Wolsty run down the street, and there was this look on his face like he might skryking too.

Everything had gone right weird. And there were so much noise.

"Frazz," Bentley was going, "Frazz, my mum says we're not

to be tight with Wolsty. Because he's having a bad do with his nerves. Honest, Frazz..."

"Eeee-eeee-aaaah. Eeee-eeeh-aaaah."

Wolsty disappeared round the corner. He never came back for two nights. It were in all the papers. He slept up on that greatbigmassive hill at the top of our street. They reckoned he might have been murdered. Just goes to show. Afterwards, though, I heard he'd built a lean-to and slept in that. Survival In The Wilds, or summat. He had all sorts of oxygen tablets and knives and stuff. From what I've heard, he filleted sticklebacks and trapped loads of grass snakes and cooked them on a fire. This one lad, Philip Frankland-Henderson – he were right weird, he had about eight names – he reckoned that Wolsty had discovered a Trojan helmet under the earth, but we never found out if it were true, because Wolsty stopped coming to school. He didn't even go to the army cadets anymore. He just stayed in the house. My Uncle Eddie reckoned he were stuck to that plastic settee of theirs.

Next time I saw Wolsty, it were just before he moved. He looked straight ahead and walked past. A bit ignorant, like. He were, sort of, marching down the pavement, making his arms go high and low.

"Charming," I said when he ignored me.

He never looked back. It made feel a bit mad, but there were nowt I could do, because I heard my mum shouting.

"Billy!"

I waited for her to shout again.

"Billy!"

One more time...

"Billy!"

I rubbed that scab on my knee. I were thinking about Wolsty, about how he never talked to me anymore, not even about football.

Soon afterwards, him and his family moved down to North Wales. I always used to think of Wolsty talking Welsh and playing rugby. I asked Bentley if they had special Welsh army cadets and he said, "Well, that's badly obvious" and it made me right mad to think that everybody were talking like Wolsty even after he'd moved thousands of miles away or whatever it was.

But I never saw him again and I hope it isn't true that he ended up in a hospital, like Frazz says. If it is, I might go and take him some flowers when I'm old. Either that or some leeks. Because that's what they eat down there, so I've heard, in Wales, where Wolsty's gone.

Lucifer Brings Light

Even as their taxi rounded the mountain road's umpteenth pot-holed bend and they saw the anvil-headed cloud rising above the trailhead, even before they'd strapped on their over-packed rucksacks, Jane was waiting for it...

... waiting as the driver aimed his rusting cab into the road's last gouge and she shuddered against her husband...

... waiting as Derek settled further along the back seat, and frowned – as he had for a week. As he continued to do now, while shelling out a thin sheath of Bulgarian lev to the driver.

That's what you did with Derek – waited, until the mood broke.

She watched him step away from the taxi, onto the loose stones of the path.

"This tosser could have killed us, you know," he hissed as he brushed by. "Sent us over a bloody precipice!"

Their cab driver shook his head, spat into the dust. His eyes were trained on the hills – hills once part of the Iron Curtain, which still marked an uneasy transition between East and West.

He hadn't counted the cash, didn't even seem to register it.

"Thank you!" Jane called.

He looked at her suddenly.

"For the ride," she said, pressing more lev into his hand. "We hike there," she mimed, voice climbing to a question. "Hiking? On the border?"

106

The taxi driver shook his head. "Bad peoples," was all he said, quietly, to the ground, in English.

Jane hurried away.

When she glanced back, the man did something strange. He put a forefinger to his arm, shyly mimicking the movement of a needle into a vein.

"Derek!" she called, quickening her pace, stumbling over rocks.

Ahead, her husband went on lumbering over the stones.

Take it, she thought.

Take whatever is sent: take Derek's moods and mad taxi rides. Take floods and rock-falls and bad peoples and all the other thrills that Bulgaria kept pushing into her face.

When she looked back, the taxi driver had gone, his cab a tiny cloud on the flanks of that great mountain.

*

Later, when her eyes wandered beyond the path, Jane felt a tingle of excitement at the sight of the clouds' anvil continuing to rise and darken.

"Look!" she pointed, but the blood of her husband's mood was still on him. She stared at the points of the anvil, risen like horns. It was no longer possible to out-run the storm. Lightning would lash the mountains.

With child-like resolve, Jane calmed herself by piecing together a face in the sky, the face of the ancient thunder god whose name lived on in these stern ridges.

"Pirin," she said to herself, the name like a taste in her mouth.

A shiver passed over her tanned skin. Old gods, strange places. Maybe that was why she'd chucked up her job, why she'd dragged Derek here to the Pirin Mountains. For wildness and danger and risk. To shake them out of their seven-year torpor by looking for signs of Jane's ancestors in the country they were said to have fled.

But on the second week Derek was already more shaken by the primitive toilets and stale mountain shelters than by Bulgaria's monasteries and high valleys – shaken by the lack of awe he discovered he felt for endless religious icons...

"... not to mention *constant bloody cheese*," he'd raged in the taxi.

At first Jane thought he'd meant it as another cryptic reference to poverty – to the shock and guilt of seeing peasants in shell-suits hand-harvesting hay on motorway roundabouts.

But, no, Derek really did mean cheese:

"Cheese on salads. Cheese on chips. Cheese on other kinds of cheese. Stay here, we'll die of coronaries before we're 40..."

"The Bulgarian word for cheese is *sereni*," she'd said quietly. But she kept her peace – looked out from the taxi, thinking: The driver knows more English than he's letting on – this isn't recklessness, it's vengeance. Vengeance on our wealth and cruelty, on the insults to his *sereni*. Vengeance on the bad peoples.

And that strange feeling had flickered again in her chest as the taxi veered across the mountain road and she stared into an abyss of rocks, thinking, This is it, *I'm alive.*

However, as so often before, she found no way through Derek's mood, no means of communicating her excitement. Their marriage was like these mountains: from the distance, a clean line. Close at hand, confused and broken.

Her eyes scanned the high passes, where Bulgaria toppled towards the Greek frontier. Beyond was the former military area, a sterile zone in which NATO forces had long ago levelled the tiny villages and laced the narrow lanes with wire.

Lately, the troops had given way to customs officers and drug squads, who stared out from flimsy booths, their dogs tense on leashes.

The tank traps lay under weeds. Kingfishers and storks stalked the banks of shining rivers.

Now the border's noise was generated not by jeeps but by crowds of Bulgarian women jostling to display lace curtains and handkerchiefs – skilful work traded for handfuls of leftover coins.

How desperate can you get? Jane had wondered a fortnight ago, watching the women lunge towards buses, hours of delicate work trailing from their hands.

She had looked back at the jostling crowds for a long time after they crossed the Greek border into Bulgaria.

Now, following a few days in Sofia, she thought she understood a little better. Desperation was a peasant standing in a busy city square selling a single bunch of lettuce for less than it had cost him to travel there on the bus. An old woman tilling the spoiled field behind a power station with a broken-shafted shovel. Two young girls tottering, white-legged and high-heeled, into the lobby of a British porn company.

People weren't dying of hunger, but life was hard. Away from the safety nets that Jane had known in the west, there seemed always to lurk another, unexpected level of misery, a deeper strata of pain...

... such as the knots of weary travellers she'd seen on the border. Albanian peasants? Displaced Kosovans? She'd watched them cleave to whatever shade they could find, and tried to guess their stories, studying the men's faces as they waited for the guards to issue orders. The traveller's clothes were scorched, their shoes broken by miles of stones.

Perhaps it was misery like this that her well-meaning workmates had been trying to protect her from when she announced she was jacking in her job: *There's a difference between being brave and being reckless, you know, Jane.*

She'd nodded as her boss spoke, appreciating his insight but doubting its foundation in experience.

When authority breaks down, organised crime takes over. People become desperate, Jane. They take risks they wouldn't normally take...

Later that day – her last at the insurance office – she walked out over the nearby bridge, musing on her workmates' advice, looked down one final time at the sluggish waters of the Manchester Ship Canal.

The old urge was on her: to throw her keys and money over the railings. To follow her purse, into the air.

"Jane," they'd said, "jacking in a steady job – are you sure you're doing the right thing?"

"No," she replied.

The answer threw them. Threw Jane, too.

"As long as I learn something from it, I suppose..."

"I suppose so..."

"Lucifer brings light," she said.

They looked at her.

"It's something my Grandmother used to say," she told them. "Some phrase passed down through the family – from the East, I think."

"Aye. Scarborough probably," said the office wag, and the moment was lost to laughter, maybe saved by it too.

They made Jane smile now: her hushed, cautious colleagues. Good people, safe in their homes, free from danger.

She stared at the Bulgarian hills, shaking her head slowly. It was beautiful here. Beautiful, not pretty. A place whose herb-sweet breezes whispered of ancient promises and sorrows.

Jane shivered in the heat.

High in the darkening sky, a golden eagle rose on a thermal, the slow coil of its ascent lifting it hundreds of metres with no visible effort. At the limit of its climb, before it plunged into the abyss, Jane imagined the bird to be pausing at some invisible summit.

Then it was gone, with one small twitch of its wings.

The air's pressure was building, playing tricks with her perceptions. She paused for breath, staring into the eagle's thunderclouds, fighting her imagination, finding that she was muttering under her breath, glancing back down the trail.

For surely no-one would follow them here? Into this wild, nameless place?

A lizard skittered away, seemingly disturbed by the movement of her eyes. As Jane slithered across a line of scree, she tried hard to hush her breath, soften her feet. "They'd have to be crazy," she thought. "Anyone who followed us *here*, into a storm, couldn't be..."

Couldn't be right in the head.

It came again, the evasive footfall that she first thought she'd heard an hour earlier – the sound of someone out of sight, holding back behind them, sculpting themselves to the mountain's contours, cleaving to hollows and cracks.

*

Just as Jane was on the verge of confessing her fears to Derek, a switchback in the path ushered the couple into a lush valley where the rocks turned from marble to sandstone, and oaks and sycamores sprouted in the red dust.

Soon, even the sky seemed to soften.

Suddenly the change was on them. They found they were talking once more, poring over the map, deciphering Cyrillic markers, pointing at symbols that could be isolated farmhouses or shepherds' huts – or their destination, the monastery.

"They built those bloody things so far out," Derek gasped.

"So they could contemplate the divine mystery in tranquillity..."

"... which is why nuisances like us traipse halfway across Europe to break it. If they'd built their monasteries in city centres, we'd have left them in peace..."

She smiled, despite herself. At cross-purposes, even after seven years, they could still work together – if Jane's will pushed Derek on, and Derek's stubborn pride dragged Jane with him.

"It'll be worth it," she promised.

But the ravines were soft and deep, and the path faltered among their fallen buttresses, and they were soon lost again, in a blind canyon.

"No-one ever comes this way," Derek said at last, wiping away insects, tipping too much of their water into his parched throat.

With a flash of revulsion, she saw that his anger had turned to self-pity. They had climbed too high on a crumbling cliff, where the trail was made by goats rather than monks, and Derek's vertigo had returned.

She set her mouth in a grim line. "This way," she said, but held her husband in place on the high rock-face as she searched the canyon for signs of their pursuer.

Below, shadows pooled in the depths. Jane wiped strands of

hair from her eyes, breathing hard. Blood swept through her legs, her chest, her head.

Unseen to Derek, she stretched one leg over the void, watched it dangle there, in space.

*

After she'd helped her husband down, Derek sank into the sands of a dead river, where the narrow canyon walls absorbed the soft sound of his weeping.

"Bollocks," he sniffed. "Bollocks!"

Jane cradled his head. Tried not to make it obvious that she was holding him down, out of sight.

Every sense in her body was stretched to its limit.

Footsteps in front of them, footsteps behind...

Surrounded, she thought. But by who? Who would follow them for miles through pounding heat, with a storm brewing? *Here*?

"Derek," she whispered.

The breath was shallow in his chest.

"The slightest sound could dislodge those rocks," she lied, pointing at the cliff-face.

He put his hands over his ears. "Where are you going...?"

"To find a way out."

He lay there, on the bed of the dead stream, his face stubbled with flies.

"Wait for me here," she told him.

"Don't move a muscle," she ordered.

*

Re-tracing their footprints, Jane searched for the point where they'd lost their way. The undergrowth was thorny, the oaks gnarled and stunted. She had to stoop and grovel.

After a long time, sweating heavily, Jane stopped and drank the last of her water. Here, the valley was striped and gouged, its narrow floor littered with huge white boulders – self-conscious strangers amidst so much sandstone.

Above, the canyon walls rose a thousand feet, roofed in by clouds. The clouds were edged with purple.

Now Jane knew this as a place of flash floods. If the storm broke, she and Derek would be washed away.

Around her, the trees of the forest hung motionless. The birds had gone on, ahead of the storm. In the silence, she found a strange giggle rising in her throat.

"Pirin," she whispered, into the canyon.

"Pirin," she called softly.

In the dead moment after Jane had hissed the name of that old god, nothing altered, not a crumb of earth moved.

Then a dark shape flitted through the trees.

"Hello?" she said, her voice cracking.

The shape seemed not to have heard her. Jane ducked low, shuffled forwards. About twenty metres further on, the shape – a small man in a purple shell-suit – stopped to scan the canyon walls, eyes narrow and tense.

Now it came, the sound she'd dreaded for hours: pursuers' feet crashing down through the undergrowth. Many feet, heavy and close.

She clung to the shadow of a gnarled bush, keeping her eyes on the man in the shell-suit. He had an unfashionable quiff, clumpy with gel and sweat. His body was stiff with tension, arms braced at his side. In his left hand, he gripped a small, thin package wrapped in a dark cloth.

When he heard the feet crashing down through the trees, the man started violently, his eyes wide and afraid. For a second, he froze. Then he knelt in the dirt as if praying, out of the line of Jane's vision.

A gang of men were rushing down the valley, shouting to each other. Now and then, they became visible through the trees, their clothes much like those of the man they seemed to be hunting: grimy shell-suits, dusty training shoes.

Jane concentrated on her breathing. The feet seemed to be all around her, breaking the forest to pieces.

Their quarry rose from his prayer, casting his eyes around the valley. A new resolve seemed to be burning in him, his arms now looser at his sides, eyes brighter and less afraid. For a moment, he stood there on the track, lips moving silently as if counting. Then he tamped down his oily quiff and plunged into the forest, and all that remained of him was the shuddering of trees.

Now shouting rang louder through the valley, and growls and curses. Rough male voices that didn't sound Bulgarian rained down like mortar-rounds from the forest.

Jane pressed herself into the undergrowth, relishing the coolness of the shadowy dirt on her lips.

Almost as soon as they'd appeared, the men were gone, leaving the forest slowly vibrating in their wake, its paths echoing with their passing, a sense that small creatures lay frozen in the undergrowth.

Jane stood up cautiously. Around her, wispy grasses whirred on the breeze. She inched along the path, absorbing the tiny noises, increasingly bold as she attuned herself to the valley's rhythms.

When she reached the place where the man in the shell-suit had seemed to kneel in prayer, Jane reached into the undergrowth and pulled out a long, thin package whose cloth covering was smeared with sweat and dust, and oil from his quiff.

Inside, someone had packed greyish white powder, which she thought was probably heroin, and a crude, hand-drawn map.

Jane knelt by the tree, as the man had done, almost laughing at the ineptitude of the hiding place. Then she slipped the package into the pocket of her hiking jacket. It seemed an easy thing to do. She put the crumpled map there too.

Her chest heaved. Tiny birds tinkled over the high branches.

In a thrice, she was gone again, back down the path, heart loud in her chest, the faces of her workmates blaring like lights in her eyes.

*

She found Derek huddled under the bush where she had ordered him to wait. He was locked in a foetal embrace with his knees. When he saw her, he flinched.

"It's me," she laughed.

His face took on a sour twist. "Where the hell *were* you?"

She shrugged. "Lost."

He bit his lip.

"I think there's some sort of gang in the forest," she said.

Derek laughed bitterly. "Oh, you *think*, do you? Well, I can do better than that. I saw them. A whole bloody herd of them, and they weren't from Cheetham Hill..."

"No. They were Serbian," she said.

Derek blinked.

"I think one of their mates must have double-crossed them – and we somehow got in the middle of the squabble."

"Squabble? Are you mad? This isn't a game, Jane."

"No, I know this isn't a game."

Derek ran his hands through his thinning hair. "We've got to get out of here. We're on some sort of smuggling route."

Jane nodded.

As they stood up, a gunshot sounded from high in the woods. Birds fell upwards into the dark sky, wings cracking like applause. Jane and Derek plunged beneath the bush.

Something was crashing through the trees.

They clung to each other.

A wild horse swept down the path, and was gone.

Derek wiped sweat from his face. "Jesus," he said. "Jesus."

They stayed under the bush, locked in their clinch. They stayed there for a long time. Then, as the sky's darkness was split by the first white flashes, Jane led Derek down the path that had been scribbled on the piece of paper in the package.

"Jane," said Derek, staring in amazement at the previously hidden village – "how did you find this place?"

Jane said nothing about the drugs, made no mention of the map.

The package seemed to burn against her skin, a small scorched place on her breast.

*

After they'd booked into a small hotel, where the owner touched their shoulders fondly and ushered them into a small, clean room, they lay down on the wonky beds, arms to their foreheads, both of them silent for a time.

Then, still without speaking, Derek padded wearily to the bathroom and Jane heard the sound of him cursing the plumbing.

She sat up, smiling faintly, glad of the linen. It was fraying at the seams, but clean and white, and seemed luxurious after a few days in mountain huts.

Outside, the thunder was close now. The air tasted faintly of metal. She went to the balcony to watch the lightning, then drew back as she was about to throw open the shutters.

A line of shell-suited men passed down the dirt-street beneath their window. The men were silent, chests heaving, black hair speckled with red and white dust.

She stood at the curtain, peeping through a tiny crack, listening to the faltering sound of Derek's shower, watching the men move away.

Later, she and her husband drank cold beer on their beds, looking out over the sandstone ravine that broke the settlement in two, and they watched the fall of a terrifying rain.

It crashed in spears over the tin awnings and ran in red torrents down the ravine. And boulders the size of horses came down on the flood, and a horse, an actual horse, brown and soft, a horse that smeared itself over the boulders, and swirled away – until, at last, a small bridge was washed out, and the rain stopped.

In the lull, Derek and Jane splashed through puddles to a terrace, where a silent waiter wiped water from the plastic seats and the ground was full of broken trees and the air was ripe with wet soil and leaves.

"Jane..." said Derek, voice quiet in the cool air.

She pulled strings of cheese from her plate with a fork.

"Tomorrow... tomorrow can we get out of here?" He cast his hands across the village, where waters still poured down the valley's red throat.

She twiddled the fork, pushing her toes against the package that now lay concealed in the dirt by her foot.

He looked into her eyes, waiting.

She thought: Tomorrow I'll put the package in the bin. No-one will ever know I found it.

But her chest went on fluttering.

"Please," said Derek. His eyes had an unappealing, beseeching quality, as if looking up at her from the bottom of a cliff.

How long had it been since her heart had heaved like this? How long since she'd felt so alive?

She ran her foot over the package. Its heat still seemed to pulse through her toes.

"Jane – those guys in the forest... we could be dead now..."

"Yes," she said, keeping her toes pressed to the parcel. "We could be dead."

"So what do you say? Can we get out of here?"

She nodded.

"Do you mean it?"

"Yes." She tipped off her sandals. Under their table, the package throbbed.

She pictured the two of them at the border.

"Tomorrow we'll cross over," she promised.

"Thank God," said Derek in a quiet voice.

Around them, tiny points of light had gathered over the terrace – fireflies, born out of the heat and rains, that stayed with them long after the waiter had turned off the lights, that pulsed in the night.

Answers

Suzanne, the angel, sits by her upset friend, twiddling a pen in her flushed cheek, saying nothing.

Calls animals aminals, dances in the alley to northern soul, eats lollies.

"If you can guess what flavour this is, I'll let you have a lick," she tells them, and the long skirt twirls.

Her glittery skin, their open mouths.

They'd burst for her.

"Will you?" they ask, *"will you?"*

Suzanne, the angel, who doesn't pretend to like football. Has warm breath. Blows bubbles when she isn't thinking of anything.

She knows what they're like. She is capable of comfort.

"They're all the same," she tells her upset friend, putting an arm around the girl's shoulder. "They're all the same."

And she watches the wet tears expand across her upset friend's cardigan. And she thinks of blue sky and a tree she's never seen.

Her upset friend sighs: "He said he'd ring, Suzanne. He never rang."

They watch the tears spread from her clothes to Suzanne's.

"I've messed up your top..."

"O," says Suzanne, and strokes the girl's hair, and a boy calls her a lesbian. She laughs like a window breaking; he goes away.

"Will you?" they ask in the dining room, before the exam.

She studies them as though they're forks.

Suzanne, the angel, who twists her long white arms round the green railings of the playground and sits on a step in the sun and giggles.

Who won't give them one straight answer.

Says: "I HATE EXAMS!"

Looks out from milky eyes, declares: "Sod this for a game of soldiers."

"Will you?" they ask. *"Will you?"*

And she flounces to the bog, wiggling a biro at them, humming Dexys Midnight Runners.

Stays in a long time, comes out smiling.

Then... teachers in brown jackets stand in the hall, where a clock ticks, and the exam starts, and I'm next to her, and I don't even have to ask.

"What have you got down there?" asks the teacher, tramping creaky boards, coming along the line of silent desks.

"Legs," she says, and everyone laughs because the teacher's a perv. He skulks to the front, moistened, clicky-shoed.

She settles again, looking into her lap, ink on her hands.

Pens scratch yellow paper. Rain comes down the glass. Outside, cars bustle puddles. The places they're going...

She blows a bubble at me – Suzanne, the angel.

Who lifts her long skirt higher.

Who gives me answers on the inside of her knee, along the length of her thigh.

The Radioactive Lowry

On our way home from school, this bloke with wispy hair tossed across the top of his head says, "Here. You two. Do you want a toaster?"

The toaster glints in his palms. Its flex dangles down like a tail.

"Take it," he says, "take the damned thing." He has a pointed yellow nose that his voice has to bustle through.

We snatch the toaster, then leg it off, as if we're guilty of something. It's a family-size toaster. The cord dangles in the wind. Crumbs fall out.

On the canal embankment Mazz pulls up, gasping. "Jesus," he says, stroking the toaster, "what a creep." He pushes the toaster under some bushes. Next to an electric kettle.

"What's that kettle doing there?"

Mazz breathes deep. "It's in a safe place."

"Who gave you a kettle?"

"That wispy bloke. Yesterday. He said it reminded him of his wife."

We stare at the kettle for a while.

I scratch my head. "His wife must be a bit funny-looking..."

Mazz cuts in. "Don't tell anybody about this stuff, Ian. They might think we nicked it. We have to wait for a while now. Wait until the coast's clear."

"Like in a film?"

He looks away.

"But we *didn't* steal it, Mazz. Plus, I'm right hungry. Can't we get it out?"

"What for, Ian?"

"To make some toast."

"It's most likely bust. I mean, otherwise, why would he give it us?"

"Maybe it's cursed," I suggest.

Mazz looks up the embankment.

"My Mum thinks she once found a cursed candle-holder on a skip," I explain. "It was a statue of a little man, but its hands had snapped off. You should have seen the bad luck after we put it on our mantle-piece..."

Mazz growls.

"... but we couldn't whizz it, because that'd have been worse... so we put it back on the skip, and..."

Mazz spits into the bushes. "There isn't any such thing as bad luck, Ian."

"Then how come our dog ran away after we put that candle-man on the mantle-piece?"

But I can see from the tight line of his lips that the subject's closed.

So we go up the bank, through the comfrey and dock-leaves, and when I look back, all I can see is bushes.

*

At the top of the slope, we run into Mazz's sister, Phyllis. She's lugging some electrical gizmo over her shoulder.

"Shine a light," says Mazz.

"This slaphead gave it to me. Look," she says: "a DVD player. Come on, let's play a load of fillums." She giggles. Her hair's frizzy and ace. It trembles in the wind.

Mazz pulls me away.

"Phyllis," I shout, "what if it's cursed?"

"Ha," says Phyllis, staggering down the lane, "a cursed DVD player! Smart!"

*

On the way home, I get this sudden craving for toast. "Mazz," I say, "maybe we should go back for that toaster."

He blinks, hard.

"For you," I say. "It'd be *your* toaster, and I'd just come round for breakfast sometimes. And I'd bring lemon curd and peanut butt..."

"There's no way that thing can come in our house."

"Then...what if *I* took it, and *you* came round..."

"With the state my Mum's in?" he snaps.

"Oh..."

"After the divorce?"

His voice falls off to a mutter. He straightens his sleeves.

"I just thought – you know – your Phyllis gets a DVD, why don't we get a toaster?"

"Ian, I put that toaster under them bushes for a reason."

"Yes."

"And I think we should leave it there."

"Yes. But what reason, Mazz? What reason did you have for putting it under them bushes?"

"So we'd know where it was."

I'm about to argue with him when a thought comes into my head:

What I'll do is, I'll go back to the canal, after dark. Just like that. I'll go back through the comfrey and dock leaves, and nobody will ever know.

Which is a bit weird, because I usually eat cereal. I'm not even that bothered about toast.

But I am going to get that toaster.

*

So at half-three, which is when it goes dark in Lancashire, after I've said bye to Mazz, I double back, right sinister, going, Heh heh heh, this taste of lemon curd in my mouth.

But halfway to the canal, that door flies open again, and it's him, The Bloke With The Wispy Hair, going, "You, lad. You. Here.

122

Come here. Take the bloody thing" – and he holds out a pocket calculator. "I never want to see it again."

He studies me for a moment with his narrow yellow eyes, then shoves the calculator into my coat pocket.

When he slams the door, there's a smell of hair cream in the street.

I go into my pocket like there's nettles inside, and take out the calculator.

Click, it comes on.

122 minus 57 equals whatever, I'm rubbish at Maths.

So, I go to myself, *now I've got a pocket calculator.*

Heh heh heh.

Then it's off to them bushes, thinking of lemon curd and peanut butter and soft crinkly toast that melts in your mouth.

*

I'm clattering down the embankment, on the way to get the toaster, when the bushes start rustling.

"Who's there?"

Nobody answers.

What if it's rats?

Then hair pops up out of the leaves, and I see who it is.

Mazz.

"Oi," I shout, "you came back for the toaster, didn't you, you bastard!" and I throw myself at him.

His throat gets between my hands, and we roll down the slope, towards the edge of the canal, where lights shines off pools of diesel.

The water smells of wet dogs.

"Get off, Ian. Bloody get off," he's yelling.

But it's as if the taste of the lemon curd has sent me mad. "You got a kettle, you can't have a toaster too!" I'm screaming. "Give me back that toaster!" But Mazz is bigger than me, he throws me off, and I lie on the towpath, panting, picking bits of white grass out of my hair.

"It's not *your* toaster," I whimper.

"It's not *yours* either," he says, and we go quiet – just lie there among the crisp bags and broken bottles, looking at the box which Mazz was shoving under the bushes when his throat went into my hands.

Photos have spilled out of the box, over the bank – dozens of pictures of Old Wispy Hair: on hills, riding dodgems, holding pints.

"I were doubling back for the toaster and he gave me half his bleeding photo album," says Mazz in a quiet voice.

"I got this," I admit, and pass him the calculator.

Mazz presses the keys softly. "Who do you reckon *she* is?" he asks.

He holds a photo to the streetlight: it's a picture of The Bloke outside a church, new bride squeezed to his side, still in her fancy white dress. There's dandruff on the man's jacket. That was back in the days when he had hair.

"Look," says Mazz, and he passes me another picture: Wispy hugging his bride, now in a tight black skirt and white cardigan. She's sharpened her hair into a beehive. It rises to a fierce point, like one of those machines that digs through to the core of the Earth.

Behind them, a sign says: SUNNY VIEW B&B. NO VACANCIES.

"You could have someone's eye out with hair like that," I tell Mazz.

Mazz ignores me. "Look at these, an' all..." He holds out a tiny pair of silver tweezers and some unladdered tights, plus another photo, this one of a baby in a pram.

I run the tights through my hands.

"None of this stuff was his to give away," says Mazz.

And he throws the calculator into the water.

Plop. We watch it float away. Then he throws in the toaster and the pictures. The toaster struggles down through the bilge. The photos lie on the surface: Wispy and his blonde bride frowning on windy beaches, hugging in sand dunes, laughing on the ramparts of a castle. Their baby is wide-faced in its pram.

The pictures crinkle at the edges as they soak water and diesel out of the canal. They look like they're developing in a photographer's tray.

Mazz stalks off up the bank, silent, rubbing his throat.

I stuff the tights in my pocket, trying to work out where I can hide them.

*

On the way home, I pass two demented-looking kids whooping like Red Indians. One of them is stamping on a dressing gown. He's got the gown's waistband tied round his head, a pigeon feather tucked under it. His mouth is so tiny, it hurts to watch him whoop. It looks like his face is going to rip.

The other lad has a long thin head, as if he's being filmed in Cinemascope. He's trying to set fire to a pair of grey slacks.

"Geronimo!" they're shouting. "Ger-on-eeee-mo!"

That's when Wispy Head pops his face round his front-door again, eyes blaring.

"Stop giving me your things," I tell him. "Your things just get me in trouble. I've got a bruised nose because of your..."

"Not that, not that. Come here. Come inside, lad. Come into the house now."

"I didn't even *need* a toaster," I mutter, but he's already grabbed me.

And now he's pulling me round the door and down his corridor. By the sleeve.

And the worst thing about it: he's not wearing anything except a huge pair of discoloured Y-fronts that say ATHLETICO INTERLOCK on the waistband.

So I try to wriggle free, but he's holding my sleeve so tight that I just drag along behind him, my arms brushing against the corridor wall, which is covered with that prickly white paint which cuts your skin. Like the icing on a cheap Christmas Cake. But old and yellowed, more like marzipan.

And there are these postcards from hot places plastered over the walls: baleful donkeys and Spanish jugs. Plus, a shelf holding a

doll in a flouncy red dress – the same doll that my Mum puts over
our bog-roll so visitors think we don't use bog-rolls.

"Let go," I shout. "I don't want any more of your stuff, you
mentalist!"

Wispy doesn't say anything. He just yanks me into the living
room. Then he shuts the door behind us. And that's when I get the
creeps, big time. Goose-bumps, the works. Because now I'm on my
own with a mental case wearing only massive underpants in what
feels like a sealed vault.

Plus, there's this whiff of hair cream. And something worse.
Rotting fruit – strong-smelling, like paint. And some sort of *thing*
sniffing round my ankles. A creature pressing its wet snout to my
ankles and shins. Up my legs, past my knees, to my...

"Get off!" I yell at the creature.

"Nancy," he shouts. "Down, boy!"

I hear the hollow sound of a snout being tapped. The creature
yelps.

"Now then," says The Bloke. "Sit down, lad. Sit down." He
pushes me into a bucket-like chair. At least I think it's a chair. It
could be anything. It could be a mouth.

"Put the flaming light on, will you," I tell him.

"Light?" he says. "Not the light, lad. You've to sit there and tell
me what you see."

"Nowt," I say. "I can't see a thing. Because you won't put the
light on."

"Darkness, son. That's the whole point. Just stare ahead of you."

The creature comes back for another sniff. A dog, or whatever
it is. It could be a wild animal for all I know. He might be one of
those nutters who keeps tigers in the bath.

"My Mam knows where I am," I blurt out.

"So?"

"So I'm just saying: she'll come and get you if you murder me."

"Murder you?" says The Bloke.

"Or rape me."

"What would I want to do that for, lad? I brought you here for
a reason."

"Yeah, they all say that."

"Who do?"

"Murderers," I tell him, as if I've met tons of them, as if it's second nature for me to be sitting here in the dark with a killer of teenagers.

"Look," he says, "I think we must be coming at each other with cross-wires. I haven't brought you here to murder you, son. Or even rape you. I've brought you here to show you this."

"Show me what?"

"This."

I look into the total blackness.

"Isn't it amazing?" he says. "It's the one thing of hers that I'm not going to give away. The one thing of hers that I'll keep. How about that, eh?"

I give him a look. Not that I can see him. Or even know where he is. But I give him a look. In the pause, his creature comes back for another go at my ankles. This time I've had enough. I give it a whack.

There's that hollow snout-noise again, followed by a yelp.

"Eeee, mind you what you're doing there, son," says The Bloke.

"Sorry, it's just that I'm having difficulty seeing."

"Even with all this radiation in the room, lad?"

"Pardon?"

"From the painting, son. From the light pouring off the painting. Are you telling me that you can't see anything at all?"

"Yes."

"Blimey. You probably need your eyes testing. What's your name, son?"

"Neville," I tell him.

"Neville? You don't sound like a Neville."

"What do Nevilles sound like?"

He pauses for a minute. "More Neville-ish," he says at length. Then I hear a loud thud, as if he's walked into something. Maybe a wall. Or a settee or something.

"Did you just walk into something?"

"Me?" says a muffled voice. "No, I didn't walk into anything, Neville."

"Only it sounds like you just walked into something."

His voice stays low and muffled. "No, not me. I can see as clear as day. Because of the light pouring off that painting."

"What painting?" I sigh. The creature's come back again. It's going to get a bunch of fives in a minute.

"The Lowry painting, son. The radioactive Lowry painting. But first thing's first, son. I'm worried about your eyesight. You should be able to see summat by now. You're very likely in need of medical attention, Neville."

"Me?"

"Who do you think I mean? There's no other Neville here, son."

"There might be. There might be hundreds of Nevilles. But I can't see them because you won't put the sodding light on."

"If there were hundreds of people in here, we'd be able to see them, son."

"From this light supposedly pouring off this painting?"

"Exactly."

I nudge the creature away again with my knee, but it just keeps coming back. Truth is, I haven't enough energy. It was bad enough fighting Mazz. My nose hurts. My eyes ache. Plus, there's this effort of trying to be a convincing Neville.

I can't get the waft up to bother any longer.

"So tell me. What do you think is its most remarkable feature, lad?"

"Most remarkable feature of what?"

"Of the picture," he says. "The picture, of course."

"I think the most remarkable feature of the picture is its frame," I tell him, staring ahead into the blackness.

"More remarkable than the painting itself?"

"Well, don't get me wrong – the painting's remarkable. It's just that the frame is more remarkable."

"I think you're missing the point, son. It isn't the frame you should be looking at."

"What should I be looking at?"

"The four figures, of course. The mutants."

I decide to let this new information sink down for a moment.

"Yes," I nod at length, "I suppose that is more interesting than the frame."

"When your eyes adjust, you'll see exactly *how* remarkable," he promises. "Because it is the only one of Lowry's paintings that contains..."

"... four mutants?"

"Well," he says, sounding slightly put out, "*any* mutants, lad. To the best of my knowledge, there are no other Lowry paintings with..."

"... mutants in them."

"Exactly. But, as you can probably tell from the light coming off it, this is no ordinary Lowry painting. This one's different."

"Yes."

"See, it's the only one that he ever did in radioactive paint, son."

"Yes, it probably is."

"Which is why," he says...

"... why it glows in the dark."

"Yes. And why I'm going to keep hold of it. Because I reckon it's going to be worth a mint in future years. See, that silly cow thought she'd just left me the tatt. But we know better now, don't we, son?"

"Yes, we do."

"So you just sit there and carry on admiring it while I put the kettle on."

"Er, you probably haven't got a kettle anymore."

"Haven't I?"

"I think you gave it to Mazz yesterday."

"Who's Mazz?"

"The mate of mine who punched me on the nose earlier this afternoon. Because of a toaster you gave me."

"I can see a bit of a bruise coming up, now you mention it," says The Bloke.

"On my nose?"

"Faintly. Because of the radioactivity. The glow. Now don't take this wrong, son. But in my opinion you ought to pick your company with a little more care."

"Yes," I nod, "I probably should. But if you don't mind, sir, I'd better be off now."

"Already?"

"It's just the radioactivity, sir. It's starting to have a bit of an effect."

"Too bright, eh?"

"Yes. Very bright."

"Of course. I should have thought of that. That's why I'm wearing these, lad."

"Wearing what?"

"These protective goggles."

"Goggles?"

Somewhere in the dark, he coughs slightly. "Well, you didn't think I normally looked like this, did you? If I normally looked like this, they'd lock me up, Neville," he says in a serious-sounding voice.

"Yes," I agree.

"And actually, son, it really isn't fair of me to expose you to these high doses without goggles of your own, so it probably *is* best if you beat it now."

I nod, struggling up from the bucket-seat.

The invisible creature growls somewhere near my feet.

"Looks like Nancy's taken a liking to you, lad."

"Yes."

"He doesn't usually show affection to strangers. You must be a bit different, son. You must have a bit about you."

The dog's growl goes on, soft and low.

"Proper taken to you. Haven't you, Nancy?"

"Grrrrrrrrrrrrr," says the creature.

"Would you like him, son?"

"Pardon?"

"Nancy. Do you want to take him with you?"

"Well, that's very kind of you, but..."

"Done. Here, boy. You're going with Neville now."

A leash rattles somewhere in the darkness. Then there's a crash. The sort of crash you'd make if you fell over a huge unseen creature in the dark.

130

Nothing happens for a few moments.

"Are you okay, sir?" I ask after a while.

"Fine," replies a strangled voice.

"Only it sounds like you fell..."

"Fell? Whatever gave you that idea? Now, look, son – take the lead in your hand. This fella's yours now. Off you go, Nancy."

*

The next time I see daylight, it's in the company of a stranger wearing nothing but goggles and underpants.

Also, I'm dragging an Irish wolfhound behind me.

"So long then, Neville," says The Bloke, patting us both.

And that's more or less it, I'm off down the street with Nancy, going God knows where, wondering what my mum will say when I turn up with a dog that's visible from outer-space. Or possibly *from* outer-space.

My luck, I bump into Mazz again.

"Got a new mate then, Ian?"

Nancy growls at him. Study the side of the dog's head. It's long and daft, and covered in slobber.

"You watch it, you," I warn Mazz. "This thing's trained to kill."

He stoops to read the name-tag. "N... A... N – Nancy! But it's got a dick, Ian!"

"I *know* it's got a dick."

Mazz laughs for 35 minutes. He isn't just laughing at the dog, either. He keeps whacking me on the back.

"It was probably the radiation, Mazz..."

"Radiation?"

"Long story."

"It must be. A very long one. *Yonks*, you were gone, Ian. I called round for you twice. There were this rumour you'd been murdered."

Nancy looks up at us.

Mazz nods. "Yeah. Nobody knew where you'd gone. So this rumour went round that you were dead."

"Which you probably started."

Mazz shakes his head.

"I'm sick of you spreading rumours I've been murdered, Mazz. Just because your Mum and dad got divorced, it doesn't mean you..."

Mazz spits onto the pavement. "We *might* be dead, for all you know..."

"What's that supposed to mean?"

He shrugs.

"I'm not dead. Look – breath!" And I breathe out. But the weather's warmed up a bit, and hardly anything comes out of my mouth.

Truth is: I'm not totally certain I'm alive. I mean, what if everything carries on more or less the same after you've been murdered? Except you drag around an Irish wolfhound and meet nutters in goggles?

I've had enough of Mazz, though. Ever since his mum and dad split up, he's been right morbid. So I wander off down to the canal. And the two of them just traipse behind me in silence, a toss-up over who looks most fed up – Mazz or Nancy.

When we get to the spot where we chucked Wispy's gear into the bilge, I reach under some prickly branches and grab the kettle.

"Ian. What are you doing...?"

"It's what he would have wanted," I tell him. And I cob the kettle into the water.

We watch it slowly fill up and start to sink, its snout rising as it goes under.

"Like *The Titanic*," I nod.

Mazz grunts. "Except it's a kettle..."

"*Her* kettle."

Nancy lies flat on the canal bank, head slotted between his paws, eyes fixed on the kettle.

"It's whimpering," I say. "It knows something."

"Maybe it can remember her," says Mazz.

We watch the dog watch the kettle as it disappears out of our world, as it sinks down into the mysterious darkness.

Another Bloody Cowboy

Some builders had smashed up our kitchen and covered it with tarpaulin.

The tarpaulin shook in the wind, and sometimes rain came in. That was brilliant, when rain came in. It was like living outside.

Until Padraig's mates sealed it. "No draught through there now, mrs!" they said. "Not long now. Just a bit of plastering."

I asked why the worker called her mrs.

"The way some people speak," said Mum.

"Which people?"

"I don't know. Cockneys."

When Dad came home, he threw down his duffel bag.

Mum studied the window. "You could drop a feather down it."

Dad frowned. "The hours that lot spent, we could've glazed the whole bloody street."

"They said it wouldn't be long now," Mum told him.

Dad looked at the window, quiet.

I was hoping he wouldn't see my fingerprints in the putty.

*

Later on, when everybody had cleared off, I played Radio One and jumped about in the kitchen. It was exactly like how you imagine a massive disco, except you had to stop dancing to click the light on and off.

*

Next day, Padraig turned up with trowels and smoothers and bags of dust. Dad looked at his watch, while Padraig smoothed down his sideburns and stared at the floor.

Mum said, "Come on then, let's make you a cup of tea."

Dad skulked away. "Another bloody cowboy," he muttered.

Padraig had ginger sideburns, speckled with paint. He tucked a fag behind his ear, wore a silver buckle belt the shape of a bison's head.

"Gracious me, now. What a cough you've got there!" he said.

I didn't tell him it was because of all the dust coming out of his bags. "This cough," I said, "it's because we used to live outside."

"Aye," said Padraig, "there's plenty of that in the world, and all."

I didn't know what he meant. He had a funny voice, Padraig. Irish, Mum said.

"Like a Cockney?"

"No. Cockneys are from somewhere else."

"Where?"

Mum looked at Padraig. "Cockneyland," she said.

"That'll be the place. Ah!" said Padraig, holding out his tea and pointing at Mum with a surprised look. He always pointed at people who made him laugh.

*

After Mum and Dad had gone, Padraig spread out his 'paper, but he didn't seem to be reading it. He just stroked his tattoos. They were purple snakes, and he looked at them, stroking them up and down, with the sports page spread out on the floor in front of him.

UNITED IN FREE-FALL TOWARDS RELEGATION

He sighed. He reckoned United should sign a few more Irish lads.

"Fellahs with a bit of go about them," he said.

"Fellahs like Georgie Best?"

He stroked his tattoo, nodded. "An Irish lad or two," he said.

Oirish, that's the way he said it. Boison buckle belt – he used to say that, too.

"Fancy one, do you, lad?" he said. "A belt with a boison on it, eh?"

"Like real cowboys wear!"

Padraig got out his tools and laid them on the floor. "Aye," he said. "Real cowboys." And he stared at the tools for a long time before starting work.

*

This is the sound Padraig's trowel made: Shhh-shhh-shhh. Like wind in the grass on the moors.

Patiently, slowly. No rush. Smoothing the plaster, shhhhh, eyes glassy, as if the wall was gone and he was plastering a big invisible hole.

Padraig had a tune inside him. He used to hum it while he was plastering. He hummed it so quietly you had to stop breathing to hear.

One time, I tried so hard to hear to work it out, I was nearly dead.

*

"Dad, when will Padraig finish?"

"Never."

"Never?"

"Course he'll finish..." said Mum. "Honestly. Filling the lad's head with rubbish."

Dad pinched Mum's leg. She screamed.

"No, the cowboys have tied their horses to the rail and that's that."

The wall was full of ripply lines. "What horses?" I said.

"What horses," said Dad.

*

Next day, I found out what Padraig was humming.

"*Stand By Your Man!*" I gasped. I'd nearly run out of breath from not breathing.

He pointed at me with the spreader. "Ah!"

"By Tammy Wynette," I said.

Padraig licked a finger and drew it down his sideburn. "A musical ear, you have..."

"*Stand By Your Man* by Tammy Wynette," I said.

"Aye, kiddo. Tammy Wynette. Auld Tammy."

And he went back to work, going Shhh-shhhh-shh.

Except, this time, after a few minutes, he turned to me and said, "The world's a desert when you're all at sea, Billy."

I looked at him.

"So it is, Billy," he said, staring at the big invisible hole. "A desert when you're all at sea."

*

Later, when he went home, Padraig slammed the new door. It shook, as if it was about to fall out, like dentures.

Mum pursed her lips, but she didn't say anything.

Then the new door came open, just a crack.

A waft of air went through the room. It smelled of wet plaster. "Draught excluders," said Mum, to herself.

For years afterwards, that used to happen. You'd be watching telly and – click – a waft of air, and the new door opening, just a crack.

Then Dad always said his catchphrase: "Come in, Padraig."

It was my job to get up and bang it shut.

One time, my mate Kev came round and the new door opened and Dad said, "Come in, Padraig" and Kev looked at me like I must have a mad dad if he said that when nobody was there.

Kev thought Padraig was cracked too. "All he does is read the bleeding sports pages!"

"Because of Georgie Best."

"Reading the sports pages with his psycho eyes."

"What psycho eyes?"

Kev gawped, widening his eyes, wide, wider. "Staring at the wall with his psycho eyes."

We laughed, but then I felt tight, so I stopped. "That's not right, that, laughing at my mate Padraig."

Kev puffed out his cheeks. He had really thin skin, so thin that when he opened his mouth, you could see the light shining through. Inside, his gums were pink, the colour of a bat's ears. "Your mate! He's too old to be your mate, he is. He's ancient, that Padraig."

I shook my head. "He's not *right* ancient. He's 31."

Kev yawned. "So what? So what if he's 31. That's not the point. The point is – he hums. He hums daft twangy stuff."

"Auld Tammy's not daft," I said. "It's a good song, is that. You can ask anybody. She's got a good pair of tonsils on her, that Tammy Wynette."

Kev's mouth opened, all the thin pink skin inside. Then he shook his head, as if he felt sorry for me. "I'll tell you what it is. He wants to concentrate on his work, that plasterer does – not spend his time humming daft twangy stuff. Folks are paying good money for work on their houses. They don't want to listen to that rubbish."

"Who says it's rubbish?"

"Listen to this. Them builders have taken you lot for a ride. You ask anybody on this street. They'll all tell you the same thing. Any bloke who gives a wall The Evil, he's probably not right in the head. He's backward, most likely. Plus, he'll be on time and a half, I reckon. They'll be paying him time and a half to hum a daft stupid song!"

"Sod off, Kev," I said. "It's got nothing to do with you, that wall."

And I stomped off, mumbling, "You don't even know what time and a half means!"

"I do," he said. "I do know what time and a half means!"

I curled up my lip, carried on stomping and muttering.

Ahead, the hills were shivery and white, and they had dark patches of soft rock in them, where people had dug massive holes, looking for coal.

One of the holes looked familiar.

Then I realised why. It was the same shape as the bison-headed buckle on Padraig's belt.

"That hole, it's the same shape as our plasterer's belt," I told this kid, Marshy, who was always hanging about on street corners, reckoning he was ace.

Marshy looked at the hole. "Except your plasterer's buckle is bigger," he said.

"It is not."

"It is," said Marshy. "It can be seen on satellite pictures of the Earth, can that belt buckle of your plasterer."

"Bugger off, Marshy. Who asked you?" I said.

Marshy shrugged. "You did," he said.

"So what if I asked you? So what if it was me?" I told him – and that was it, off stomping again.

There were a lot of tight people living in our town.

*

Even at home you couldn't get any peace.

"Out from under t' feet," said Mum, dragging the Hoover about, banging into the settee with it. "You'll end up a plasterer, you will, lad!"

"Padraig's helper," said Dad, darting a look across at Padraig, to make sure he couldn't hear.

I should have told Dad – Padraig couldn't hear a thing when he was plastering; it was as if he was miles away across the hills, too far off to hear, with all this wind blowing.

Mum whacked the settee again. "Padraig's helper," she said. "Don't talk daft..."

Dad shook his head. "I'm not. Our lad's 11. Padraig's managing about an inch a month. By the time Billy's ready for leaving school, he'll be able to join in, cut a few corners. Save Padraig a bit of time."

Mum sighed and pushed me off the settee with the Hoover.

I traipsed over to the other side of the new kitchen, miles away, and carried on watching Padraig work.

You couldn't explain it to them – Mum or Dad or Kev or anyone. Shhh-shhh-shhh, like wind in the grass on the moors. And Tammy.

Padraig humming Auld Tammy, sometimes stopping to stroke the purple snake tattoos, or hoist up his trousers by the buckle, or pat the fag behind his ear.

Sliding his smoother down the wall and up it again.

Down and up. Up and down.

Hypnotising you.

*

He did finish eventually, though. I remember him putting down the sports page and taking his last glug of tea.

"Your mother makes the finest cup of tea in this town," he said to me.

Foinest.

"Get on away with you now!" said Mum. She never liked you saying nice things about her.

"Ah!" said Padraig.

He dragged his sack down the corridor. Mum looked at the dusty white trail he'd left over the carpet.

"So long," Padraig called.

"Bye," we shouted.

There was a bang, and he was gone.

Two seconds later, the new door clicked open.

Mum pursed her lips.

"Come in, Padraig," said Dad.

*

It was quiet in the house again after Padraig had gone. You couldn't even smell the plaster by then; it was covered in yellow paint. Our kitchen really looked like a disco after that.

"Dad, will Padraig come back?" I asked.

Dad nodded. "He will if I find he missed a bit."

I don't know why, I felt sorry for Padraig. Man United were rubbish that year, and Georgie Best said he was going to retire. He was only 26.

"Bloody waste," Dad said.

I wondered what Padraig thought about it.

Then Winter came and it rained every day, and I was glad we'd got rid of that tarpaulin. I never even pretended the kitchen was a disco anymore. It had loads of kettles and stuff in it, and you looked at it and thought: So what, a big kitchen.

Until, one day, my mate Kev comes up to me on that bit of concrete outside school and says, "I'll tell you what it is, Billy. Your plasterer's a murderer."

"Sod off."

"He is. Read the `paper!"

I started to run. Over my shoulder, Kev laughed and shouted: "Not the sports page, though!"

I ran so fast it was a PB, Personal Best.

By the time I got home I was gasping, like I'd gasped when I ran out of breath trying to work out what Padraig was humming.

Inside, Mum and Dad were staring at a photo of Padraig on the front page of the local paper.

"Let me see," I said, "let me see."

I squeezed through their arms and hands.

In the picture, Padraig had on a wide-brimmed hat and brown suede jacket with stringy bits hanging from under the sleeves.

He was pointing a gun at the camera.

COWBOY KILLER GUNNED DOWN FORMER LOVER

"Shocking," said Mum.

I looked at the gun. "It's only a toy," I told her.

Dad frowned.

Mum kept quiet, stared at the walls.

Unemployed plasterer Padraig Reilley yesterday pleaded guilty to the slaying of Oldingham supermarket worker Susan Flenders, 29...

Eyes flitting back to Padraig.

Second paragraph: *Reilley, a keen member of several local Country & Western societies, stood motionless as the charge was read out.*

Underneath the picture, it said: *Reilley in full Country & Western dress.*

"To think," said Mum. She felt the kitchen wall with her hand. I ran. I went up the hill and stared at the town from the moors. The moors stretched on and on, like a desert, and there was wind in the grass going: Shhh. Shhhh. Shhhh.

*

Kev and me were talking about it last night, and he said Padraig deserved it. Said they should lock him up and chuck the key away.

"Because he'll do it again," he said. "See." And he pointed at the picture of Padraig in full country and western dress. "Look," he said. "Look at his psycho eyes."

"Them are ordinary eyes, them are," I said, and I stomped off again. It was getting like a full-time job, all that stomping.

Going down the street, I had this mad thought about my shoes, how the stomping would be wearing down the leather, and then I stopped thinking about that and I wasn't thinking anything at all, just staring at the coal-digging on the hill, until it became amazing, how it was dug in the shape of Padraig's belt.

I tried hard to feel sorry for his girlfriend. But I never knew her. I wished he hadn't killed her. I could imagine she was a nice lass. On her picture, she looked right happy. Then again, Padraig always seemed happy, the way he hummed.

Without knowing it, I'd walked home, so I went in and slumped down on the settee.

Mum and Dad were watching a documentary about the Royal Navy.

The bloke doing the voice-over said, "Every six months, Ronny comes home from sea to fix the washers for his wife and mend the boiler."

Mum said to Dad, "Our tap's allus dripping. Happen you could join the Royal Navy."

Dad squeezed her leg, more of that carry-on.

The kerfuffle made the new door come open.

A waft of cold air crept across my neck, blew through the room.

We all looked round.

"Come in, Padraig," said Dad.

Voodoo Address Book

After she rubbed my name out of her address book, people saw less of me. I wasn't in if they called and I was in if they didn't.

Then they didn't.

I lay in bed with shoes on, on the off-chance, waiting. They were brown shoes with frayed laces. They leaked.

All I could keep down was packets of birdseed, which I laid on the dresser, just looked at them. Stupid budgie pictures.

Then I was sacked for absences, even though I'd been going to work, and, when I went to complain, before I'd even started to talk, my boss said, "Next!", and e-mailed a bloke about draught excluders.

After she rubbed out my name, the light started to shine through me. I looked like I was standing behind glass, but there was no glass – not even in the windows of my house, which was, soon afterwards, repossessed by double glazing bailiffs.

"I paid the mortgage," I told them.

But it seemed that all records of my bank details had gone.

"You bastards," I screamed. And they beat up the part of me they could still see – my ear – and then locked me up, because I was starting to scare children.

"I'm just an ear!" I pleaded, but the warder was searching for where he'd put me on his desk, and had become distracted.

Days he searched, under folders and magazines, as I slowly thinned away into the air, until I was the size only of a single word, calling upwards, "Please. Under the paper clip."

But by now, my voice had faded so low that the warder mistook it for his own paranoia and had to be calmed with large amounts of tea before submitting a written explanation of my disappearance and how it had fetched him to the point of madness...

... which is how I came to be here now, the size of a wished-away thought under the warder's pencil on an incident report form...

... as small as a gap between words, between letters, the inside curve of a comma, last flick of its tail...

... while the warder proofreads his report, deciding that *voices in my head* sounds over-dramatic, and reaches absent-mindedly for the rubber.

The Maker's Name

Saleem held the cricket bat under the strip-light in the kitchen. Light gleamed from its edges.

His father was solemn. "Linseed oil," he ordered.

Saleem nodded. His feet crunched across the gift paper. He imagined himself out of the dark European winter, into the heat and light of summer.

First, he would sleep beside the bat.

That night, under the sheets, he breathed in the smell of willow, felt the cool sheen of the bat's blade. Its handle smelled of rubber, thick and sour.

He raked a puny flashlight beam across the maker's name. The writing on the bat was a mystery, like its smell.

How many centuries would he score with it?

For many days, Saleem went through a ritual as solemn as the expression on his father's face, applying layer after layer of linseed oil to the bat, toughening its surface so that it would be ready when summer finally arrived.

Each morning before school he fired imaginary shots across the carpet. The bat gleamed like a jewel.

His father said: "A batsman is great in his head, not in his arms."

Saleem nodded. The linseed's rich smell hung in the air.

His father said: "Watch the ball. Always watch the ball."

He taught Saleem to wait in stillness for the ball, to keep his head perfectly still. "The eyes watch. The body waits."

144

Days went by. Summer was coming.

"Today we can use the bat," his little brother told him.

But Saleem shook his head. "No, Mohammed. It isn't ready yet. I'll know when it's ready."

His mother, Jusna, watched as he worked. First he dipped a cloth into the linseed and then he smoothed it across the bat. Saleem knew that the crushed flax would protect his bat. His father had taught him to sandpaper the bat after each layer. "Not hard. Sand it lightly," he had instructed him.

Jusna hung at the door, listening to the paper's fizz, studying her son's frown.

When enough linseed oil had soaked into the wood, Saleem told Mohammed the bat was now strong enough to take the ball's weight.

"Today," said his brother.

"No. First we have to make it soft."

"But you spent all that time making it hard!"

Saleem was as patient as his 12 years allowed. "If we played with it now, it would split."

Mohammed gaped at the bat as if he had found a flaw in the earth's crust.

Saleem took his brother's hand and guided it across the bat. He wanted Mohammed to feel its subtle knots and hollows, where the maker had worked with the wood. "Feel the grain," he said. "This is an expensive bat."

Mohammed struggled to break free. "Smells!" he said.

"Of the oil."

"So now it's hard."

"Too hard – it could split. We have to break it in."

"Like a horse," said Mohammed.

Saleem pretended to smack him. "Or a naughty brother's head."

Mohammed rocked backwards, out of the way.

Saleem said, "Perfect. If you moved like that on a cricket pitch, you'd duck the bouncers."

Mohammed giggled. "No. I let the bouncers hit me."

"Oh, yeah?"

"Yes. Look. Crash!" He hit himself in the chest with a tiny fist. "See. Not hurt at all. And that was even a bouncer by Wasim Akram." He rapped his chest. "Bang!"

This time he knocked the bat out of Saleem's hand.

The bat fell backwards and cracked against the wall. Saleem gazed down at it, unable to move, his feet rooted like a tail-ender's.

"I didn't mean it," Mohammed wailed.

Saleem grabbed Mohammed's arm and shook it. Mohammed began to cry, the tears as thick as linseed oil. Finally, Saleem had no more patience. "Get up," he commanded his brother.

Mohammed rose, wiping a bubble of snot from his nose.

"Get the bat," he ordered Mohammed, scared to do it himself.

His brother rubbed snot into his knee. He gave Saleem a terrible, hard glare, then laughed. "Here," he said. "Nothing wrong with it."

Saleem seized the bat and ran his hand down it. The spine hissed. He shouted with joy: "This is the greatest bat! It will never break!"

"Not even from a Wasim Akram bouncer!" said Mohammed.

"Or a thousand bouncers."

"You'll smash them all for six."

"I'm going to score a century!"

Mohammed cheered. Saleem dragged him to the window. They stood in a brittle shaft of northern light.

"There," said Saleem, pointing across the derelict factories and light industrial units. His finger came to rest on a green space tucked between broken allotments and a dirty brown mill pond. "That field, next to the lodge," he said. "That's where I'll score my century, Mohammed."

Mohammed laughed, then became serious. "But you said the bat wasn't finished."

"It isn't. We have to find the bat's middle. That's why you break bats in. To make their middles as soft as soap."

"Soap..."

"Father says a good bat is like good soap. Hard until you work it, then soft."

Mohammed turned up his lip.

"The bat has springs inside it, Mohammed." He feigned a shot, imagined the ball rushing to the boundary beyond cover. "The better you break the bat in, the better the springs work. You get a feeling when you whack that ball in the middle of your bat. Father says it is like a taste."

"A taste of soap?"

"You should not be disrespectful towards your father," Saleem told him.

But Mohammed had grown restless. "Why can't I have a bat like yours?"

"You will," said Saleem. "When you are 12-years-old. That's what Father said. For now, you must help me." He gave his brother a cork ball. "Throw it to me gently, I hit it back. You catch it. We do that. That's how we break it in."

*

All afternoon, Mohammed sat on the bed and threw the ball. All afternoon, Saleem hit it back. When Mohammed went to bed, Saleem worked alone in the back yard. He worked until the sky turned black and his mother called him in.

That night, he stared again at the bat, marvelling at the dark simple letters of the maker's name.

The letters were a signal to him from an unknown, faraway place, the place where the bat had been made with chisels and planes and paint.

He clicked off the torch and kneaded the bat with supple fingers.

His father had told him, "Your work doesn't create the bat's middle. The middle is already there. Your work allows the middle to reveal itself."

Now, for the first time, as he lay in the dark with the bat by his side, Saleem sensed where the bat's true middle lay. Slowly, it began to glow with his heat.

When his eyes closed, that same heat was flowing miles away

147

in a place where eighty thousand fans had risen to their feet.

"Saleem!" the fans shouted, "Saleem!"

*

In the morning, the summer holidays began. Saleem ate breakfast and went outside. The weather was blue and blustery. Gripping the bat, he set off across the wasteland between his house and the green field.

His father stood on the step. "Watch the ball. Keep your head still," was all that he said.

Saleem nodded, and walked on.

Mohammed chased after him, through trails made by kids and dogs. "My brother's going to score a ton!" he told his friends.

They struggled through the burdock and comfrey, shouting, "Saleem will slog them!"

Saleem looked across the wasteland, to their terraced street. Pale faces looked back at him. The weeds had already scratched his arms. He held the bat like a scythe, but he pushed at the nettles with his hands.

Finally the boys came to the mill-pond. Beyond, stretched the townfolk's allotments, their meagre turf picked to dirt by chickens. Saleem breathed in the acid stink that wafted from the pens. He wanted to register every detail, to be so wide awake that it became a trance.

As he walked onto the pitch, Mohammed and his friends tumbled after him. Dandelions furred their sweaters. They were quiet now, their faces set in concentration.

The players examined Saleem's bat. He gripped the handle.

Mohammed watched from the boundary as sides were formed and a coin tossed. The coin wobbled in the wind and came down tails. The teams ripped open a kit-bag. It smelled of leather.

Sudden gusts ripped clouds into little pieces. The sun made quick, dazzling thrusts. Saleem's bat gleamed like steel.

Wickets were driven in, run-ups measured. The biggest boys put their hands in their pockets. Some of them began arranging the field.

Stephen was the captain. He was Saleem's schoolmate, a serious, ginger-haired boy with patterns across his face. Saleem, he decided, would bat at number three.

Then Stephen's freckles puckered. A tall youth – mature for his age – with hair already sprouting above his top lip, had walked slowly across to them.

Stephen looked down into the grass.

"Number three is where I bat," said the youth, his voice as slow and sure as his stride. He had hard eyes which never blinked or flitted. Batsman's eyes. The youth was called Tariq. "I am one year older than Saleem," he said. "He bats below me."

Stephen shrugged.

Tariq stared into the kit-bag without acknowledging the other children. It was as if he had made the world into a corridor. The muscles pulled tight under his white shirt. Saleem noticed that Tariq wore shoes rather than cricket boots. The shoes were slip-ons, old and scuffed, their heels low, the soles smooth from too much wear.

"It's not fair!" said Mohammed.

Saleem shushed his brother with an umpire's finger. Tariq strapped on the pads and waited, staring ahead.

Each time Saleem tried to concentrate on the game, his eyes drifted to the bat, then to Tariq. He remembered his father's words. But he could not keep his head still.

When the first wicket fell, Tariq strode to the centre of the pitch. He did not acknowledge the dismissed batsman. He made one single helicopter whirl with his bat, then settled.

His bat was a wall of wood. It blocked, deflected, and battered. The fielders splintered across the pitch.

Tariq's hands were soft on the handle. He did not sweat, nor did he lift his head.

*

Eventually, another wicket fell.

Now Saleem's gloved hands drew tighter around the bat. The

149

smell of the bat rose up. He breathed the linseed like a holy scent, walking slowly to the wicket. He tried to copy Tariq's measured gait.

But he said *bad luck* to his dismissed teammate.

Mohammed cheered from the boundary.

Saleem was conscious of the stinking mill-pond. His heart pounded. The bat seemed a long way off – at the end of his arm, but far away, in someone else's hands. He knew suddenly that his head would move, that he would be unable to follow his father's one simple instruction.

As Saleem approached, Tariq nodded almost imperceptibly. Saleem took a breath, in admiration of the older player. Then a pang of resentment rose in him. Why should he appreciate one moment of unexpected kindness?

He took guard, scratching a line from leg stump, the way professionals did. His bat's first contact with dirt astonished him. He wanted to reach down and wipe away the stain.

Saleem was still thinking of the stain when the first ball came down. It beat his unprepared thrust easily. The stained bat was not the perfect clean thing he had cared for. He had lost something.

The second delivery beat him, too. Fielders gasped, the wicket keeper cursed. The bowler returned to his mark, breathing deep.

Tariq stared at Saleem, through him.

The bowler came back. Yellow light glanced through clouds. Saleem saw a diamond of blue. The ball fell out of it, a red apple with stitched seams, shivering. He saw the manufacturer's silver stamp. The ball hit the ground hard, and then rose. Saleem's back foot put down roots, his front foot moved forward. His head stayed still.

The bat was soft and hard in his hands, like soap.

Mohammed's childish shouts went with the ball to the boundary.

Saleem examined the red welt in the willow. He ran his fingers over it, feeling the seam's soft indent. Now the dirt didn't matter. It seemed as if he had recently been given a taste of something delicious which he could no longer recall.

Mohammed shouted: "Smack it again, Saleem! Smack it for four!"

But Saleem blocked the next delivery. His head was still. He watched the ball. He was calm, as clear-headed as he sometimes became at night when falling asleep.

The ball was following a track which came to his bat.

Saleem played the rest of the over like a memory. He knew, before it came, where each new delivery would land, and sensed, ahead of time, the angle his bat would make.

Over after over, he drove the ball across the turf. The ball glinted as it crossed the boundary. It thrummed through weeds. And Mohammed and his friends jumped and danced – just as Saleem knew they would when he reached his century.

*

The boys must have come out of the weeds. When Mohammed first saw them, they were thrashing the air with sticks, shouting in voices that sounded leathery and worn-out.

As they spilled onto the pitch, Saleem thought they must be new fielders. But they were hitting the air and thrashing it with their sticks.

Mohammed fell suddenly into the weeds as they passed him. The boys with the sticks laughed. Their lips were grey.

"Pakki lover," they said to Stephen. His freckled face looked puzzled. They knocked him down and stood over him.

"Mohammed!" Saleem called.

Sticks swished, the comfrey-field shook. Wind traced flashes in the long grass.

Mohammed was gone.

A stick came down on Saleem's face. He felt nothing, then a pain like cold milk between his eyes. The boy who had hit him said: "Stand still!"

Saleem backed away.

"Stand still," said the boy.

Tariq came to Saleem's side. "Hit him," he said. "Hit him with your bat."

Saleem looked down the length of his arms. He saw the red

welts in his bat, felt its power in his hands. He raised it, as Tariq said he should. Then he stopped, unable to risk breaking it.

In the time it took Saleem to lower the bat, Tariq's attacker had swung round and put his stick in Tariq's face. Tariq fell like a broken stump.

Blows rained down upon them. Saleem looked for his brother through gaps in his hands.

Rough hands pulled at his bat. He knew it would come to this, he was ready for it. He held on. But the bat slipped through his fingers, and was gone.

A tall boy with a dark helmet of hair held the bat in the air, above Saleem. His hair was glued with gel, a heavy dull gold chain swung at his throat. He shoved the bat into the kit-bag and dragged it to the edge of the mill-pond.

The others held Saleem down while the boy piled stones into the bag.

"My bat!" he cried.

The boy pushed the bag. It floated across the pond, then began to sink.

Saleem watched it go under, tears brimming in his eyes. The boys kicked him again.

Then they ran.

The wind blew. It dragged brown spume off the pond. Narrow cuts stung Saleem's face. He lay on the shore, staring at the pond, listening to distant whoops. He imagined his bat among cans and mattresses, broken glass and old fence posts, his bat settling in the secret underwater mud.

*

Mohammed found his brother lying on the shore. He put an arm round his shoulder. Saleem drew away, wiping tears.

"They have gone now," Mohammed reassured him.

Saleem said nothing.

"Tariq and his brothers will get them," said Mohammed.

The wind tore in. Saleem looked into his empty hands.

"Your face is bleeding," said Mohammed.

Saleem pressed into the gravel. "They took my bat," he said in a muffled voice. He wanted to press harder into the gravel, to go in, to disappear out of his life.

"The bat?"

Saleem pointed to the exact spot. It was fixed in his mind like a pitching ball.

Mohammed blinked, embarrassed by his brother's tears. "Under the water?"

Saleem remembered the hours he had spent, the sandpaper he had wasted. "Father will never forgive me."

Mohammed shook his head. "We'll tell him. About the boys. Their sticks."

Saleem shook his head

"Maybe the water will send it back out," said Mohammed.

Saleem said nothing.

"Yes," said Mohammed. "Maybe. If we wait."

Saleem said, "Little brother, this isn't the sea. It's an old pond. Nothing moves down there, it's mud."

Mohammed thought hard. "No," he said. "Remember King Arthur? It's like King Arthur."

"They put rocks in the bag," Saleem told him. "They weighed it down, Mohammed. It's sunk. It's sunk to the bottom."

His brother shook his head. "Don't you know the story of King Arthur? He was the king, his sword went into the water. But the Lady of the Lake found it. She brought it out of the water and King Arthur became strong again. The sword's name was Excalibur. The Lady of the Lake saved Excalibur."

Saleem stared at the dirty pond. He was angry, then calm. He laughed. Mohammed giggled.

Saleem rubbed his brother's hair. "King Arthur," he said.

*

Afterwards, Saleem wandered the streets, kicking walls, dabbing cuts. All the time, he thought of his father and of the bat settling deeper in the mud. He rehearsed excuses, forgot them, tried to remember again.

Eventually, he found himself by the side of the pond again. Twilight had turned the water grey. For a crazy moment, Saleem considered diving in, then remembered the deep mud.

A figure sat below him on the bank. With a shock, Saleem realised it was Mohammed. He scrambled down the slope. "What are you doing here?" he demanded. "Don't you know how late it is?"

Mohammed said nothing.

"Brother, what are you doing here?" Saleem asked.

His brother was small and huddled. He didn't move. "Waiting," was all that he said.

*

Each day for the rest of the summer, Mohammed returned to the pond. Even long after their father had come to terms with the loss of the bat, he went back there.

At first, his friends walked with him. Then, slowly, they became bored of his silent vigil by the shore.

"Mohammed," they said, "come to the swings."

But Mohammed shook his head. "I am waiting," he said, and they went away, twisting fingers against their temples, saying, "Crazy boy."

*

"Mohammed," said Saleem, finding his brother once again by the pond, "it's time to go home. You have to leave. The bat has gone down in the bag. It's under the mud."

Mohammed shook his head. "It will come back. Like in the story."

Saleem looked at the side of his brother's face.

They stared together over the water, until gravel and splinters had pressed little holes in the backs of their legs.

*

As it was growing dark, Tariq came to the top of the slope. He kicked the dirt. His shoes were grey with scuffs.

Suddenly Saleem felt pity for Tariq – for the best cricketer they knew, who didn't have the money to afford boots.

Mohammed spoke. "We are waiting for the bat to be returned, Tariq."

Tariq stared into the starless night. The sticks had left thin red marks on his cheek.

"Like in the story," said Mohammed. "In the story of King Arthur."

Tariq's eyes probed the corridor he had made of the world. He turned and went back up the slope, stiff-backed.

At the top, he spat into the dust.

Saleem kept his eyes on the water.

Tariq said, "Remember that day when they came out of the long grass – those boys who beat us up and threw away our gear? King Arthur is *their* story. Their story, not ours, Mohammed." His eyes bored into the darkness. "Saleem, you should have hit those boys with your bat. That is why it is under the water now. Because you were weak. Not because of some stupid story for English people."

He turned and went back over the wasteland. The long grass swished in his wake.

Saleem stared at the water. It was depthless and grey, like the Lancashire sky. He thought about his bat, imagined the mud. He wondered if the maker's name had been washed from the blade.

For a moment, he believed with all his heart that the pond would return it to him.

Then the feeling went away again.

He sat beside his brother, staring across the dark water, empty of faith or anger.

His head was still. His eyes did not flicker.

In The Path Of The Comet

It must have been autumn when he first started going on about the comet, although I can't recall exactly because I was having growing pains at the time and couldn't think straight.

Touched, my Mum said. Shatter-pated, she said.

But my guess is autumn.

In those days I was usually to be found slumped in a damp shed which our Head Master called the *Senior Pupils' Club*, pretending I didn't mind a tiny sci-fi nerd following me everywhere going on about The Edge of Known Space.

The shed was opposite our canteen and made a perfect spot to spy on Sonya, this lass from the other side of the valley.

When she ate, a calmness came over her, she nearly closed her eyes, and you could imagine she wasn't thinking of Todd.

It made me feel safe.

But, like I said, Mission to Mars always followed me, so the peace never lasted.

Like that day when the growing pains were making lights flash in my legs and he came up behind me snuffling like a poodle, poking me with his telescope, going, "We're in its path, Carl. Not long now."

The usual smell of tinned salmon was rising off him. He had on the normal kit, too: grey sweater seemingly made out of old trawler netting; grey nylon trousers, worn as shiny as ice; grey blazer, chewed at the elbows.

And his skin so grey it was almost blue.

In the canteen, Todd went on mumbling, stroking his baseball glove. He was close to Sonya, almost touching.

"Yep," said Mission To Mars. "Any day now, Carl." His hair was a frizzy black clump, as dry as a sponge.

"*What* day?"

He tapped his telescope. "The day it touches our orbit, Carl."

I sighed. Wherever I turned, he was there, going on about The Maverick Scientist Sir Fred Hoyle and Ancient Peruvian Batteries. "Is this about that comet again, Michael?"

"I get it, Carl. You're angry with your hormones again."

"No. I'm angry with *you* again."

"Because your goatee won't grow. Because your balls have barely dropped. That's why you're angry, isn't it, Carl?"

Rain pattered the window. I moved my chair.

"I know all this because I looked at your chin through my telescope," he nodded, tapping the telescope on my arm.

I studied the place on my arm. It was unnerving. He hadn't blinked since he came in. There was no evidence he'd *ever* blinked.

"I bet you'd like to study *Tonya* through my telescope, eh, Carl?"

I mimicked his weird little voice. "*Unfortunately, however, that cannot be allowed, Carl...*"

He nodded his tiny head gravely. "I didn't buy this for pervs to letch through, Carl. As you well know."

Silence fell between us. Dust swirled through it. Dust made inside stars.

"I'll tell you what it is: at this rate, you'll end up like one of Tonya's Fancy Men."

"*Sonya.* It's Sonya, Michael."

"Fancy Men called Kenny. Kenny Probably Richardson. Who's a fireman, most likely. A cocky fireman that picks up jailbait in clubs. Who preys on young women in their boob-tubes. And probably plays left-back for the Spread Eagle. Some stupid pub like that. One of them blokes: no skill, kicks it miles."

"Boob tubes?" I said.

"Kicks it out miles. For corners," said Michael, quieter.

In the canteen, across the car park, Todd leaned closer to Sonya.

157

They nearly touched, but there was still a space. You could see light through the space.

Kids came and went between us, through the car park. There was a small pain behind my eye.

That must mean my eyes were growing.

Flecks of dust whirred in the autumn light. I think it was autumn light.

Michael said, "Don't sigh, Carl."

"What's it to you if I sigh?"

"It bugs me when you sigh."

I sighed louder, to make him go away.

He said, "Very funny, Carl. We'll see who's laughing when it grazes our orbit."

"Yes," I nodded. But I hadn't a clue what he was on about.

*

On the way home, I saw Sonya. Sonya and Todd.

I turned off down the wrong street, where two little lads were shooting each other with ray-guns. One of them had on a red plastic cape. It flapped in the wind.

"I shot you," he said.

The cape-less boy shook his head. "It missed. Your laser's defective."

Cape-boy threw a stone at his head. "That didn't miss," he said.

When I went to help the other lad up, blood trickled onto my fingers. Then his Mum bustled round the corner. She saw my hand on the boy's head.

She didn't say anything, she led the boy away, staring at the blood on my fingers.

*

"Honestly. Fifteen-years-old. And that *leaden*," said Mum.

I slumped on the couch.

"Is that fluff on your chin?"

158

"Fluff, Mum? Why would there be fluff on my chin?"

Mum shrugged. A damp smell filled the house. I watched her ironing.

Eventually, though, it was exhausting watching her work, so I went to sleep. While I was asleep I dreamed I was in the space between Todd and Sonya. It stretched for thousands of miles.

*

The next day, it was like I was still asleep. Walking to school, I ended up behind Sonya. Sonya and Todd. So I turned down another street, past the allotment-gate, where two pensioners had been moaning about soil and rain since The Year Dot.

"'T' worse year I can remember."

"Aye, Bill..."

"Slugs. Flies. Blight. Whatever next, ay?"

"Comets, so they say."

Bill laughed. "Comets, eh!"

"A visitation of comets," said the other one.

They laughed so hard I was glad to walk away – except, further up the street, I was somehow walking behind Sonya again. Sonya and Todd. So I had to double-back.

Luckily, this time, the pensioners had gone from the allotments gate, and there was just a shovel leaning on the fence. The shovel's blade was wet with mud. There was a snail halfway up its shaft. When I knocked the snail off the shovel, one of the old blokes shouted, "Oi!"

"I were just knocking off that snail."

His face looked through the weeds in the fence. "It's not your shovel to *be* knocking snails off..."

"I had to double-back, though."

"Lad. Don't touch what isn't yours," he said.

*

By the time I got to school, I was tired from the extra walking, so I decided not to bother with the first lesson. I went to the pretend club and sat down.

Then Michael came in.

"That showed them, didn't it?"

"What did?"

He tapped his telescope. "Don't play innocent with me, Carl. I saw you knock that snail off."

"Which snail?"

"They reckon they own them allotments. Strutting about with their buckets. But the County Council is the official proprietor."

"What are you talking about?"

He tapped the side of his nose. "This is it, Carl. There are people *watching* old blokes like that."

At the shed door, he gave me an 'OK' sign, which he looked through with one little red eye. "I'll tell you what it is, Carl: I might let you use my telescope soon."

Soon afterwards, Old Mardy, the Geography teacher with the lumpy arse, came to drag me from the shed. "I received a report you were loitering in here," he said.

"Report from who?"

But Old Mardy was deaf as a post, he never answered.

*

On the way home, I stepped into line behind Sonya. Sonya and Todd. I was in their orbit, creeping through the murk, hiding behind bollards and dogs... until eventually they reached the cinema, where I joined the queue's tail, casual-like, watching Todd toss a baseball, checking the glove didn't touch Sonya.

Then Michael was in the queue, jabbing me with his telescope. "Smart," he said, "you've come too. Is it because of the surprising reviews? Because sci-fi films don't get good reviews, do they, Carl? Because the critics are biased against sci-fi, aren't they?"

"Stop saying Carl," I said. "And don't tap me with that telescope either. It's bringing up a bruise."

Michael shivered. I was craning my neck, trying to look like I wasn't craning it.

He droned on. "Have you noticed they've stopped calling me Mission To Mars, Carl?"

"Hmm?"

"At school, Carl. They don't call me Mission To Mars. It's worn off. They call me *Uranus* now. Because it sounds like Your Anus. Which is tight, isn't it, Carl?"

"Yes."

"But – have you noticed, Carl? They still call you *Sonya's Stalker*?"

"What?"

"The big lads – they..."

"Look," I said, "it isn't my fault if Sonya's always in the places I go. If Sonya and Todd are always in those places."

"That's what I tried to tell them, Carl. But..."

I looked at him, a tiny figure as white as a star under the black sponge of his hair. "Michael," I said, "why are you talking about me when I'm not there?"

"Well, they were going on about your goatee, Carl. And I told them they were tight, so they called me Your Anus. And then I lost it. I said it was none of their business if you stalked Tonya. Carl can stalk whoever he likes, I said. Besides, I said – she goes under-age clubbing, so if people want to..."

"Michael," I said, "the only stalker round here is you."

He stared up at me. "That's a tight thing to say, Carl. I'll expect you to apologise for that."

Thankfully, the lights went down then and the film started, some stupid thing about an organic spaceship – a sort of outer-space whale.

Light swarmed over Michael's tiny face. "Ppphh," he said, "pppppppphhh."

It was impossible to watch the film without thinking: *Mission To Mars is next to me. And Sonya is somewhere behind us. Sonya and Todd.*

Plus, the way Michael watched films.

When the hero argued with his girlfriend, he groaned, "As if."

Then the hero checked his watch and Michael said, "As if."

161

Whenever the hero walked or drank or just sat still, Michael said, "As if."

Eventually, he started shuffling in his seat, the tinned salmon smell rising off him.

Then a girl in the audience laughed. It sounded like Sonya. It sounded like Sonya laughing somewhere behind us in the dark.

When the cast were eaten by alien wolf-reptiles, I looked across at Michael. That and the shots of the whale-ship, they were the only times he didn't say, "As if."

My ears tingled.

The credits rolled.

Michael read the names and said, "As if."

On the way out as I craned my neck into the dark cinema, he jabbed me with the telescope. "Excellent. Night has fallen. Perfect conditions."

"Yes," I said.

"The film has whetted our appetite, hasn't it, Carl?"

"Yes," I said. My neck was aching from constant craning. There was a tight feeling in my chest. I was like an animal creeping out of its burrow.

"So if we go on the hill, we'll see it, Carl."

"Yes."

I went with him into the wet grass. And when he passed me the telescope to search for the comet, I pointed it at Sonya's house on the other side of the valley and stared at her window until the aching in my chest became like a white light and I passed it back to him.

The wind tugged at our clothes and hair. It was dark above town, a faint orange glow on the clouds.

"Disappointing conditions, Carl."

"Yes," I agreed.

I shook my head for 15 minutes.

"Very disappointing conditions," I said.

"I'll tell you what it is, Carl: with these clouds, we'll miss that comet."

"Thanks for letting me have a go on the telescope, anyway."

"It's the least I could do, Carl. After what those lads said about you."

"But don't go on about that."

"I won't, Carl. Because it's tight they laughed at your goatee. And called you Stalker. And criticised your unsteady voice. And called you A Late Developer. So I won't go on about it, Carl. About how your goatee won't grow. And how your voice wobb..."

"And could you try saying Carl a bit less, too?"

"Yes, Carl," he said.

We sat there in the grass, looking down on the dark streets.

"Light pollution," said Michael.

"Yes..."

"I'll tell you what it is, Carl: there used to be thousands of stars visible with the naked eye. And now it's dozens. Because of light pouring into the sky."

I sat there thinking about that, saying naked eye.

Naked eye. Naked eye.

Michael said, "When that comet comes back, we'll be dead."

I stared at Sonya's house.

Michael scanned the clouds with the telescope. "A limited opportunity, Carl. Then – whoosh – gone. Plunging into space, dragging its tail. Or sometimes the tail goes in front. A beard of ice, flying out in front of it. Imagine that, Carl."

"Yes."

"And I'll tell you what it is, Carl: without comets, nothing would ever have happened round here."

"In Todmorden?"

"Not in Todmorden. On Earth. Nothing would have happened on Earth, Carl."

"Please try to stop saying Carl," I said.

"I will definitely in future try to stop saying Carl," he promised.

"And could you stop saying *I'll tell you what is*, too?"

Michael pursed his lips. "No," he said, "I'll keep saying *I'll tell you what is*."

I decided to let it go.

"But imagine it without comets, Carl. The Earth. See, according to The Maverick Scientist Sir Fred Hoyle, that's how intelligent life started. On spores from comets. Flung out when they went past. Which brought intelligent life to this barren rock."

"What intelligent life?" I said.

Michael telescoped me in the rib. "Ha. *Intelligent life!* Good one, Carl."

I rubbed my rib.

Michael sat in the grass saying, "*Intelligent life!* You're a card you are, Carl. They should call you Card, not Carl. Shouldn't they?"

"Definitely," I said.

"Ha," said Michael. "Card, not Carl."

"Ha," I said.

We sat in the grass, looking up at the stars, saying, "Ha. Card, not Carl."

After a while, Michael said, "Anyway. If we miss our chance – if we never see the comet – don't worry, Card. Because it'll still happen."

The wind blew against my head, left a cold feeling between my eyes. Or maybe it was growing pains. You never knew what was making you hurt.

"What will? What'll happen?"

"The comet will spread its spores whether it's cloudy or not. And then the change will happen."

He was staring up at the sky, the frown closing his face to a slice, as if he was peeping out of himself through a crack in the curtains.

When he started droning about The Maverick Scientist Sir Fred Hoyle again, I stopped listening. I stared at Sonya's house, thinking: One chance. The next time, you won't be here. You'll be dead.

That was when I made my momentous decision.

All I needed was an opening. Maybe an accident. Say, I found Sonya underneath a crashed car. Then we'd be able to have a conversation. And I'd drag her twisted body out and we'd fall in love and buy a dog together. And take it for walks past Todd's house.

Michael's voice drifted through the grass. "I'm going to help you to get off with Tonya, Card."

I sat up straight. "No..."

Michael nodded. "Nevertheless."

"I don't need help, Michael. See, she's going to have an..." I stopped. It seemed I'd been hoping Sonya would be crushed underneath a car. "Please, Michael."

"Well, we'll see," he said.

We sat in the wet grass, shivering, until I got sick of the "pppph, pppppppph" noise and told Michael I had to go.

On the way down the hill, Michael said, "I'll tell you what it is, Card: when I grassed you up, I did it for your own good."

"Yes."

"See, you shouldn't be sitting in sheds during lesson-time. The County Council could come down hard."

"Right."

We walked on further.

"Some people," he said, "would have the manners to thank me for that, too."

"For grassing them up?"

"And letting people look through their telescope."

"Michael, thanks for letting people look through your telescope."

"*And...*"

"And what?"

He looked at me, not blinking. Never, ever, in his life blinking. "*And...*"

"And?"

"The little matter of that apology."

"What apology?"

Michael sighed. "You can't call someone a stalker and expect to..."

"But it's true. You're everywhere I go. Even that film tonight. Because I once listened when you went on about Arthur C. Clarke. About some stupid twigs that might have been Ancient Peruvian Batteries."

He shook his head. "You need even more help than I thought you did."

At the foot of the hill, we parted without speaking. But I followed

Michael. I followed him down the cinder track to the house where he lived with his Dad, a skinny little man in a dirty shirt who mended shoes on the market.

The windows were flecked with grey dirt and had been sealed with plastic sheets to keep the heat in. The curtains sagged like knackered old dishcloths. The gutters were full of weeds.

It was the only house still standing. The neighbouring property had been reduced to a shell, its rafters poking out, strips of wallpaper flapping like bandages in the wind. The rest of the terrace was a demolition site. County Council bulldozers had crushed dark tracks through the cinders.

It looked like the last house in the universe, like The Edge of Known Space.

When I saw Michael's Dad tapping away with a shoe-mallet in their kitchen, I put down the rock I'd planned to chuck at their window. I went home. I needed to think about my momentous decision.

But all I could think of was Michael's dad and his dirty shirt.

*

The next day, I got up early. Even if I didn't save Sonya from under a twisted car, I was determined to show off my winning personality. I pulled my goatee to make it longer and washed my hair. Then I put talcum powder down the front of my underpants, a trick from a dirty magazine. After that it was tooth-brushing for an hour to make my teeth look American and white. Like Todd's.

Next, I whistled for a bit. Whistling's good for your confidence. That's why milkmen do it. So they don't drop the bottles.

Then I was scared, so I put on my snorkel-hooded parka. Zip-entanglements or busy roads posed problems – otherwise, it was an excellent coat. Like a corridor on the front of your head. You could hunker down in it, nice and quiet, off the beaten track.

Then – whoosh – out the door. And no feet ever danced down that street like mine. Even if I did step in a lump of dog-track. That wasn't a sign, though. There are no such things as signs. Otherwise, we'd still believe that comets were omens and visitations. And comets are just lumps of rock and ice. They don't mean we're doomed. They don't mean anything.

"But stop thinking about comets, Carl," said a voice in my head. "Why are you thinking about comets? You should be thinking about Sonya."

"You're right," I said, "I'm touched. I'm shatter-pated."

I scraped off the dog-track, trying not to think about comets. Trying as hard as I could to think about Sonya.

*

I found her in the library, sitting on a squashy plastic chair, hunched over a pile of books. Her thick black hair fell in coils around her. It was quiet, just her pencil going sssss over the page. Ssssss over the page.

I put my hood up. But Sonya saw me as I turned away. She stared at the hood.

"Hey, what's up?" I gulped.

"Your hood."

I shrugged. "In case it rains..."

"Inside a library?"

"Flat roofs," I gestured, trying to get the hood down, realising in panic that there had been an entanglement.

She'd written in her exercise book: *The Earth's highest point is approx. 30,000 ft. – as is its lowest point. Since the distance between the two is only 60,000 ft., the Earth, comparatively, is smoother than a snooker ball.*

I tried to act casual. "What's that?"

"A fact," she shrugged. "A Geographic fact." She eased the zip from the fur. It took two seconds.

Her fingers had passed within a centimetre of my face.

"Free at last, free at last," she said.

That was when Michael came in.

"Ah, Tonya, just the person," he said. "There's an important matter I want to discuss."

Sonya peeled a strand of hair to one side of her face.

167

Michael prodded the telescope into my ribs. "Did you hear what this lad did up the allotments?"

"What allotments?" said Sonya.

"He knocked a snail off a shovel. Without asking the old blokes."

Sonya said, "Right..."

"They reckon they can treat the County Council like shit. And another thing: he told a brilliant joke. About intelligent life on Earth. Go on, Card. Tell Tonya that joke."

I stared at him.

"But the thing is, Tonya: I also want to warn you about so-called Americans."

"About Todd?"

"If that's his real name," said Michael. "He could be called anything. I mean, once you've got away with pretending to be American, you can..."

"But he *is* American. His Dad moved here on business."

"Tonya," said Michael. "Tonya, Tonya, Tonya. Wake up, love. It's time to get real. Take a closer look at his teeth."

Sonya shook her head.

"No teeth could be that white," said Michael. "Most teeth aren't white at all, Tonya. Normal teeth are green. Or maybe even yellow. Like Card's."

"Wait a minute," I said.

Michael winked. He put his hand on Sonya's shoulder. She looked at him out of the side of her eye, like a bullock in an abattoir.

"And as for them clubs you go to," he said, drawing close, "you ought to know better, love. You could pick up STDs. Blokes like Kenny Richardson don't care where it's been, you know, love..."

Sonya gathered up her books slowly and left the library, not looking at us.

I was thinking of comets. Of the one chance they get to make contact. Then – whoosh – gone. Into the coldness and dark. Darkness darker than a cinema. Voices in the far stalls, no way of reaching them...

Michael nodded. "I reckon it's the coat. Women never fancy

fellahs in daft coats, Card. I had one like that once and the zip was always getting entangled."

"Why the hell did you tell her about snails?"

"She'll come round again."

"Yeah. In about ten thousand years."

"At least she knows who you are now. Even if she probably thinks you're called Card. But I'll tell you what is: if she *still* won't go out with you, I'll let you look at her through my telescope."

That was when I took the telescope off him and tried to break it over my knee. Which didn't work, obviously. So I kicked it under a desk. And it hit the librarian's foot, so we had to leave it there and leg it.

Outside, Michael said, "Whatever. We don't even *need* telescopes. According to my calculations, the comet's overhead. Which means we can take advantage, Card."

"And stop calling me Card."

"First Carl, then Card. It seems to me, young man, that you don't want to be called anything at all."

"I'll tell you what it is, Michael: I wish *you* were a comet. I wish you were million of miles away and I couldn't see you anymore."

"And if I was that comet, I'd deliberately fling my spores onto other people. I wouldn't drop a single spore onto you. How about that, eh? You'd be the only person on Earth to miss out on The Change!"

"*What* change?"

"The next big evolutionary step, of course. Tonight's the night, Card. The night when everything gets changed."

"Including your Dad's shirt?"

I felt tight as soon as I'd said it. His face flickered. He blinked for the first time ever. He looked like he'd been tapped with his Dad's shoe-mallet.

"Sorry," I said.

Michael didn't speak. He turned away, went up the hill. And I followed him at a distance. Followed him, like I followed everybody in those days. Because I was shatter-pated. Because I was in their orbit.

*

At the top of the hill, Michael stood staring into the sky. It was drizzling as usual, the orange streetlights spreading their glow over lumps of cloud.

I watched from a wet ditch as he checked his watch, pulled out a notebook and scribbled in it, frowning.

Wind flashed through the grass.

He took his clothes off. He took them off slowly, like an old man. And even though they were worn-out clothes – dirty and grey, riddled with holes, sagging and thin – he folded them carefully and rested them next to the patch of green moss where his skin ached in the night as he lay down.

Then I crept out of the ditch.

"What the hell are you doing, Michael?"

He looked at me out of the moss, shivering. His body was tiny, just ribs and elbows.

"Can you feel them?" he said.

"Feel what?"

"The spores, Card." He gazed into the night. "Lie down with me. Let them settle on you. Then you can rub them in."

There wasn't a single hair on his body.

"Don't worry," he said, "There's no way the County Council will find out. They stop the patrols after dark."

I started to laugh. I was shivering and laughing, looking down at his tiny, hairless body, watching him run his hands over its skin and bones.

"You're as white as a comet," I said.

"As its tail," he corrected me.

"Or its beard."

He sat up, touched my chin.

I flinched, grew calm, let him do it. I didn't care. I took my clothes off. I just wanted to be touched, I didn't care who by.

170

Above us, the wind fumbled to break holes in the clouds. Beyond, a few stars flashed.

The night was massive. Who knew what might come out of it? We lay there, tiny white scraps in the grass.

"This is it," he said. "This is the change."

Speedbone Sauna Blues

"This music you're listening to/Let me tell you why I don't
like it" — Ken Smith, 'Poem to which the answer is no'

On Friday afternoon the graffiti on the school desks looks pointless.
And the clocks tick for no-one and the bells keep ringing.

Steve scoops up exercise books, drops two. Sighs. Tipples the
books from the crook of his arm into a carrier-bag. Curriculums to
discuss, team-meetings to attend.

Margaret is dabbing and scratching with an old-fashioned pen.
VG. Good. Fair. See Me.

"No departmental meeting this week then, Steve?"

"Cancelled," he lies.

Seems he's forgotten how to leave a room. He pretends there is
an important document on his desk:

POLITE NOTICE.
STAFF KINDLY RETURN MILK BOTTLES TO CRATES.
THIS IS A STAFF-ROOM, NOT A BIOLOGY
LABORATORY.

Margaret lays on another full-stop. Forty years in the same
seat. Her eyebrows arch. "They've been giving you a rough time,
eh?"

The full-stop quivers, plump and precise.

Steve rotates the milk-bottle memo. "Who do you mean, Margaret?"

"That lot. 3B."

"3B," he repeats.

"Little swines," says Margaret, kindly. On the wall behind her is a calendar featuring a photograph of a jeep in a jungle.

A large clock clunks. In the departmental meeting, chairs will be scraping closer to tables.

A large blue nought in the register. Absent without explanation.

Margaret lays down the ink-pen. Everything around her is the colour of old envelopes, but she shines for Steve.

He remembers his Grandmother's old saying: *Eyes are the light of the body*. He tries to post a smile back to her across the staff-room's brown tundra.

"Anyway, I thought I'd use the free time," he explains. "So it's the sauna for me now, Margaret. A bit of a wind-down..."

Margaret's eyebrows do their thing. "Whatever lights your candle, Steve."

"Candle!" He hoists his marking. The strain turns his shoulders square. He looks like Honey Monster loping through the corridor.

"Bye!" says Margaret. Says her voice. The door sweeps closed, a horizontal wipe.

Keys jangle. A technician brushes past, the metal bunch bouncing on his hip. "Bye," he says without interest, and vanishes beyond the fire door.

"Bye," says Steve.

Closed doors down the corridor. Far-off voices in the gloom. Items on the agenda: 1.) Classroom control. 2.) Skiving Teachers.

Like an actor in *The Great Escape*, Steve inches to the perimeter fence, emptying tiny amounts of soil from his pockets.

The car park is deserted. Trees beyond its fence make black tangles in the sunset. People in meetings will look out, and perhaps report him to the sinister milk bottle authorities.

Dull thud of hatchback. Keys, engine, handbrake.

Waving. Steve is waving. Plus – one little toot. Just that, just once.

Toot if you support Steve sneaking off early from work.

Towards the exit, not waving. Frowning. The last of the sunlight makes freckles out of the mud on his car's windscreen. He squirts water at it with a fierce prod, then clicks on a tape, hoping it will fill his head as it does at night when he cooks. Warming the kitchen, somehow rounding off its sharpness.

The tape whirrs, then kicks in.

Robert Johnson. *Hell-hound on my trail...*

"3B," he thinks, "a record about our relationship."

Jesus – that voice, the load it carried. And the person it travelled through – gone from the Delta for six years, whereabouts unknown.

Great Skivers Of Our Time.

In the car park, the trees are stripped to the trunk. Winter-bare. As dead as the Dada which Gresty this week told him was shite.

And Gresty is battered each night by Platt, and Platt each morning by Trent. And Gresty dishes his pain back to the teachers and the bus shelters of Lancashire. And these are the Blues we are all singing.

The branches break the sunset into confusing patterns. Steve closes his eyes, but their lids are too thin; the sun continues to throb and dazzle. Plus: it's best to keep your eyes open while driving.

Gresty doesn't care about the Blues. Techno, that's what Gresty likes. He doesn't want music that makes sense of his life. He wants music that sounds like it. Machines, traffic, arcade games. Noises going round and round, not getting anywhere. The tedium is the message.

Steve thinks about the sauna, what it is about the sauna. Once he thought he went there to feel alive. Now he wonders.

The sun is going down. A burning has been lost. The stars and moon are fixed against a darker sky.

Another car park, this time the one at the municipal sports centre. Queues for pools, courts, mats. No-one else for the sauna. Steve pauses. A strange thing: the same jeep in the same jungle on the same calendar.

"And still the same day," he thinks in the cubicle, studying his legs. They are white, his socks navy-blue.

He kicks his underpants into the cubicle wall, doesn't even send his eyes down for a look. Stays North of the Cods.

His clothes fit snugly into the locker. Then he remembers his coat, so he takes everything out, crams in the forgotten item, and slaps shoes and wallet on top.

Now there's a problem with mud.

He takes the shoes out again and examines the clay footprint on his coat. Sighs. Removes everything from the locker once more. Crumples and bundles. Wipes his coat. Puts the shoes into the locker, lays the coat and his bag and his wallet on top.

The damaging effect of weight on shoes.

Steve ignores this stray thought.

He gathers up his corduroys, whistling. Coins spill out of their pockets. He has to go down on his hands and knees, and grope.

Two coins – a sum of exactly 22 pence – have disappeared from the world.

Drains and gutters gape under his fingers. He imagines his 22 pence lying in a sewer, floating out to sea, settling in a trench.

"At it again, ay!"

Steve judders. When he looks up, he sees the sauna attendant high above him in the sky. He nods, somewhat guiltily. Thinks: how come Lancashire's sauna attendants are always Cockneys?

"You must lose fackin paaa-aaahnds down there, mate!"

Nods, noddy dog, nodding. "These trousers."

"I'll tell you if I find it, mate." The attendant hitches at his tracksuit. "Yeah, 'course I will!" A wink for Steve's nodding. The attendant's muscles pull on his T-shirt. Bunches of hair gather at his neck, as if pushing up to the light.

"My last 20 pence piece," Steve tells the assistant.

But the man is already halfway back to his official position behind the little gate.

"For the locker..." Steve explains to the steam.

Nothing for it but to follow.

Close to the attendant's official position, Steve passes the shower-block. He's studying a swirling plughole when he realises that an old man has tracked his progress down the aisle through the steam.

The watcher has ponderous grey eyes. His soap hangs suspended in its loop. When Steve walks on, the old man finally drops his gaze and slubs the soap deeper into his midriff.

The attendant has gone on somewhere beyond the official position. Steve stands naked in the open-plan foyer, waiting, drawing his hands around his chest like an adolescent girl guarding her breasts. Steve tries to forget that he has a penis.

A door bangs. Keys jangle. Everybody's got keys these days. Finally, the attendant comes back, purpose in his nonchalance, frowning as he has been taught.

He unfastens the little gate without speaking. Steve thinks: If he finds my 22 pence in the sewer, he'll put it towards a pack of condoms. My coins will play a part in the violation of a young girl.

"The 20 pence piece," he explains again. Pauses. Re-crosses hands on chest. "For the locker. It went... there."

Imagines: the attendant sneaking down into the sewers after work to look for it. To make the coin his own.

"So you can't shat your locker, ay?"

"No."

"Right. I'll keep a watch on it."

"Actually I was wondering if you could lend me 20p. Till later."

"Eh?"

"Well," says Steve, "it might be safer that way. See, my wallet is in there, and..."

The attendant runs a finger along the horizontal line that divides the back of his head into two hemispheres. He has thicker legs than Steve's waist.

"I'll *watch* it, I said."

"But if you have to go away. If you have to come through the little gate..."

"I won't," says the attendant. He snaps a button below the counter.

The alarm! thinks Steve. The Cockney attendant has pressed the alarm. I am to be arrested for wantonly repeating questions to an employee of the municipality.

Music comes on in response to the attendant's finger. Roxette. Steam curls. The attendant begins to tick boxes on a list. Steve still has a penis. It's hanging there between his legs. It persists.

The attendant hums to Roxette, banging his free hand on the desk. There is a Roxette quota in UK sports centres.

"So you'll watch it? Watch my... my wallet?"

The Cockney attendant goes on ticking boxes. Makes an angle to the wall. Locker open, transaction closed.

A nightmare flash: *"The management regrets that, owing to the theft of your clothes and wallet, you must walk home in the nude."*

Steve sighs. There is a word in his head. The word is: "Bollocks". He sloshes back through the shower section.

Trust. A better world would have more trust.

In the showers, the old man has almost disappeared beneath his soap. Great white suds weep from his body. One, unblinded grey eye tracks his progress as he walks past. Steve doesn't respond. He wants to forget the eye, forget its object. Forget nakedness. Forget bodies.

He yanks the sauna door with a grunt, and steps inside.

*

Bang.

He tooters into the little room, eyes adjusting to its gloom, and steps over the out-stretched leg of The Man Who Is Always On The Floor, groping a path to the bench. The wood is hot and soft under his hand. He sucks in air, holding it deep, lowering himself onto the slats. The luxury of it. A great heat, which must be slowly conquered.

Outside, the grey-eyed old man passes the window, stooping awkwardly for his towel. Two soapy points hang suspended from his upper body. Breasts. The old man who watched Steve grope for his locker-coin has grown breasts!

But try not to think of that.

Or the wallet.

177

Hush. Lie still.

Slowly, Steve arranges his body over the planks, lying flat with his eyes closed, a forearm pressed to the sockets.

He listens for gulls, for the sloughing of distant waves.

"'Ot 'un today, lad," says The Man Who Is Always On The Floor.

What he always says, when he always says it.

"Aye," Steve murmurs, "hotter than John Prescott's arse!"

His sauna-mate laughs, repeating John Prescott's name under his breath, holding it there in his mouth like a taste that he can't quite work out.

Steve settles in, comforted by the routine, relishing the hatching of sweat on his skin, enjoying the sensation down along his belly and abdomen, his penis and his thighs.

He chooses a drop at the back of his knee and falls with it, breaks on the floor with it...

... and then slowly rises as steam to rejoin himself.

Energy cannot be destroyed. He tries to imagine that – tries to picture his personality steaming away from his body, into the sky.

Then he no longer knows if he is thinking in pictures or words, or whether he is thinking at all. The gloom of the sauna, its one weary yellow light, is lodged between his eyes. The place and his perception of it seem to merge.

Whoosh.

Steve's steam bolts for the exit. There are shapes against the light. Loud hard voices. A sharp, cool waft of air.

"Come on, Baz. Get a fucking move on."

Steve's eyes open. He thinks: Not now. It's *my* turn...

The shapes wait, hold the door.

"Baz! The cold's gonna get in!"

Teacher Steve snaps to attention. Cold doesn't enter, heat leaves.

A rough voice reverberates beyond the door. "Keep your fucking hair on, lads."

Baz, finally. The three of them. Bandy-legged, thick-limbed, squat against the light.

BANG.

"Like a fucking furnace."

"Told thee, Baz. Shouldn't have come if tha couldn't take it!"

"I can take it," says Baz. "I can take it all right."

They settle in, their bodies jostling for space. Two of them squeeze together on the upper deck beside Steve, while Baz straddles the lower tier, his back forming a giant wedge of muscle against Steve's foot.

Baz wipes the tattoo of a rose on his upper arm. "Have you farted, Terry?"

"Them beans at dinner," says Terry, a slit-mouthed man, the narrowest of the three. He talks into his chest, a fixed, far-off grin on his face, as if everything's a joke but nothing's funny.

"Jesus. That's disgusting, that is!" says the youngest, a fresh-faced kid with the word YOUTH stamped over his wide shoulder.

"Can't take him fucking anywhere," Baz groans.

Steve tries to close his eyes again.

"What you doin' down theer, old fella?" Baz asks The Man Who Is Always On The Floor.

The man tries to pretend he wasn't eavesdropping on their shouting. He shrugs, humming under his breath.

"Chased him off, did you?" asks YOUTH, his stiff neck turning to Steve.

"No," Steve replies, copying the smile.

Classroom control.

"Then why's the old boy down there?"

"Escaping from our farting," says the slit-mouthed man. Smaller than the other three, less muscled. Older. Having a laugh, eyes not laughing.

They cackle. Baz dips his head. "And happen I had beans too. Happen you ain't seen nothing yet," he warns the Man Who Is Always On The Floor.

"Ey," giggles YOUTH – "I've 'eard that the lasses say that an' all, Baz!"

Baz takes his dick in his hand. He holds it like a length of pipe. "I'll tell thee what, YOUTH: I draw the full family allowance, me. I'm not sure I can say the same for thee, though, lad." He peers into the gloom, putting on a squeaky voice: "Did you put it in me, YOUTH? Have you started yet, son?"

YOUTH shuffles on the slats, tested, nervous. "Cheeky bastard."

Baz strokes his chest. There are muscles on his fingers. "And I'll tell thee summat else: it were plenty big enough for yon bloody Sharon the other night. No complaints theer, like."

"What bloody Sharon?"

"*That* bloody Sharon," says Baz precisely. He spits through his teeth onto the heater. It hisses, once.

"The lass in the office? Sharon Dunkley?"

Baz almost nods.

"Sheesh. That's a big lass, that is," says YOUTH. "Tits like astrodomes..."

"Man alive," says Terry.

"Where did you take her then?"

"Any place she'd let me."

Animal noises in the sauna. Steve hates their machismo, shares the same needs, thinks of breasts swinging. Decides it's time for the pool...

But can't go.

Because he would have to step over them, risking their scrutiny and laughter. Laying bare his failures and vegetarianism. And, anyway, they slammed the door so hard, it's possible he isn't strong enough to force it open.

Trapped.

In an extreme survival situation, who would they eat first? Shhh. Shhhh.

Steve grips the wooden slat as if the sports centre is crossing an ocean, as if it may be about to pitch and roll.

"I bet you took her down Martham Grange, didn't you? Into that lane behind the club?" Terry chuckles. "You dark horse, you..."

Steve feels a foot pressing against his leg. It's Terry's foot. Terry's foot against his leg.

Terry speaks to Steve.

Terry says, "Them Catholic birds, eh? The worst of the lot –

aren't they, eh? The worst of the fucking lot."

It comes out like a threat.

Steve nods.

But YOUTH shakes his head louder. "Hold your horses. If you supposedly shagged Sharon Dunkley, how come you never said owt about it till now?"

He taps sweat off his finger-ends, waiting.

Baz's voice stays low. "Because I couldn't speak for three days, could I? Shagged me senseless. I'm only surprised me hearing didn't pack up."

Their laughter thuds for a while, then slowly dies.

Heat builds. They sway with it, chewing their knees, relishing the taste, polishing their arms like cars.

Quietness prevails.

Then:

"No, though. Why are *you* sitting on t' floor, old lad?"

The Man Who Is Always On The Floor looks away from YOUTH. Makes eye contact with Steve.

Steve contemplates his schooling. Bullies swarming over the earth, breaking wind, things, hearts...

His eyes droop, he lets the man go. In this on his own. Why *does* he always sit on the floor anyway?

"Well," says the man.

YOUTH's thick neck comes round. His thumbs jabs Baz. "I reckon they're *puffs*, these!"

Steve and his tendons work together to construct a smile.

"Aye, arse-bandits, " says YOUTH. "Which is why this 'un can't stop grinning, eh! I bet they were *at* it before we came in!"

Baz keeps his eyes on Steve. His voice is level and low. "I'm right though, aren't I, pal? They're dirty bitches, them Catholic lasses, aren't they? Or is YOUTH right? Would *you* not know?"

Steve's strategy is calmness, a sense of the classroom around him – the ground he must hold, the spaces he must not enter.

Sharon's shagger faces this new prey. Sex has failed him, filled him with hunger only for more sex. Put sex everywhere, in everything. Even in Steve.

They drip together on the wooden rack, inches of heat between their nakedness.

"Ah, ignore him, lad. He's been working too hard," Terry tells Steve. He gives Baz a quick push. "Haven't you, Baz? Been working too hard?"

Sweat falls off Baz for a time. Like a goal-frame struck by a football, quivering after the event. A sad thing, and lovely. The crowd fixed on the counter-attack, rain dripping from a forgotten bar.

"We've *all* been working too hard," says Baz quietly.

"Amen to that," Terry grunts. He grips the wood tighter, arms flaring.

"Fucking speedboning for you," Baz nods. "Does your head in, man..."

"Count the brass, though," says YOUTH.

"See if you still feel that way in six months. When you've got hernias in your eyeballs," Baz promises, rubbing his arms tenderly, as if they're someone else's, the arms of a lover. "I thought today were never going to fucking end. About two o'clock I'm thinking, Only another four or five. But, Jesus, they kept on coming..."

Terry wipes his torso. "Plus, that stun gun weren't working proper..."

"Aye. If that thing goes on t' blink one more time..."

Baz looks at his hand, at the conglomeration of sweat. "Well, they don't care if *we're* half-dead. So I can't see 'em worrying if yon cows are still breathing when we gut 'em."

"I'll tell thee what," says Terry, aiming his words at YOUTH: "it'll be *us* on t' blink if they keep working us like this. It'll be us gutted. You'll see, lad."

YOUTH shakes his head. "You knew t' game before you signed up, Terry. Commission, man. Piece-work. Get 'em skinned, peeled, boiled – all that bollocks – here's another fifty quid. Ta very much, that's me down the Cat's Whiskers. Pint in my hand, brass in my pocket. And all the women I can eat!"

"Hark at him," says Baz. "Only been doing t' job 10 minutes!"

"That's what it is, though," says YOUTH. "And look! Here's comes The Quiet Man! He knows his eggs. He'll tell you the rules!

Isn't that right, Quiet Man? What do you reckon?"

The door has come open without much effort on the part of the fourth slaughter-man. He stands in the frame, reduced to vastness by the shadows, apparently constructed from a single muscle.

"Where've you been? Soaping yourself down in the bogs?"

The Quiet Man says nothing.

YOUTH puts the question to him. YOUTH says, "Which do you prefer? Speedboning or ordinary slaughter?"

The Quiet Man stares into the sauna. "Which do I prefer? I'll tell thee what I prefer. I prefer 6 o'clock. I prefer clocking-off time."

"Well, I get all the beer *I* need," grunts Youth, flicking his eyes at Terry, "and the totty. See, if you ask me..."

"Aye, and nobody's asking you," puts in Terry. "You think you get women? I've news for you, cock. Compare it to the lads on the oil-rigs. Or plumbers or brickies."

"Or even a fucking teacher," says Baz.

Steve has a Winston Smith moment. Big Brother staring straight at him out of the video screen. In the form of Baz.

Baz lets out a sigh. "Aye, well. It pains me to say it. But at the end of the day I'm with YOUTH on this one. I'm not saying we're paid right. No way. T' pay's shite. But it takes more than brass to bag birds. No point flashing your wallet if you can't flash this." He takes hold of himself, shows it to them. "Eh, Terry?"

The Quiet Man nods in refusal. "Shut your mouth for once, Baz. YOUTH asked me what I reckoned, so I told him."

"When?" says YOUTH. "When did you tell me?"

"It were so long ago," says Baz, "that I can't remember the fucking question."

Quiet Man waits while the three of them finish laughing. "Seeing as you missed it, I'll tell you again," he says at length, in that same level tone, his voice tuned to the sauna's inner workings. "I reckon we kill stuff all day. I reckon we get home knackered, play wi' t' kids, shag t' wife, and black out. Then I reckon we get up, and it's supposed to be a different day. But it dun't seem any different. I reckon it seems like t' same old, same old. Because it doesn't matter whether it's speedboning or ordinary slaughter, it's all the fucking same. And I reckon they pay us just about enough to drink and shag ourselves stupid. So we can't think straight. So we want more of the same thing that's makes us stupid. And I reckon that if you don't like it, you should get another job."

A pause, as if everyone is frightened.

Then Baz sings, "Fucking hell. Jesus wants me for a fucking sunbeam!" and, among the laughter, Terry shouts, "Right. I'm off out!" and that's it, they're leaving, like buffalos migrating, and the door is swinging open behind them.

The Man Who Is Always On The Floor pulls it shut.

He scratches his shoulder blade, mumbling tunelessly under his breath. Tum-te-tum, te-tum-te-tum. Tum-te-tum, te-tum te-tum.

Lancashire Blues.

"I know one of that lot," he points, pinching a blob of sweat with his other hand. Tum-te-tum.

Steve studies the timer. Studies it very hard. Sand goes on spilling into its bottom half. Time, and more of it. As if time has nowt else to do, as if it's got all the time in the world.

"Aye. That young lad," says the man. "The one they call YOUTH. Used to live up our road."

Steve rubs his shin. He doesn't want to talk about the man's embarrassment, to make it more embarrassing.

"A nice lad, he was," says the man.

"Aye?"

"Mind, he's fallen in with a hard lot there..."

Steve inspects his arm, checks his midriff.

"I suppose they don't mean any harm, like," adds the man. "Unwinding, you might say."

"Aye."

"Thing is, they've supposedly got of a bit of a tendency to nick stuff..."

"Who does?"

"Them lads. Slaughter-men. I read it somewhere. In the 'papers. A legal case, or summat. They reckoned it goes with the job. Ripping heads off all day. Makes 'em a bit.... y' know." The man twists a finger at his temple.

These are the things that flash through Steve's head:

A locker.

The Cockney attendant.

His wallet.

He gets up fast, aware of contact between the soles of his feet and Terry's sweat. Then he's gone, out into the world beyond the sauna, funny bits of his body bouncing as he rushes to the official position.

The Cockney attendant isn't there, the door to Steve's locker is open.

He thinks: They've stolen my clothes because their jobs are so horrible!

But when he checks, the clothes are still crushed inside the locker, the same muddy footprint slowly drying on his coat. And his wallet there yet, balanced as neat as a stone on a cairn.

Only his shoes are still in danger.

He hurries to relieve them of their burden, the weight of his clothes, aware of other punters filing in, getting changed, taking showers.

His body throbs with the heat, with the noise.

He thinks of Margaret laying her ink-pen on the desk in the staff-room, chairs creaking along the corridor as the departmental meeting winds down.

Imagines the yellow lino in his kitchen, the hob that he fusses over, its bright rings shining for no-one.

And Gresty, laying into a local bus shelter with both feet.

Thinks: poor me, poor speedboners, poor animals.

Somewhere not far away from where he's standing, the slaughter-men must be swimming in the pool, the sauna still throbbing in their veins.

Steve tries to concentrate on that, on the thought of the men stroking paths through the pool, their arms as pink as a calf's belly, the water as clear and as pure.

He picks his sock out of the gutter, surprised that it's still navy-blue, that his life hasn't changed while he's been gone. Above his head, the Roxette CD goes on spilling itself into the air, gumming its traces in the damp corners.

He closes his eyes and listens to the blood pumping through its channels, thinking how near it sounds, how far from yourself you must travel in order to notice it.

In That Brilliant Village

Billy's mum had warned him about Brussels. But Brussels had a plan:
"That village, on Mischief Night... it's BRILLIANT." Rain splattered him. *"It'll be on the News!"*

"Look, Brussels..."

"Colin," he hissed. "Call me Colin."

Billy looked down. A red double-decker trundled past. Puddles swayed. "Alright," said Billy, at last.

Brussels punched drizzle. "Ye-s-s-s-s-s-s-s-s-s-s-s-s-s-s."

"Wait," said Billy. "Tomorrow's..."

Brussels dared him to say it: Friday. School. Skiving.

The pavement was cracked and wet. Billy tried to think.

"It's your mum..." said Brussels.

"No," said Billy.

"Yes, it is. She hates me. I think she talks about me behind my back."

What Brussels looked like: freckles in the shape of Finland; fog-coloured eyes; white ears which the light shone through. Red face, small hands. A dad who'd run off to Belgium, which was like Cheshire – but no salt.

Billy frowned. "It's just – she'll know we're skiving."

"ACT NORMAL," Brussels ordered.

*

187

The Last Days of Johnny North

Billy held a fork, and thought she could tell.
He watched a volcano programme.
"Pressure builds relentlessly..." said the commentator.
When Billy scratched his head, it was a giveaway.
"Billy," said his mum – and *she knew* – "pass the remote."
It was a relief to get rid. The way he'd been pressing it...
Even the direction of his head on the pillow.
Signs. Tokens. Omens.

*

"'Bye, mum," he said, next morning.
Look at his stupid NORMAL WALK.
Skiver, said passers-by. Said their eyes.
Billy imagined another Billy, Billy No. 2, who was good. Who
got House Points.

*

"Why'd you bring *that*?" said Brussels.
Billy's satchel had wet seams. "So she'd think I was..."
Brussels blinked. "Stuff it in the bin. And your uniform – put it
in a hole."
"What hole?"
"In a hole or bin or tree."
Billy shrugged.
Their bus pulled in.

*

The kids on the bus knew secrets. They wore grey blazers, not blue.
They had different laughs, different skin.
Brussels said, in a loud voice, "Be like me. Be dead quiet."
They crept to the upper-deck, pretended to read Billy's
Chemistry textbook.
Behind, a kid talked about the volcano programme: "Pressure

builds relentlessly. Tectonic plates. Massive underground forces."

Brussels told the boy, "You go to a right crap school, you."

They pushed each other into the aisle. Everyone shouted, "FIGHT!"

Then the bus driver appeared.

*

The boys stood under a tree, watching it drip. The tree's leaves were nearly gone. The sky was suet-coloured.

"Walking's better, anyway," said Brussels.

"How far, though?"

Brussels pointed to a wet cart-track. "One mile."

The track wriggled into the hills. Billy moved his satchel to the other shoulder.

Brussels said, "The way you moved that satchel. Like you don't believe me."

"No, it's just... can't we go by road?"

"Too far."

Billy looked at the hills. "My mum says there are Bad Men..."

"Believe that? Go on, take your books. Miss kids doing *anything*... in that brilliant village."

Wet stones slithered under their feet.

Brussels said, "It's easy, it's one mile."

*

"... like the back of my hand," Brussels was saying.

It had been hours.

A tall, thin figure plodded towards them over the hills.

Billy smiled. "We can ask him!"

Brussels kicked stones sulkily. "Pointless asking walkers... walkers are useless."

The walker had a knobbly nose, watery blue eyes. He was wearing tight red shorts. Mud on his shins. Flaky grey knees.

"Morning," said Billy.

"Afternoon," said the walker. He was smoking. He stared at Billy's school badge. "Free as birds, eh?"

Billy didn't speak.

"If birds were ever free." The walker breathed out smoke. "Not as empty as they look, yon hills. Not at all. I've seen sparrows taken by wildcats out there..."

Drizzle fell between them.

The walker's eyes were like hands on Billy's chest, "They're *wick*, them hills. A boy could go lost. Disappear."

"Not us," said Brussels, kicking stones. "We're off to this brilliant village called Rivvington. Where kids can do whatever the fucking hell they like. Have you got a drink of water in a flask?"

The man closed his eyes, then smiled coldly. "Rivvington? Straight on. Over the ridge." He picked at his rucksack zip.

Billy took a step back, pulled Brussels with him.

"Can I not offer you something?" said the man.

*

Brussels said, "I didn't want a drink of water, anyway."

"The way he skenned at my uniform..."

"Pointless asking people like that for a drink of water. Walkers. Walkers who say actually! Actually and basically! Ought to be put down. Pull a trigger. Bang. Out of our misery."

In the distance, the walker had lit a cigarette. He watched them.

"Not to mention – his legs," said Brussels. "Swirly hairs all over them – like pubes."

"Don't..." said Billy, walking as fast as he could.

"Walkers are wankers," said Brussels.

The rain fell a little harder.

*

The track fizzled out in a bog. Beyond was a bleak brown ridge, littered with boulders.

"Them are Ice Age rocks," said Billy. "Thousands of years old."
Brussels never answered.

Past midday, Billy thought about spuds. Butties. Crumble. Pop. Double Chemistry. Mr Butler – mental with a ruler.

He hopped over a brown tuft. It quivered. He daren't readjust his satchel in case Brussels took it wrong. The grass was tough as wire.

Between tussocks, black pools glinted. Billy had heard of sheep being sucked down.

Brussels whistled 'Colonel Bogey'.

In conquering severe concentration difficulties, he will score higher marks.

"Look at this," Billy had told Brussels on reports day.

"Huh?" said Brussels, kicking a bush.

*

"Top of this ridge..."

"Top?"

"Just ower."

"How far?"

"One mile."

An oily stain crept up Billy's shin.

"Piece of piss," said Brussels. "Legless people could manage it. Daleks. Cats, even. Cats through cat-flaps – easy! Like trees. It's windy, you don't tell trees to shake... they just know." He tipped up a boulder. "The Next Ice Age! Ha!"

They scrambled up, hearing rocks fall.

*

From the ridge, they had a grand view of the moors.

"Down there," said Brussels.

Billy followed his finger. "In that reservoir?"

"Next to it."

Billy screwed his eyes: another bog, a shed.

Brussels laughed. "Mischief Night. Doing *anything*. In that brilliant village. You'll see. Heard about it on a train."

"On a train. When did you go on a train?"

Brussels fiddled in his pocket. "Go on trains quite a lot, me. On business."

Billy's shoulders ached. The satchel had bashed his hip. He imagined textbooks sunken in black pools, like sheep. They'd dig them up in four hundred years, perfect!

An expert, striding to the camera. *Archaeologists believe these primitive chemists worshipped books...* Cut to a bog... *which they buried alongside sheep.*

Billy snorted.

"That's tight, that is," said Brussels.

"What is?"

"Laughing. How would you like it? Your problem, you're like them lads on that bus."

"I'm not. Watch."

At the bog's edge, Billy took out the textbook. Even if Billy No. 1 did it, Billy No. 2 would still have the book. "We are gathered here in this House of God today..."

"... to commit this book..." Brussels broke off, giggling.

Billy held his sides. "Ashes to ashes...."

"... bog to bog..."

Plop. The book into the bog. Going down slowly, as if it didn't want to die.

Bubbles.

"Amen," said Billy.

They held their sides.

"If we could bury Mr Butler...," said Brussels, rubbing camouflage into Billy's cheeks. Billy kicked him.

They wrestled.

"Woooooooooooooooooo!" Billy shouted, a Native Red American Indian.

Brussels lay back, gasping. "White man speak with um-forked tongue!"

"Wooo," said Billy.

"Smoke-um peace pipe," said Brussels, "in um-happy hunting grounds."

They settled back on tussocks, quiet, thinking. Currents twisted in the reservoir.

A crow flapped overhead.

Brussels fidgeted. "He said *wick*."

"Who did?"

"That walker. What's *wick*, Billy?"

"Crawling with stuff. Like if you get nits."

"You saying I've got nits?"

Billy sighed.

A shape looked back from the ridge, the first person they'd seen for ages. "What's the time?" said Billy. He was hungry.

Brussels watched rain fall on a black pool. "Reckon this water's wick?"

"Only with books."

"The weird thing is, you could've put anything in your satchel. But you put in the books for today's lessons..."

Billy didn't answer.

"All the right books for today's lessons..."

Billy looked up at the figure on the ridge. He bit his lip.

Brussels rubbed his trousers, started to get to his feet. "Must cost a packet, them text-books," he said. His eyes followed Billy's to the ridge. "What's that tosser skenning at?"

The figure on the ridge didn't move.

Brussels made megaphone-hands: "I-UM SCALP YOU!"

"It's that walker..."

"Bet he's lost. What does he think we are – St Bernard's? Ought to buy a map."

"He was going the other way."

"What did I say? They're allus lost, are walkers! OY! SCALP-UM!"

Billy looked at the bog. "He said straight on."

"It *is* straight on," said Brussels, trying to balance. "It's about..."

"... *one mile?*"

Water swirled around Brussels' ankle. His mouth opened. "I

were going to say that exact distance, Billy! One mile! Psychic. *You read my mind!*"

Billy was shin-deep. He looked into the bog. It moved.

He went down.

It was a soft-spot.

"Past my knee..."

But it was past his shoulder.

Brussels grabbed Billy's blazer. Threads unravelled. Billy went down fast, peat in his throat. Suddenly, he understood: *I'm going to die*. He looked for the book; to stay out of trouble. He was cold, he was warm.

Then Brussels came up close and stared at him. It made sense.

"Close your mouth!"

Brussels grabbed Billy's throat. Billy remembered Tarzan films. Struggle in quicksand, it sucks you faster.

Water touched Billy's lip. He came to the edge, pulled by the Adam's apple.

Then he was on a tussock, gasping. His vomit came out black.

*

Brussels said, "People die up here. Don't you believe me? It's true, it's on the News. They die. But mud, you rub it in – it isolates you."

"Insulates," said Billy.

"From the cold," said Brussels. "We should rub more in – to isolate you."

Billy stared into Brussels' fog-coloured eyes.

Brussels had pulled Billy to the cabin. The cabin was black and windowless. Its roof was mossy. There were dents in the door.

Billy shivered.

Brussels started to batter the cabin with a stick.

"Don't..."

Brussels said, "How else am I supposed to get in?"

"You're not supposed to get in."

"Then why leave this stick here?"

Across the bog, Billy's satchel lay on an island of bent grass. A textbook had slithered out. Its white pages turned.

"The wind's reading," said Brussels, whacking his stick against the hut.

The cabin's door fell backwards off one hinge.

"Mischief Night," said Brussels.

A jacket swung on a wire hanger.

"Avon calling!"

Inside was a camp-bed with a yellow pillow, split along the seam. Its pillow was stained.

"Sleep slavver," Brussels grimaced, taking things off the stove. "Look, Billy – tectonic dinner-plates. *This beat is tectonic, this beat is techno-tonic!* Mad acid rave in a cabin."

He fell onto the bed. It collapsed. The pillow spilled feathers. "This cabin. They ought to fix it up, it's a death-trap."

"Who should? Who should fix it up?"

"How would they like it if *I* had a dangerous cabin?"

"You've knackered everything..."

"I'll sue them."

"We're not even supposed to be here. You broke in, Brussels. It's bad enough skiving, but..."

"What did you call me?"

Billy looked at him, afraid. Creosote throbbed in his nostrils. He bent double, vomited. Black water trickled down his chin.

As he straightened, the light in the cabin thickened. A shape filled the doorway.

The shape was long. Dark. Thin.

Brussels opened his mouth, as if to swallow light.

The shape came over the threshold.

Tiny feathers fell. Brussels ran through them. "Want some of *these?*" He held out little fists – as frail, as easy to break, as wings.

The shape fled into the light.

Brussels flung himself outside.

The shape faced him. It was the walker. Grey legs, wet eyes. He took a breath, like a swimmer about to enter a wave.

Rain flurried.

"Thought you shouted help..." said the man.

"Scalp," said Brussels. "We shouted *scalp*."

The man showed empty hands.

Billy fell out of the cabin. His face pressed the dark peat. He heard an angry voice, then a scared voice – then nothing, except wind as it moved in great flashes through the grass.

*

Billy lay in a hollow, listening. Dry cold hands rubbed his arms, his legs. A voice said, "Warming you up, aren't we..."

The hands moved over Billy's chest, down his stomach.

"Warming you up," said the voice.

The man's hands kept him in the hollow.

"Well – what are you waiting for, boy? Find help!"

Brussels' feet faltered on the hollow turf. "Billy..."

"Want him to die of cold, boy?"

Feet, stumbling.

Through the man's hands, Billy saw Brussels stumbling backwards over tussocks, his mouth a dark slash.

"Now then," said the voice, "now then..." Rich breath wafted over Billy's cheek. It was close to his lips. On them. "Now then..." Billy felt a weight come down. He tasted something as bitter as nicotine, or coins – and moist, like liver.

Then Billy was rising and running, and he'd found Brussels. He had pushed the weight away and the voice was calling, but he was with Brussels and they were stumbling towards the reservoir, rain in their faces.

The walker knelt in the grassy hollow where Billy had lain. His head was tilted to the blank sky. Billy washed his lips in the reservoir. Brussels pulled him away. Billy tried to go back down the slippy cobbles to wash his lips again.

They couldn't bear to listen.

The man was howling.

*

196

"Don't worry – apples," Brussels promised Billy.

But they passed no orchards.

"A shop, then..." said Brussels, breathless, running.

The hills were bare.

Billy rubbed his lips with a thistle rubbed his lips with a thistle rubbed his lips with a thistle.

"...In that brilliant village, on Mischief Night... robbing shops – for mints and chewy... Not a blind thing they can do... And... blind people. You can rob blind people, too...one night a year..."

Billy said, "My blazer's ripped."

"Lucky it weren't your knob... our neighbour caught his knob in his flies... that were that... he went mental."

Brussels kept talking as he ran:

"...mental like Butler... Imagine Butler getting his knob stuck in his zip in a Chemistry lesson... The Periodic Table – Ouch... Imagine grabbing his ruler, Billy... Can you imagine that?... Leathering Butler with his own ruler... on Mischief Night... In that brilliant village...."

They saw lamps. The village was wedged in a valley. It smelled of smoke and cold water.

*

In the main street, teenagers stood chatting and pushing each other under a dim streetlight.

Brussels said, "Can we come with you?"

They laughed when they saw the state of Brussels and Billy. "Come where?"

"Doing A Load Of Mischief."

A skateboarder with blond streaks said, "Why don't you ask our little brothers if they're playing out...?"

The teenagers laughed harder. Cyclists pulled wheelies. The blond lad made his skateboard climb a wall. Three girls chanted rap. A radio whined. One girl whispered something and then grabbed the others' arms, giggling, watching the blond lad.

197

*

Going home, Brussels scooped a bin-lid from a garden. He carried it for miles along dark country lanes, then threw it in a field near the wet cart-track. "Short-cut?" he said. Wet feathers winked in his hood.

The long flat moors were like animals, crouching. Billy shook his head. Something howled.

They looked at each other.

"A dog," said Billy.

Brussels nodded. "I thought that. Psychic. Like when you read my mind before..."

Billy walked faster.

"...before you chucked up... and he... what if he meant us to sink... so he could pretend to be helping... and..."

Billy said, "Brussels..."

"*Colin.*"

"Colin. Want them to talk about us behind our backs?"

Brussels frowned. "It could've been the kiss of life, couldn't it, Billy..."

Billy stared into fields, mile after mile of them – wick with secret creeping things. Weasels, rats, voles.

The fields stretched to the hills. Further. Even trees – there were eyes in the trees.

"There was no bloke," he told Brussels. "Those kids, they were other kids. We were in Manchester."

Brussels looked as if he might cry.

"We were shopping," said Billy.

Far off, the dog went on howling.

Brussels said, "There wasn't even a cabin, was there, Billy..."

"No," said Billy, "because Mischief Night's for kids."

"That's exactly what it is," said Brussels. "For bits of bloody kids."

Their shoes made wet slaps on the asphalt.

"We were in Manchester," said Billy

"We went shopping."

"Then they won't laugh at us."

"Behind our backs," said Brussels.

They walked towards town.

Slowly, the sky turned orange.

Faraway, the dog went on calling to something in the night, something beyond its reach, which it couldn't have, which never answered.

Birds

The driver's grey eyes move in the glass. "Off anywhere interesting then, kid?"

I follow his eyes into the mirror, nod.

"I'm up this guy's arse for a reason," he says. He takes a hand from the wheel of the truck, pulls a packet of cigarettes from the pocket of his denim shirt. A practised flick, and his mouth reaches down.

The lorry trembles over concrete.

"Want one?"

I shake my head.

His words are flat in their vice, the cigarette a straight line. "Good on you, lad. Wish I could pack 'em in, really. Tried it, like, but you know..."

He holds the box tight against the wheel and uses his free hand to bang a match off it. Sulphur flares up. He lowers the cigarette into the fire, takes a deep breath. The nicotine sighs through him. He slides up the seat, yawning.

The truck stays at 70, stays locked to the rear bumper of a Clio.

"Cancer-sticks, these things, kid."

The windscreen is cracked on my side. Concrete ridges go bump-bump-bump. A sign says: *London, 115*.

"That's the thing with this lark," he says, in his Midlands drawl. "Start off killing time – end up killing yourself, ay."

"Well, beats working in a factory...."

"Yeah, beats that lark," he says, sucking in smoke. "Bleeding dark holes, them places, ay? At least you get around a bit in a lorry." He stamps on the gas, moves up in his seat. "Get over, you bloodyoldfart."

The veins stand up on his arm as he yanks the gear. I look down, into the Clio. Its driver is turning to shout at us, his mouth scrambled by the cracks and whirls in the lorry's windscreen.

"They give any tosser a license these days, y'know..."

"Yeah."

"Any old tosser. I saw one old boy going the wrong way down the motorway a while back. Wrong bloody way."

"I read about that, I think."

He shakes his head, brings out another match. "Here."

"Like I said..."

"It isn't a fag, it's a match." He folds my fingers round it. "You might need to strike it, kid."

I look at the side of his face.

"For when I fart," he says. "Poison gas attack, eh. No, really – if I fart, use it. You never know, ay?"

"If you fart..."

"Ha." He shuffles in his seat. "Only joking!"

I smile.

"You hope," he says, shaking his head. "You hope I am, don't you. Christ, ay. Truck drivers. What are we like. I'll tell you this though: most of 'em wouldn't bother – they'd go ahead and fart. Just like that. You'd be dead in your seat, kid."

I study my fingers folded round the match.

"Burns off the smell, like," he says. "Not that I'll fart." He settles back. "Just if one pops out, like."

I turn from him and stare through the windscreen's cracked web. *London 110.*

"Way I see it, you've to be nice to your hitchers, kid. I mean, it's a deal, innit. You get where you want to go to – in your case..."

"... Spain."

"Spain, like. And I get the benefit of the company. Plus, y'know, it helps cut down on *these*." He studies a new cigarette. His other arm is lazy and flat on the wheel. "I must be wrong in the bloody head, ay."

Through the crack in the windscreen, the other cars and trucks look like splinters of metal and paint.

"I'll tell you what, kid. Have a look at this lot, ay, you'll like these." He reaches into the glove compartment, pulls out two Polaroid photos.

One of the photos is of a woman, white-skinned and English-looking, with long curlyish brown hair. She's leaning against the front of a lorry, this lorry.

Her black leather gear is studded with silver buttons. The studs have been pulled open to reveal her breasts.

"Cracker, ay? Her idea, an' all." He jerks his head to the right. "Wanna race, do we, ay?" The other photo slides out of my hand as he yanks the gear. "Up me arse for an hour, then all of a sudden he's Evel K-fucking-Nevel." He pulls out, looks across at me. "Careful with them pictures, like."

"Sorry."

The photo trembles on the floor of the cab. Someone has written "CROTCH SHOT!" on the back, in blue felt-tipped capitals. I turn it over. The woman is leaning on the fender, her gloved hand pressed to the dark fur between her legs.

"Here," I say.

He ignores my hand. "Watch this," he says. The truck spurts forward. We move ahead of Evel Knievel, overtake the Clio. Its driver makes a gesture.

"Ha," says the truck driver.

"Your pictures..."

He looks at me suddenly, raises his blond eyebrows. "Oh, aye. Them – crackers, ay. Didn't I tell you. Just got 'em out. There and then." He shakes his head, lays the photos on the armrest between us. "Course, that was a while back, kid. Just after we first met." The cigarette moves through the fingers of his free hand, as if it's a thought looking for the words. He shoves it into his mouth. "Young love, ay."

I smile.

He says, "You're wasting your time down there – in that Spain, like."

"How come?"

"They don't want to know, do they, eh? Stuck-up lot, the birds down there. Better off in Brum, lad. Didn't anybody tell you? Legs right up to their arses, the lasses in Brum. And none of that stuck-up carry-on. Plus, y' know what else they say about Brum, don't you? We've got a Bull Ring twice as big as Pamplona's but four times more dangerous." A cough brims on his lips. "That's Brum for you."

Through the warped glass, white-paint graffiti stretches for six lanes across the motorway bridge: I'M AFTER REBELLION BUT I'LL SETTLE FOR LIFE. I shift my head to read it.

"Having a bit of trouble with that window, ay, kid?"

"Yeah."

"Glad it's not on this side, like."

I nod.

"Only it's better staying out of the ditch if you can help it, innit."

*

Wheels, tarmac, gear changes.

I stare through the cracked glass. *London 64*. The sign seems to hold itself static, and is then suddenly gone.

"How did it happen, then?"

He taps the windscreen. "That mess? In Germany, kid. Bird hit it. Good job it's tough stuff, ay? I'll have to get it seen to in London, though. A mate of mine can probably fix me a deal. Cockney wanker, like. But he'll see me straight."

The M1 rushes under.

"I thought it must have been a stone – you know, a pebble or a bit of grit."

"A pebble? No, this was a bird, kid."

"Only it happened to a mate of mine twice in the same week. Two separate stones."

"O, aye, did it." The lines of his grin run tight on his face.

"Funny," I say. "Nothing for two years, and then two in the same week. Still, I suppose it's a shock whatever it is."

"Ah, you know what it's like. You get used to all sorts in this game, kid."

The truck bounces over the asphalt.

"What sort of bird was it then?"

He stretches. "How do you mean?"

"Well, you know – was it a big one? Looks like an ostrich must have smacked it to make a mess like that."

"It was a *bird*," he says, looking across at me, frowning. "Daft bitch walked out in front of me on the autobahn. Near Dusseldorf."

The Polaroid's glisten in his armrest. His cab sways. "Her car had broken down, hadn't it? So what does she do? Only walks along the side of the bloody road, looking for help. Busiest fucking street in Europe. Next thing I know she's bouncing off the window." He looks at me. "Never even had time to get the brakes on. Bang. Just like that. Three hours I was held up."

I stare ahead. Specks whirl in the glass. Scraps of tyres lie scattered over the hard shoulder. The crash barrier is broken into pieces by the windscreen.

Cars move out of line, into line. There are dark marks on the asphalt.

London 56.

He flips open the cigarette packet and waves it at me. I reach across the trembling gear housing, take one.

The Coming Attractions

They showed good ones down the Fleapit on Sundays: double-bills starring David Carradine and Burt Reynolds.

Usually, they smashed cars up.

If they didn't, the four of us shouted, "Come on – smash cars up!" Except for Jeffrey, Our Deep Mate.

The usherette had a time with us. It was probably bad enough working there, anyway. For a start, the place *hummed*. Our mate with the bristly eyes said you could hear the smell.

"They must have hundreds of cats, eh, Douggie? For it to smell this bad?"

"Or one massive one, Matt," he replied, rasping his stubble.

"DOUGGIE AND MATT – TWO REGULAR GUYS," said Keith, huskily.

Everyone groaned. "Oh no – The Trailer Voice..."

"Shhhhhh!" a pensioner warned us.

Keith Could Not Be Stopped. "EARTH'S ONLY HOPE AGAINST THE MASSIVE PISSING CINEMA CAT."

"*Quiet!*"

"It's Keith's Trailer Voice. Because they're not smashing cars up," I explained to the pensioner.

"Also because of them pubes," said Keith, pointing to where giant shadows of hairs trembled on the screen.

"Possibly because they haven't cleaned the projector's gate possibly," said Jeffrey.

Keith shuffled. "I can't concentrate for them pubes – they're dangling in that actor's face!"

Next thing – the usherette points this huge pole of a torch at us. In the bright foyer, she looked tired. "I've thrown you out before, haven't I?" she asked Douggie.

Douggie straightened a lick of hair.

"Aren't you getting a bit old for this carry-on?"

He stared at her legs. "I might be," he said.

The usherette watched him strut away. She straightened her apron. When she turned to go, her heels made little dents in the carpet. The carpet was thick and soft and blue, and it seemed to glue her down.

*

When we caught up with Douggie, he was swigging a can.

"Where did you get that?"

"A place with a tinkly bell over the door, and tills inside."

"Shops," said Keith.

"Not where... how..."

Douggie narrowed his eyes like Clint Eastwood. "My mistake – two cans," he said.

What an afternoon. We ended up underneath a bush.

"What are we doing under a bush!" I said.

Keith growled, "FOUR YOUNG SCHOOLMATES BENEATH ONE EXTRAORDINARY BUSH..."

"I'll drink to that," said Douggie, and we did, because it turned out he had four cans!

"This week," he said, looking into the quiet branches, "I'm going to cop off with that usherette."

Under our backs, the whole planet was spinning.

*

Later, at the bus stop, Douggie said he was offsky.

"But your fossils will smell your breath!" I said. "It's... it's..."

"... against the law," laughed Douggie.

Everyone sniggered, even Jeffrey, Our Deep Mate.

"I'll tell you what it is," said Douggie: "you ought to relax, Matt. Forget *rules*. Take the weight off."

He sauntered away. All our eyes were on him, six eyes on one back – his broad, strong, hair-covered back.

"He even probably shaves his eyes..."

"He's going to get off with that usherette," Keith slurred. By now, he was greener than green. Emerald.

"That usherette? She's about 30!"

But Jeffrey was looking into a drain as usual, and Keith had fallen over.

"When's this bus coming, anyway?"

Jeffrey said, "It's Sunday, Matt. There aren't any buses on Sundays."

I scratched my head.

Later on, we had to slap Keith around a bit, until he went from emerald to burgundy. Then he woke up and became 'fridge-coloured.

"You're `fridge-coloured," I said.

"MEET KEITH – AN ORDINARY JOE WITH A DIFFERENSH: KEITH'S TURNING INTO A FRI..."

We told him to stop doing The Trailer Voice, we were sick of The Trailer Voice. "Why can't you act more mature, Keith?" we said.

Keith belched.

*

On the way home, Keith told us the world's best films. "Fifth, obvioush: *Shmokey and the Bandit*. Fourth: *Gone in 60 Sheconds*, them cop cars they wreck. Third: *Convoy*. CB Radio. Second: *Carquake*. Winner, shtands to reason: *Death Race 2000*."

"What about *Westworld*?" I asked.

Keith rolled his eyes. "*Westworld*! *Westworld*'s rubbish."

"Possibly *The Time Machine*, possibly," muttered Jeffrey.

"*Westworld* was slow," said Keith.

"When smoke comes out of Yul Brynner's eyes..."

"When smokes comes really slowly out of Yul Brynner's eyes," said Keith. He teetered on the kerb. Steadied himself. "*Death Race 2000*. When they squash that old biddie under..."

"... the spikes," I said, "the spikes on the tyres..."

"Which you pretend you've seen, don't you, Matt? Except you've never been to an X-cert. Because you look too y..."

"At least I can hold my ale..."

"Fffff," said Keith.

"And I'm not 'fridge-coloured, either."

Jeffrey and me left him underneath another bush.

"It must be summat I ate," he groaned.

*

At Jeffrey's, his little brother came out – Jeffrey II, we called him, because he was sort of a sequel to Jeffrey.

"Has Our Jeffrey been on about black and white films again?" he asked.

"Monochrome actually," said Jeffrey. This way he spoke.

Jeffrey's brother said, "The best film's *Logan's Run*. These crystals they've got in their hands, right. Red crystals. But the crystals blacken when you're 30, and you've to report to Carousel, to be killed."

"*Westworld*," I said. "*Westworld*'s good."

"I haven't seen that one," said Jeffrey II. "It's most likely rubbish. In *Logan's Run*, this bloke – he gets past 30, right – and he runs off. To Sanctuary. And the police, right – they're called Sandmen. Because they put people to sleep. And..."

Suddenly I legged it. I was offsky.

Heh, I thought: *Matt's Run*.

I imagined a crystal in my hand that went from green to emerald to burgundy to 'fridge-coloured when people talked shite to me.

*

Then it was Sunday again, and we were staring into the usherette's torch.

"You lot," she said, looking at Douggie.

"It's this film," we told her, "it's right boring."

"Do you want throwing out again?"

"No."

But Douggie stared at her legs and said, "Yes. Throw me out please."

He kept his eyes wide in the beam.

The usherette smoothed the bum of her uniform. "Alright," she said quietly, "follow me to the exit, please, sir."

We leaned back in our seats, watching. The door closed softly. Dust whirled. Keith tapped his fingers. "He'll come back in a minute, and he'll have a full beard."

"Because he hasn't shaved since the film started..."

"ON A FARAWAY WORLD KNOWN AS PLANET PUBE," said Keith, in The Trailer Voice, "LIVES AN EXTRAORDINARY YOUNG BEARD..."

"Ha," said The Girl Behind. "That's a good impression, that is. A right good impression of your fit mate."

"What fit mate?"

"That fit mate of yours with the deep voice."

"He's *well* fit, he is. He's a right manly voice," said Another Girl.

"See the arse on him when he went out!"

Keith swung round. "Douggie? That's not an impersonation of Douggie – it's The Trailer Bloke. Are you deaf, woman?"

"Shhhhhhh," said everybody else.

"But *everybody* recognises The Trailer Voice!" Keith protested.

"Keith," I said, "she'll throw us out again..."

Except the usherette never came back, she'd disappeared. I studied the door's seal, trying to work it out.

"Why did Douggie ask to be chucked out?" I said.

But nobody was listening, because, by now, *Beneath the Planet of the Apes* had come on, this amazing film about bald mutant priests who lived in a ruined underground city, who hated monkeys.

"Punch them in the head!" Keith yelled.

"Keith," we warned, "she'll come back in – she'll..."

He'd gone off on one. "Monk – EEES!" he was shouting.

"This is potentially ruinous," Jeffrey muttered. Something like that. "The usherette will have no option but to confiscate our ticke..."

"Monk-EEEEEES!" shouted Keith.

"Mut-ANTS!" shouted some kids from the other side.

Keith shook his fist.

"Keith..." we hissed.

But still the usherette didn't come. No soft footsteps, no torch in the face...

... until, eventually, Keith must have thought it was pointless making a racket if we weren't going to get thrown out, and he settled down.

Soon the whole cinema was quiet, watching.

When we found out that the mutants worshipped The Bomb, Keith gasped. He didn't mention the projector hairs anymore. He just gawped.

"Let there be light!" the mutants cried.

And the world blew up.

"They mistook The Bomb for a deity," whispered Jeffrey, through his hands.

"Phew," said Keith. "Phew-eeeeee."

"It just goes to show," said Jeffrey.

Outside, afterwards, we were stunned into silence. We walked through evening sunlight, kicking stones.

Keith said, "Bloody mutants, worshipping rockets. Them monkeys should've twatted the bald idiots..."

I didn't tell Keith and Jeffrey, but out of the corner of my eye I'd spotted Douggie. He was in the queue at the Chinese, with the usherette. She was looking up at him as he spoke – spoke in that quiet, thin-lipped way, one hand rasping bristle, the other looping his belt.

Then we turned the corner, and it was like neither of them had been there, like I'd not seen them, and the kebab shop had never existed.

"Against the laws of nature..." Keith was saying.

He shook his head.

We ended up by the bus stop, watching Jeffrey stare into the drain.

"This time last week we were rat-arsed," I said.

"Because of Douggie's ale."

"It's ace when Douggie gives us ale."

"He's right generous, is Douggie."

"Possibly because he can gain ready access to it. Possibly because he looks 27," said Jeffrey.

"He doesn't *have* to give us ale, Jeffrey. He could go under that bush and drink it on his own."

"Or the pub," said Keith. "Or wherever he wants. Because he's massive."

"And bristly. And he looks 27."

We rubbed our chins. Nothing happened, no buses came, even the birds had stopped singing. It was Sunday. Everybody was slathered in their houses, imagining Monday.

"Why are you allus looking in that drain, Jeffrey?"

Jeffrey shrugged. "Don't you ever wonder where the pipes go, Matt? The sewers and tunnels? Which only a handful of engineers ever see? Or the hairs and bristles and skin? Don't you ever wonder where it all goes?"

We stared at him.

"If it goes into rivers?" said Jeffrey. "If it falls off people's bodies and travels possibly into oceans?"

He stared into the drain. "It's like the film, Matt. It's *beneath*."

*

On the way home, two girls were on about the usual subject:

"He's well fit, that Douggie. He's Fit for Britain."

I walked on aimlessly – until I reached the amazing bush. Where, guess what, Douggie was lying on his back again!

"Here," he said, and threw me a can.

"Smart!"

I got under the bush, and had a good drink.

Douggie said, "Sozz for blowing you out in the flicks, Matt..."

"No problem, Douggie."

"I'd things to sort out." He scratched his head. "You know what they're like."

"Yeah."

"More trouble than they're worth."

"Hmmm."

"Ask me, Matt, we'd be better off without all that hassle, wouldn't we?"

I watched a jet cross the sky, heading north out of Manchester, for the Pole.

Douggie said, "She's on the market again, anyway. If you fancy a poke, like."

I turned to face him.

"The slapper in the flicks," he said. "I've binned her off. One afternoon of *that's* enough for me. Weren't even up for a proper shag, like."

"No," I said.

Douggie said, "She doesn't know yet, though."

"That's right."

"Couldn't be arsed to tell her, like."

I looked away from him, towards the jet. Imagined I was on it, stretching back with a beer, looking down, thinking: Good riddance to bad rubbish!

"Like I said, Matt – if you fancy a do..."

"Yes."

"... she'll be in the foyer at knocking-off time."

"OK."

"Waiting for me, like."

Bristle poked through Douggie's chin. *It comes from inside*, I thought. *From beneath*.

"Not that I'd bother, if I were you," he said. "She's dowdy when you get to know her."

"Yes."

"I mean, you think you've met a nice one, and there's always... always this one little thing."

He watched the jet.

That's my jet, I thought.

He followed my jet with his bristly eyes. "I'll tell you what it is, Matt. I wish my bollocks hadn't dropped. I wish I was a late

212

developer, like you."

Maybe it was the beer – I did a thing that Jeffrey calls the Umbrage, or something. I snarled, "Piss off, Douggie!"

"Hold on, Matt..."

But I was completely Umbraged. I shouted at him, "What have my bollocks got to do with you? You stupid big hair-covered alcoholic!"

Then I threw my can into the road, and it hit a bus.

That was typical – a bus coming. When did a bus ever come on Sundays unless you threw a can in the road?

*

After that it was Umbrage, big-time. I chewed my teeth to splinters, chugging the streets, shaking my pathetic little fists at traffic lights and shops.

"Who's he reckon he is?" I asked a ladder.

I saw my reflection in a shop window.

"The big ape," I said.

I kicked a dustbin and two pigeons – except the pigeons flew onto the town hall. So I booted the town hall. Not the whole town hall, just the steps.

Then I wrote HAIRY BOLLOCKS on three pieces of paper in bold capitals and set them loose. Watched the papers fly up into the sky.

People would open up the papers and read HAIRY BOLLOCKS, and be really shocked. They'd probably write to the local newspaper.

*

I'd calmed down by the time I reached the Fleapit.

COMING ATTRACTIONS, it said on a poster in the glass case: *THE EROTIC SIZZLER... EMMANUELLE.*

The usherette was standing in the foyer, staring out into the street, frowning, checking her watch.

'Serves you right,' I thought...

213

But it was something to do with the carpet, the marks her heels had pecked in it – the days and weeks of tracks she'd laid through that pissy building. I went in. I stared at her legs. I said to her, "Douggie isn't coming, love."

She wouldn't look at me. She just studied her hand quietly, as if there was a crystal there, a crystal turning black.

"He's pissed under a bush," I said.

On the way home, I tickled a hair I'd found on my chin. It was thin and short but I played with it until it became important under my fingers, like a hair does when it's stuck in the projector's gate – a tiny squiggle of hair that swells up into a question mark under the light.

And the question mark's the size of a wall and you sit there in the dark, staring up at it, waiting for an explosion or a crash or a fight.

Waiting for something to finally happen.

Crumbs

Phil's on a train, and he's tired because he slept badly and he's been working hard. Then he got up early, drank too much coffee and now can't finish the newspaper crossword.

He's sitting alone on a double seat (and thank God for that), and there's a couple at a table across the gangway. The man is talking about the Russian Revolution.

When he looks down at the crossword, Phil thinks: I should be looking at the scenery. But looking out of the window irritates him because it puts him off the crossword. Plus, he has a cold and his joints ache.

The man in the couple is saying, "Of course, Tolstoy wrote about it. He romanticised the Cossacks."

Phil turns his achey neck to look at them. They are eight or nine years younger than him, just enough of a gap for them to be recognisably like him and for him to be jealous that they are younger but not much different. He thinks: They shouldn't talk about things they don't know anything about.

The woman in the couple is eating crisps. She crunches them, then puts more crisps into her mouth before she's swallowed the mouthful she's eating. She does this a lot. There are crumbs on her newspaper. The woman is further on with her crossword than Phil is. It's the same crossword. Phil dislikes stupid people who are more intelligent than he is.

The man is thin, with a long neck. His Adam's Apple works

like a lift in a shaft. He says, "Yeah, Tolstoy's short stories are incredible, you know. It's hard to imagine the Russian Revolution without them."

There is another world somewhere in which Phil can lean across to the man and say, "That's bollocks, that is, all that stuff you're going on about." But Phil is not in that world.

The train creeps through Rugby like it's ashamed to be seen there. A seven-letter word for 'everlasting', ending in 's'. Not eternal. Phil looks out of the window at a low bridge composed of many arches. The guard clicks a passenger-counting device. Not passengers, customers. Drab fields of scrub and grass stretch away beyond a blur of embankments and fences.

Then: a steel-grey sports car takes a humpy bridge over the railway. Phil's train rushes towards it. The car is near, nearer, there. Gone. Drama in its passing. Phil is stirred.

The girl reads from the newspaper: "Millions of pounds are still unclaimed from the lottery. That's unbelievable, isn't it."

The man says nothing. He is looking down, silent about Tolstoy.

The girl says to him, "There's a bloke here," shuffling the newspaper, "who refused to give his wife half of his lottery winnings." She looks at the man. "If I won £50,000 I'd give you half of it."

The man is looking at the crumbs on the tabletop. Tons of sheds whizz past. Phil finds them objectionable. He orders more coffee from a trolley with squeaky wheels and drinks it without pleasure. He is aware of the position of the tongue in his mouth. His joints ache. There is a skeleton inside him. Rape fields spill over the field's high edge, on into the thickening clouds.

The girl says, "Did you know they're planning to build another runway at Heathrow?" She has opened a flask whose contents smell like burning tyres. Phil looks at the woman. She has dyed black hair. She is too pale for it. He thinks: She is about to slurp her soup.

The man puts up his arms and stretches. He is wearing a grey T-shirt, stained at the armpits. He yawns like a man who knows he's being watched. The book on his lap slips off. He retrieves it. It's *The Third World War* by General Sir John Hackett.

The girl slurps the soup. "Dante was born today in 1265," she

216

tells the man. He keeps his eyes on the rows of redbrick houses beyond the window. Their roofs shine in the fading morning light.

Further down the carriage, a man is telling his two female companions the names of all the members of Parliament in the North West of England. At certain moments, the women interrupt, and he laughs in exactly the same way at everything they say. Then he starts to talk about the BBC in an authoritative voice.

"The German economy collapsed completely today in 1927," the woman tells the man. He presses his arm against the window, then rests his face on the arm.

"Harvey Keitel is 63 today. Sixty three. He looks younger than that. Richard off *Richard and Judy* is 46. Forty-six. He's not 46. He's older than that, isn't he. Stevie Wonder's only 52. That's not very old, is it. I think that's funny."

The man speaks into his arm. He says, "Forty-six."

She chuckles. He turns his head to look at her.

"Do you want a yoghurt? she asks him.

He unsticks his forearm from the window and smiles. There is a gummy trace on the glass.

Phil looks down at his crossword.

That clue. Everlasting.

He is tired of being alone.

The Spike

First she had to wet the handkerchief with old woman spit.

Flenky took a crafty peek from the yard, leaning on the cracked sill, staring into the camphor gloom.

His Gran piffed politely onto the cloth, then lost her patience. She keeked round – even though she lived on her own – and started really pelting the hankie.

After that, she twisted the moist cloth into a sharp, tight point, occasionally piffing more spit. It took about a week.

Then the corner of the handkerchief was a spike.

The spike would have glinted in the sun, except the sun never shone. Just the grey flurr scraping across, adding grey to grey, keeping cotton supple.

"Puts me in a job, that sky," said Flenky's Gran. And the other old women on the street nodded.

At first, when he was little, Flenky had always forgotten – banging on the door with his dad, waiting for her to answer, thinking of school or footy or trees, and then he'd see the spike and remember... and it would be too late.

She always attacked him in the doorway.

"Come here, lad! Come here!" she yelled, her voice made shrill by clanking looms, the need to shout.

The spike drove into his ears, spearing wax.

Her eyes bulged. "By heck, thur's potatoes in theer!"

Flenky's dad was a traitor – went along with the torture, lips

218

curling, eyes finding cracks to dwell on, cobwebs that maybe made him wonder: Is the old girl slowing down?

"A! Ah! Aaaah!"

She leapt back as if ashamed of her dirty relative, fearing that news would spread about the stuff he kept in his head.

"He dunt care, tha knows..." they'd be saying, twitching lace curtains, widening mouths to make giant Os and Es, the mime they'd learned in mills where machines mauled words. Factories of gossip.

"And you'll never guess..."

Flenky would never guess. Never guess how much wax he contained. Never guess how it shamed his Gran to see it. Never guess what Them At No. 27 would say if they saw it, too.

"Saw my wax?" he said.

"COMIN' OUT THI LUGS!" she explained – as if the wax was running down his face. He imagined the scene at his funeral: *You'll never guess... the lad's brain wur meltin' or summat... all down t' side of his face... thowt we'd die of shame.*

He complained to his dad.

"Dad," he said.

"Quiet."

"I haven't said owt yet."

"Just in case."

"But, Dad, it hurts when she pokes in my ears..."

The sports page twitched. "What dust ta expect, lad?"

"Eh?"

"It'll happen larn thi for bein' such a mucky pup."

"I can't help having that stuff inside my head."

"Course tha can, lad. Wash 'em out!"

Flenky tried. He balanced on the edge of the bath, trickling in water from a plastic measuring jug.

Afterwards, he was convinced he'd gone mad.

"All the sounds are weird," he told his dad.

"Balance on one leg and hop wi' thi head on t' other side."

When Flenky did what his dad said, Sandra Billings saw him through the window. She was trudging down the street with her underwater walk.

It was because Flenky slept downstairs in the front room. People could see in.

Sandra Billings pointed a big, rooty finger through the window. Flenky hadn't got a clue what she was doing walking down his street. She was supposed to live miles away.

"Ha! Look!" she mimed, moist lips making the OOO like his Gran, like his town, divided by walls, connected by shame.

Flenky's cheeks burned. He ran outside. "It's 'cos of me Gran," he told her.

Sandra Billings laughed, twisting a loony-finger at her temple.

The streets seemed wide and bright and empty. Flenky had a funny taste in his mouth.

Stoop-shouldered, he caught a flash of himself in the window of his room, saw his cheeks' embarrassed bloom, imagined his Gran advancing with a brush, Skewerer of Ears, Scourer Of The Flush.

The taste in his mouth was carbolic soap.

"Dad, why doesn't she use *ordinary* washing-up liquid on the plates?"

His dad was on with the sport. "Gran's generation doesn't like waste."

She was four foot, ten inches tall.

"How come Gran's like that?" he said.

"Like what?"

Flenky couldn't say dwarf. "Small," he said.

His dad thought for a minute. "She wur squashed," he said.

"WHAT?"

Dad, back to the sport. "In an experiment."

Flenky fled. His dad was reading about Bob Latchford, Paul Mariner, Joe Corrigan. Tall men. 'Keepers. Strikers.

He paced the drizzly streets, trying to work it out. He was scared that Them At No. 27 would find out about the experiment.

There was still water in his ear. Everything sounded gurgled and squashy. He couldn't even stand up straight.

"I can't do it," he confessed to his dad.

"Do what?"

"That Bouncing Thing."

"Bouncing's hard," said his dad.

"It's my balance."

"Balance is to do with your ears."

A horrible flash swept through Flenky: his Gran advancing with a massive cotton spike, saying: "Come here, I'll sort thi balance out, y' daft article!"

For a time, he considered going to live in the hills.

"Up theer, on them moors," he told Sandra Billings.

"What, hopping?" she said.

He scowled at her. "How come you're always over here these days, anyway?"

Sandra Billings twisted a bulky foot, got out a fag, pointed it in the direction her words were going to go. "I'm shagging your neighbour."

"Martin Jackson?" he said.

She shoved in the fag, nodded with tight lips.

Everywhere Flenky went there were people smoking and shagging. Up the swings, on the back yard coyts, down the back-alley. They were belching fumes and humping in the dock-leaves and dog shit. Flattening grass, knocking back nettles.

"That's disgusting, that is," he told Sandra Billings.

She got out her loony-finger again. He ran off. He imagined that he was a nomad over the cobbles. Drizzleman. The Rain's Avenger.

Then he decided that he was soaking to the sodding bone, so he went home.

The old woman was waiting behind the door in his house this time.

"A! Ah! Aaaah!"

"Stand still, lad! Stand still!"

Drizzleman (The Rain's Avenger) got a pounding.

"Full o' spuds!" she screeched, holding up the brown-stained spike after she'd pulled it from his ear.

"Bits o' black," she said. "Thur's even bits o' black!"

Afterwards, Flenky hid under the bed for three hours, then got up to watch *Garrison's Guerrillas*. They had a jeep that skidded around in circles on some foreign wasteland, and then they won the war. It was because they blew up a shed.

"Turn it over now, lad," she ordered.

"O, Gran!"

They had to watch another circus.

"Burt Lancaster might be on later," she explained.

"He's an actor," he told her. "He doesn't do circuses any more."

She stabbed a needle into some wool, yanked and tugged, cut off the knots with her false teeth.

"Burt Lancaster hasn't done circuses for thirty years," Flenky told his dad.

The sports section shivered. "Nil-nil," said his dad. The needles ticked and clittered, ticked and clittered.

"She's not even watching, dad!"

"I already told you. Nil-nil."

Flenky grimaced. "Not football. Telly."

The 'paper came down. His dad's tired head loomed out.

"He gave up the circus yonks back. He's a film star," said Flenky.

"Stop oinin' her," said his dad.

"But Laurel and Hardy are on t' other side!"

"They're dead, them two," said his Gran. She was knitting boiler cladding. Or a coat for a horse. Or something to cover a bungalow with.

"So?" said Flenky.

"*Dead folk*," she shuddered.

Flenky gave up.

"Meks me feel funny," she said. "Watching them who've passed on. Gives me a turn. 'S unnatural."

Rain streaked the window. A clown was throwing buckets of feathers around. It was remarkable, for some reason, that the circus performers came from Romania.

"I'm bored," said Flenky.

"If you're bored, it means you're boring," said his Gran.

"Go out and kick a ball around," said his dad.

"It's pouring down."

"Puts me in a job, that sky," said his Gran.

Flenky snatched his ball, and went out.

Drabbins was waiting for him on the spare land.

"Aya," said Drabbins.

"What are you doing here?" Flenky asked him, watching the rain.

"Waiting for you."

"But you didn't know I was coming."

Drabbins shrugged. The rain had tangled his hair into greasy loops.

Flenky bounced the ball, once. "How long have you been here?"

"An hour."

"An hour?"

"Two hours," said Drabbins.

"Two hours?"

Drabbin's buff-coloured jacket was stained from the downpour. He looked like he was made out of old cardboard boxes. "I've been here for two-and-three-quarter-hours," he said.

Flenky shrugged. "Let's have a kickabout."

The ball sluiced through puddles. As soon as they had begun, Drabbins fell over.

"Dog-shit," he said, pointing at his trousers, scraping it off.

Rain had plastered wet stripes over the pebble-dashed sub-station wall that they used for goals. Flenky picked up the ball, bounced it, waiting for Drabbins to clean up.

A man in a black cap was fiddling with the sub-station door. He had to put his clipboard next to a puddle because the hinge was stiff.

DANGER OF DEATH, it said on the door.

"That bloke's going inside our goals," said Drabbins. A big piece of dog-shit was stuck to the back of his hand.

Flenky gave up, went home. There was water inside his head, water outside it. Their town's steep streets funnelled streams down the valley sides. Drains gurgled. Gutters groaned.

He was thinking about the man in the black cap. Thinking about his clipboard.

In the alley, he passed his Gran. She was wearing a shiny red raincoat. Flenky heard the old woman muttering as she splashed past. She didn't look up.

Some big lads on the corner aimed laughter in her direction.

"Ey up. It's *Don't Look Now*," they said.

His Gran stamped past, grinding her stained false teeth.

"Hallo, Gran."

She beat on through the deluge, out of Flenky's life, into her own – to the doctors and to the back yard shed where she kept 600 brushes. To dark grocery shops where they sold mainly potatoes. Flenky could barely understand it. In his mind, when she wasn't with him, she was working on the spike, piffing spit and twisting. Preparing.

"Just seen Gran going home," he said when he got back.

Flenky's dad dragged a weary palm through his hair. "Not drowning, wur she?"

"No."

His dad's heavy eyelids came down. "She's taken the huff. And it's your fault, lad."

"How come it's my fault she's taken the huff?"

"I told her about yon carbolic soap."

"Why did you do that?"

"I don't know. She slung her hook soon enough, though."

Flenky pictured his Gran's downcast face. "Some lads were laughing at her," he said.

"T' streets are full o' bloody hooligans. Lakin' about, doin' nowt."

His Dad went back to the sport with a scowl.

Flenky said, "What does Gran do, Dad?"

"Works in a mill."

"I know that. What for?"

"What dust ta mean, what for? So she's food to eat, you dish-cloth."

"But what's her job?"

"Weaver."

"What's a weaver do?"

"Weaves. What's this, *Twenty Questions*?"

"What stuff, Dad?"

"Stuff."

"Yeah, but *what* stuff?"

"I don't know. Clothes probably. Shirts and that. Blouses."

"Why does she say that weird thing about the sky, Dad?"

"Say what about it?"

"How it keeps her in a job, summat like that."

His dad sighed. "Cotton's got to be moist. Stops it snappin'."

The glass trembled. "I hate rain," said Flenky.

His dad said nothing, tracked cricket scores. Rain stopped play. Players off for bad light. Match abandoned. There were chips of steel in his hair. Curls of metal. Oil fumes deep in his skin.

"Dad?"

"Hm?"

"What do you do, dad?"

"Rob trains. Bloody hell. Don't start on me."

Flenky went upstairs. He crawled under his bed, lay there on the floor. He looked up at the saggy under-belly of the mattress, thinking.

Dust gathered. Fluff settled.

Then he thought: What am I doing under the bed?

Time passed.

Soon it was time to go to sleep. But he decided that he would sleep under the bed to see what it was like.

A long time later, when it was dark and the must keened in his nostrils, Flenky woke up and decided to get into bed.

As he slid out across the glassy carpet, something made him go the window. When he looked out, he saw the same old streets bearing their dark load, a distant crack of purple in the East.

Then a tiny part of the blackness broke away from the rest of the night. It came floating towards him, all glistening and red, grinding splinters out of its own teeth.

The figure kept its head down, went on chunnering at the cobbles, mumbling at the moss which grew in the cracks, complaining to the few straggly blades of grass that wriggled free from the wilderness beneath their town.

The tip of Flenky's nose met the cold pane.

"Gran," he said.

She battered on down the street.

He jerked up and chucked on the first clothes he could find, trying in his haste to remember the order: socks over toes, never put jumpers on legs, only one shoe per foot, flies at the front.

By the time Flenky was in the back yard, pressing the sneck, trying to shrug off sleep, his Gran had vanished.

He stood in the alley, trying to see through the dark. But it was like a screen.

A cat skenned at him from the dustbin door. Flenky stared back at it. The cat's alien gaze didn't even flicker.

Evil eye, evil eye...

"Gran!" he shouted with a shudder.

No-one answered. The moon had found a hole in the clouds. It seemed to be flinging itself head-first through the blackness, as if bent on smashing itself to pieces. Its light was cold on Flenky's chest.

The back-alley looked like it was waiting for something.

Flenky yawned at the staring cat. He wondered why he'd slept under the bed. It seemed a bit mad all of a sudden.

"You daft pillock," he said, but quickly shut up when he remembered that only loonies wandered alleys in the middle of the night muttering to themselves.

"Like Gran," he thought.

As he turned to go back to bed, Flenky became aware of a faraway humming. He held his breath. The humming continued. Somehow he knew that he had been hearing the humming for a long time, that it had been there when he first entered the alley.

The low drone kept on, as if it had something to do with the darkness, a part of the night that worked on your ears rather than your eyes.

Then, standing in the back-yard's doorway, thumb pressing hard on the sneck, Flenky could no longer work out where the humming came from, and wondered maybe if its source lay inside his head, in that strange black place where dreams stirred.

Dreaming. Or awake?

If not dreaming, then how could he be here now, going bog-eyed at a cat in the middle of the night under a racing moon?

He let go of the sneck. It was as if he was imagining two separate people, the Flenky who went back to bed to please his dad and the

Flenky now pelting across cobbles in untied shoes, in search of his Gran.

He was out of breath when he found her on the other side of the garages. She was still bearing down through the blackness.

Flenky stopped, held his sides. He had a stitch, which was typical.

"Wait," he said.

Sealed in her plastic coat, she didn't hear him. She went on clouting through the puddles that covered the garage-land's gravel paths.

The humming was louder now. Flenky felt it move through him, a part of the blood that pounded in the far-off channels of his head, behind the wax and the dirt.

Suddenly, by the threshold of some enormous building, she turned, framed by the door.

The door swung back to reveal the clattering black maw beyond.

They stared into each other's dark shapes, the old woman and her Grandson. People flitted past. More shapes. More banging of the giant door.

"Ian Flenkinson," she said. "What the hell are *thee* doing rackin' about at this time o' neet?"

Flenky's mouth opened and closed, a rhyme with the building's blackened door. "I don't know. Where are *you* going, Gran?"

"To work, lad."

"What work?"

"My work," she said. "Here. In this bloody place. Mornin', Betty."

A hunched woman grunted in their direction before vanishing into the building, as if swallowed.

"But..." Flenky tried to concentrate. "But it's dark," he said.

His Gran took down the crimson hood. Her face was lined. She turned her head to the racing moon. A little light fell upon her frown.

"And what did tha think I did every morning, lad?"

Flenky shrugged. "Went shopping..."

227

His Gran's tiny frame moved with laughter, as if she was a weird new bird shaking off dirt.

"For carbolic soap, and that," he said, embarrassed.

The old woman reached up and straightened a lick of his hair. He flinched. It had been a bit close to his ears.

Now she was tying Flenky's shoelace, bony hands a blur of motion, face upturned to his.

"Tha's gettin' a moustache, lad," she said.

Flenky looked away from the bones and wrinkles, down to the sunken cobbles, where black boots trudged.

Suddenly he thought: Even stone won't last.

"Get along home with thee now," she said. "I'll not tell thi father."

Flenky nodded.

"Sithi, lad," she said.

She yanked at the door. It groaned shut.

Afterwards, as heavier, hairier hands heaved the handle, Flenky lingered there for a little while, watching the mill swallow an entire crowd.

He half-expected the building to bulge with the mass of all those people. But nothing much changed. Machines hammered, smoke billowed. And that same humming went on from within, loud and even.

"Bye, Gran," he said.

On the way home, as dawn's first light broke over the stained garages, Flenky touched the fur above his top lip.

By the side of the gravel path, he noticed weeds struggling to find homes for themselves at the tidal margins of little pools.

He splashed in and out of puddles, keeping his eyes on the wooden garages. Some of the oldest ones had collapsed, as if flattened by the sky and its rain. Flenky wondered, briefly, whether his Gran's house would still be there when he was old, or whether there would be a gap in his life, like gaps between garages.

Then he imagined her advancing with a cut-throat razor.

"What a bloody beardy mess! Hold still, lad, hold still!"

He pressed the sneck on the back door.

"Weirdo," he said to the staring cat.

Upstairs, he peeped through a crack. His dad's prone shape stirred under the sheets.

A big white clock ticked on the bedside. Soon it would clunk, then ring.

Before he got into bed, Flenky looked out through the window.

In the alleyway, fuzzy through dawn's first drizzle, the cat was still staring at the place where he had been.

In The Home

I'm in the bath, terrified. I want to get out.

"Please," I beg my angel, "help me."

My angel lives in the tap but refuses to show himself. He's shy.

I slap water. Steam rises, there are big wet pools on the lino.

"You promised you'd call," says my angel finally in a tiny, reedy voice, "you never called."

"I'm calling now," I moan.

The plastic duck spins.

"Never for nice things, always for business," he says. "Would one little call have broken your neck?"

My fear emboldens me. I go at the tap with the one limb I can still move, my big toe. I bung my big toe into that tap. I really bung it up there.

Now everything's muffled, unclear.

"You're just making things worse," says the angel.

"See if I care," I tell him, "you're a weak angel. And shy and small. When I think of the angel I had when I was young, I could weep. My angel then, he was man-sized. The size of a house. With wings. The whole wardrobe. He had a harp. Are you telling me you even have a harp!"

My arms collapse into the suds and swirl.

"Well?" I ask.

"I have a mouth organ," the angel croaks.

"That's my point," I say, voice fading, arms useless flippers by my side. "Back then, there was no end to it, the feasting, the wine. We used to share our spoils between us. Mortals and angels, side by side. Once, we had a gourd. A gourd, I tell you! There was sweetness in my angel then. But more than sweetness. Strength, besides."

"Back then," says the voice from the tap, "you needed a strong angel."

I want to say: *And I don't now? I don't need strength now?*

But my voice has gone.

"Once," says the angel in the tap, "you were sweetness worth saving."

I take a final breath, forcing water out of the tub in a long, rolling wave – then fall back, and go under.

The water sways – the only sound is its roar. I look up from under the suds, which pass like clouds across a sky.

My eyes are open, I can't even blink.

The angel in the tap says, "Lie still now. Be calm. Soon, even I will be strong enough to carry you."

The News At 10

A door's about to bang. My Mum's going out, my Dad's staying in. The thunderous sulk.

"Your Dad's got a monk on 'cos I'm off out."

I don't look at her. I don't look at him. I concentrate on the TV. Three kisses, one for each child, two of them sleeping, me still glaring at the idiot-box, afraid of my Dad. My Dad's Rasputin. I don't say a word. I think, "How selfish, to leave me here. My poor Dad, too."

Three kisses, three children. Three jobs. He has one of them, Mum has two: "Down on hands and knees, scrubbing men's urinals in pubs. Day in, day out. Why shouldn't I go out? For a bit of fun?"

I wipe off the lipstick and stare at its trace on my hand.

He doesn't say a word.

"Three nights a week breaking my nails on boxes in a bloody factory!" Then. Lingering by the door. "Working with mental cases," she tells the side of his face. "People who can't even count."

Most days when she said that we'd hum the *Hovis* music. Dah-de-dah. Dah-de-dah. Dah-de-dah-de-daaah. *Aye, there wur no alarm clocks in yon days...*

Not tonight. Tonight the door gets its bang, and there's a space at the side of my head, and now that she's gone, I want to look at her.

The Sweeney starts up. Rasputin and me stare ahead. No "Time for bed, lad"; no "Stop moaning and go" – just hard men battering doors, flipping couples out of bed. Sticks, alleyways, teeth. *"Put*

232

your vest on, Sid. You're nicked, mate..."

Unspoken words fizz as the title cards flash up. Part one. Adverts. Part two. He doesn't say a word. Between parts two and three, the *Hovis* advert comes on. Dad-de-dah. Dad-de-dah. If I smile and Dad sees me, he'll smile too. We'll be able to talk about football.

The News at Ten is next. He watches it come and go. For the first time in my life I go to bed without being told.

*

At 2 a.m. I hear the door, and get up. Bang. Bang again. Bang bang bang. Slamming to go out, slamming to come in. Don't break the glass...

Shouts. Two people shouting, one listening at the top of the stairs. "... jealous."

"Jealous?" His only word all night.

I squash my ears under my hands. If I press hard enough, it'll stop and they'll make friends.

"It's alright when you come back and fall down the stairs, spend all Saturday playing cricket. But I go out once, and..."

One word all night. I want him to shout back – tell her what it's like at his work. He never says. Sometimes I smell oil and metal on his duffel bag and I ask, and he says, "Nowt you need fret about, lad." But the curly filings that cling to his jacket seams... He should shout, and then I'll know.

My sister starts to cry. The living room squeaks, light stripes the landing. I bolt away. My mother comes upstairs. Under the sheets, breathing hard, I listen to her in the next room, saying, "Back to sleep. Back to sleep. Back to sleep." Softer and softer.

I fall asleep and wake up and fall asleep and she bends over me and kisses my face and I smell alcohol and flowers and I want her hand to stay in my hair.

Round and round. Up and down. Back to sleep. Back to sleep.

*

233

Three days later we go out shopping in the car. Rain on the windscreen, wipers chop it off. Saturday mornings it always rains.

It's Ken Goodwin, I tell my brother, he's the best on *The Comedians*. Rubbish, he says, Norman Collier, he's the best. Is he heckaslike, it's Ken Goodwin. Rubbish, Norman Collier – that chicken he can do.

"Stop chuntering, you two."

I look at the back of my mum's head. Dad's hand tightens on the wheel. One word in three days. Our sister squashes between us, singing, "So what, so what, so what, so what, so what."

At the supermarket, we stuff her in the front of the trolley. Dad hangs at the back, looking at packets. Pretending. Saturday crowds tipple into the cramped store. There are pillars to bang into, cans to knock off. "SO WHAT. SO WHAT. SO WHAT."

"Grand Prix!" says my brother. "Nicki Lauda!"

"Careful. Your sister," Mum warns.

He pulls out of a swerve. "This trolley's got crap wheels..."

"Don't say that."

"What?"

"That."

"Well," he says. "Wonky, then."

"So what," says my sister.

At the tills, a long line stretches away. Trolleys go into the back of you. Mum ticks off beans, Weetabix, toothpaste, soap powder, jelly.

"Behave, will you! What have I told you!"

My brother retreats around the trolley, towards Dad, who's bumped into a bloke from the factory. Mum glowers through the checkout as they talk.

"Got lumbered too, eh, Harry?"

"Aye, well," shrugs the man from the factory. He coughs – not a proper cough. "Tha knows. What wi' t' wife, and everything..."

Dad looks down. A horrible floor, black and white, black and white – squares covered in scratches. "Still badly, Harry?"

'Fridges waft out warm air. Trolleys roll by. "Nowt much to be done for her, lad."

Dad's voice is as flat as the floor. "I'd no idea..."

Harry smiles. "Still. If I can handle *this*, eh?"

"Aye," says Dad quietly. "Pandemonium."

"Woss than bloody work!" He tries to laugh.

Dad tries, too. "Tha'll not be saying that on Monday, Harry."

"Well. Happen I won't." He throws something absent-mindedly into the trolley. A packet of rusks. "Your cricket'll be off too, like as not, eh?"

"Two weeks running," says Dad. "I'm just down here, helping..." But he can't say the next word. He looks through the checkout, to where Mum's loading up.

"Helping t' wife with a few bags," says Harry, trying to smile. "I'll not keep thi, mate."

Dad nods at the floor.

We go through to where Mum's filling bags.

Bag. Thing. Thing, thing. Bag.

"Not there. There," she tells my brother.

He takes it out. A sauce bottle. "Just trying to help..."

"Then push your sister." She runs a finger over his frown. "There's a good lad."

"Only helping," he repeats, quietly.

On the way out, tills open and close, like doors, like mouths, like wallets. Fingers press buttons, hands press heads. Trolleys struggle in the narrow Saturday aisles. When Harry goes by again, Dad nods self-consciously. But it's bad. Meeting twice.

A woman scowls at some jars. Mum hoists bags.

"Give them to me, give them to me," Dad tells her.

"Alright, alright, don't moither me."

"Give them to me, give them to me," he says.

"I'll take two," I tell him. To prove I'm strong. He nods and takes one off me. Now he's got seven bags, all close to the ground, pulling tendons in his arms.

I concentrate on keeping a good grip. They walk on ahead, my brother dragging my sister.

"Not so fast," Mum tells me, but I walk faster to hide the pain. She studies me as if I'm an idea that's never crossed her mind: "Doesn't he look serious when he's carrying summat?"

To her astonishment, the question's for my Dad.

He nods, closing the boot. As his hand smooths the seal, it touches her leg. She wipes her eye and reaches for him.

"They're making friends," I tell my brother, like a grown-up.

The Only Fruit

When university ended, Jimmy drifted for weeks around lifeless bars, knocking about with a dwindling band of like-minded souls – mature students, wary of a return to the treadmill.

While waiting for something to happen, he ate baked beans and white bread, and paid the rent by shining a torch at empty seats in the campus cinema.

Under-occupied by his work, he watched seasons of old classics, staring up at the stars' gigantic faces, sharing in their yearnings and fears.

He was unsure whether he was running away from his problems or facing them. Rivers and hills looked more real in the dark cinema, as did streets and buildings. In Jimmy's everyday life, people and things seemed vague and far-off by comparison.

"Because you've been studying so hard. Thinking," said Louise, one of the last of his fellow stragglers. She bobbed at the knee as she laid down their drinks, a habit Jimmy had noticed from the start.

He looked up from his seat, as if watching her on a screen. "My favourites are the musicals," he confessed.

Meet Me in St Louis had fetched him to tears. Even the mean-spirited *Singing in the Rain* had done its job on him.

"How come I only ever cry in films?" he asked her.

"A few months back in the real world, Jimmy. That'll clean out your ducts."

"The real world," he said, gripping his pint. He'd made no plans for life beyond his studies. To have done so would have been to accept that he was going back there – to the working world he'd fled.

Butlin's with books. That's how he'd thought of university. "Let's stay here," he proposed.

Louise frowned. She reorganised her long legs, as if suddenly aware that they were in danger of touching his. "Jimmy," she said, "there's something I've been meaning to tell you.... it's an offer I can't refuse. They want me in London."

"Who do?"

"That legal company I mentioned. Anyway, we can't stay on campus forever..."

"Why not?"

Louise shrugged. "It's dead here."

But he could feel something brimming up. "Things are starting to happen..."

Louise threw back her hair. "In the usher's job?"

He wondered if this was the moment.

"No," he said, "in life."

But the moment had already passed.

"Get real, Jimmy," she said with the smile that had haunted his sleep. In dreams, Jimmy escaped his shyness. In dreams, he told Louise the truth – that he often dreamed of her.

He waved her off from the city centre coach station. Her hair shone as the bus to London pulled away.

It was time to go.

Back on campus, he took a pile of books to the meadow for the final time and rang his mate Malcolm, a factory manager back north in their home town.

"I need a stop-gap," he told his old friend, leaning back in the grass with his mobile.

"Back to reality, eh..."

"If you can give me the directions," said Jimmy. He imagined Malcolm running a hand through his frizzy hair, frowning.

"Well, there's nowt in our office," said Malcolm. "Nowt at all."

Jimmy lay back in the grass and looked up at the sky. "What about the shop-floor?"

The line fizzed.

Eventually Malcolm said, "It won't pay off your loan – you know that."

"Better than haunting campus like a ghost..."

Malcolm's voice faded away. "What...?... Oh, *bollocks!* Look, summat's come up. I've got to go. Listen: get the train. Meet me at the gate, 6 o'clock, Monday."

"Monday evening?"

Malcolm sighed. "The other 6 o'clock. And, Jimmy – don't be late."

Jimmy grunted into the mobile, then his credit ran out. He lay for a time studying the sky, watching jets hang their bunting over the Midlands.

Clouds passed overhead, spilling their shadows across the fields beside the cycle-path where he'd lain for hours as a generation of confident girls whizzed by, their faces turning into Louise's, melting again.

They sang in loud voices as they passed on their bikes, and were unafraid of using their bells. And now they were gone to kibitzes and legal offices and The Next Step Towards Where They Needed To Be.

On the other side of the meadow, the last slanting sunlight glinted off Jimmy's window. Beyond, he made out a few peeling posters of Nastassia Kinski and Miles Davis and the patch over the door where rain had seeped through a faulty seal.

He half-expected to see himself at the desk.

Wind blew harder through the field. Jimmy watched it turn the pages of his book, in the grass, in the sun.

*

Malcolm greeted him at the gate. Another new boy was waiting too – a man with collapsed cheeks and thick-rimmed glasses who said his name was Brian. Age-wise, he could have been anywhere between

20 and 60. For all its many ravages, Jimmy noticed that Brian's skin looked surprisingly soft, as if old age had visited itself upon a toddler. But there was a strong smell coming off him. And black stains under his arms.

Jimmy was glad when Malcolm ushered him a little further away.

"Good to see you," his old friend frowned.

Jimmy scowled narrowly into the dawn.

"Aye, it's early," said Malcolm. "But a few shifts in there, you'll be sleeping like a babby... waking up terrified, desperate for milk. No, I'm only kidding. But – listen," said Malcolm – and he glanced over his shoulder – "there's been a change."

A few yards away, Brian had gone on standing where Malcolm positioned him. He was staring at the gate like a cow in a field.

"I want you as supervisor," Malcolm whispered.

"Me?" said Jimmy.

"There was a bit of trouble..."

"What trouble?"

Malcolm sighed. "The trouble you get in factories." He sounded tired, impatient. "Look. You'll be on twice the money. Like we said, it's a stop-gap."

"I've no experience; I wouldn't have a clue."

"A supervisor doesn't need a clue; he needs eyes. A supervisor keeps things moving. You've got eyes, Jimmy. Any slacking, thieving..."

"... I grass on them..."

Malcolm nodded. "For an honest wage." He looked over at the new boy, who stood before the gate, unmoving. "I've taken on new hands – lads like you and Brian – because of what went on. This bother I mentioned. So now it's a new slate. A fresh start. And you're a clever lad, you've a Degree..."

"In English Literature," said Jimmy. "If I get it."

Malcolm rooted in his hair. "It has to be a lad I trust. Do me this one favour, Jimmy. You'll be out of here in two months with some debts paid off. I need to square things off, side a few things away."

Jimmy looked into the yard, where grass shivered between broken slabs. The sight of these few strands of grass put him on a trail that led him down a cycle path to his flat on campus. He thought of girls on 'bikes. He thought of Louise's hair. Faced by this smashed-up yard, the chain of associations struck him as ridiculous.

"What's so funny, Jimmy?"

"This," he told his friend. "Those" – he pointed into the yard, where piles of wrecked pallets lay splayed across the flagging. "That" – at a damaged-looking pigeon, pecking scattered fruit. "What the hell *happened* here, Malc?"

Malcolm frowned. "The main thing is it never happens again. I've warned Brian, I'll warn you: casual staff get a rough ride. They're a threat to the regulars."

Jimmy laughed harder. It came back off the factory wall, returning to him hollow and strange. He stared into the factory's black mouth. A machine had been switched on. It made a gushing sound.

"Mature students don't go down too well then, eh?"

Malcolm tried to find a place for his feet. "Not especially."

"So we'd best draw the curtains over that little partition then."

"Yes," said Malcolm. "No unnecessary attention. A supervisor's like a good football ref – he disappears while the game's on." He talked quickly, efficiently. Jimmy imagined him 'phoning in stock – doing it well, by the book.

"The main thing's not to make enemies," he said.

"How about friends?" Jimmy asked. "Can I make friends?"

"Just keep things moving."

"That it?"

"No," said Malcolm. "There's a bloke called Rocco. Make sure you rotate him every hour. Otherwise, stay away."

"Stay away from Rocco?"

Malcolm's eyes were darker and more hooded than Jimmy remembered. As he nodded, a few workers came down the street.

"If you need me," he said, "I'll be in the cabin."

"Right," said Jimmy.

"The cabin inside the factory," said Malcolm.

*

By the time the new boy clocked on, his name was gone. "Brian," he told the juice boys. His voice made the sound of chewed cloth, but there was a surprisingly bright tone within it, as if he couldn't believe his luck to have found himself such a position in such a place.

"This shop," he told the juice boys, "it looks proper nice."

The juice boys' eyes turned cold. They laughed behind their fingers. In the early light, their hands were raw and white.

"I were just saying to these lads. It looks a right grand shop, doesn't it?" Brian said to Jimmy. Beneath the glasses his eyes were huge, yet murky and distant as if peering up from the bottom of a pool.

They walked together across the yard, where a forklift truck trundled over broken pallets. Its driver pointed at Brian. "Who's this gormless-looking bastard?"

"Benny Hill," the juice boys replied, "his name's Benny Hill."

Brian didn't blink. The factory rolled across his lenses. He stood by Jimmy's side. The others stared.

Then Jimmy knew that if he didn't lose Brian it would cost him dear.

"To work now," he said.

In the changing room, he took the supervisor's uniform from a rusty peg. It was a one-piece outfit the colour of blown cream, two sizes too small. When he reached for his hat, the uniform pulled on his balls.

*

The factory's job was to process juice. It came in as sap at one end, went out as a thin fluid at the other. Sour-smelling fluids dribbled down machines, lay in pools on the concrete.

No-one who worked there ever saw an orange.

The noise was like cars crashing, all the time.

"Start on the same jobs as yesterday," Jimmy told them. "We'll rotate later."

Someone gave him a clipboard with columns of mysterious blank spaces.

"Where will I go?" said Brian.

The forklift driver looked over at them from the far end of the factory.

"Box-stacking," said Jimmy.

Brian wandered down an aisle to the pallets.

"Show him," he told Rocco, the juice boy with the smallest, greyest hands.

"Show that smelly bastard, Benny Hill how to stack boxes?" A spanner was tucked into the creamy folds of his uniform.

"His name's Brian."

Rocco wiped his hair. It had the dull shine of a machine. Jimmy decided Rocco wouldn't be rotating much that day.

*

Deeper inside the factory, bottles trundled towards women with hair tied up in net bags. The line grinded at their waists. They stuffed the boxes and tape-gunned the tops. Then the boxes were swung by Rocco to Brian, who was now called Benny.

"*Fly Me To The Moon!*" sang Margaret. She had a long horse's face and mauve lips.

"When Benny Hill smiles," said Rocco, "I think of Texas."

Brian blinked. Half a set of dentures bulged in his mouth.

"Because of all those wide open spaces," said Rocco. His laugh made the sound of buckets scraping over concrete.

Jimmy pretended to be filling in figures.

The air was sourer for Rocco's passing.

*

At the end of the line, a long, thin man laboured over cardboard. His skin pulled papery over his hands. But his cheeks shone like English apples, his deep-set eyes widening each time he finished a box.

"Who's that?" Jimmy asked Margaret.

243

She was singing too loud to hear.

The thin man placed boxes on the production line and watched them in their procession away from him, as if each new one was a miracle.

Jimmy had the strange sense that the thin man had been watching him. "Margaret..." he tried again, "who's that tall fellah at the end of the line?"

"The Skeleton, love?" she said. "Never mind him, love."

"*My dead mother! My dead mother!*" the juice boys called after the thin man.

The Skeleton went on working, stooping to each new box as if in prayer.

"*Fly Me To The Moon,*" sang Margaret. In her mouth, the song made the sound of pulley wheels.

*

Incredible things happened in the factory.

Once, an external door opened. For three seconds, Jimmy saw streets that seemed more beautiful than Malham Cove. As the door scraped shut, it exposed a yellowy warning. HYGIENE NOTICE: COVER HEADS AT ALL TIMES.

Brian Who Was Now Benny swiped his face with his cap, went on stacking boxes. Sweat had made the shape of Australia on his back.

"Keep your hat on, Brian," said Jimmy, pointing at the sign.

Brian's eyes swelled: big enough to burst and run down his face. *Decision: sacked. Reason: burst eyes.*

"The hat," said Jimmy.

Then he knew that Brian couldn't read.

*

By mid-morning, Brian had begun to lag. Juice boys glanced across the factory. "Fat Tom..." they said. "Fat Tom's coming."

"Hurry *up*," the juice boys urged Brian.

244

Fat Tom didn't stop when he reached Brian's boxes, he didn't change course. He walked straight through, crushing most of the boxes, knocking the rest sideways. His tool kit bulged.

Then he was gone, like a tyrannosaurus vacating a clearing, leaving the smell of saturated fats behind him.

"We warned you," said the juice boys. "Didn't we warn you?"

Cardboard lay strewn across the shop floor. Boxes inched towards the end of the line, fell through Brian's hands. Watching closely, Jimmy noticed Brian's fingers. They were as stiff and thick as carrots, the nails unbitten.

Margaret broke off from singing, briefly. "Fat Tom's bowels are regular as clockwork," she said.

Brian looked at her with huge, baffled eyes.

"And When He Goes, he always walks in a completely straight line," she explained.

*

Noon came up on them like a beach.

In the canteen, women with white triangles in their hair fussed over the tea-urn. Jimmy watched the steam rise. He envied it, and sorrowed for its fate. They sat at a table, where Brian crammed in oily eggs and cracked beans as his sweat spread. Pity was far off, a place Jimmy couldn't go. When Fat Tom pushed through, his elbow went into their backs. It was an obese elbow.

He ordered double chips and double eggs and treble kidney and double liver.

His job was to say fuck to broken machines.

*

"How old are you, Benny?"

"24." The beans were wet on Brian's lips. Behind the gums, a black hole.

Rocco said, "You look 50."

The juice boys laughed.

"24," Brian repeated blankly.

Rocco looked at Jimmy. His neck was wired with long white tendons. "If *he* reckons I'm working all day next to that smelly bastard again..."

Brian loomed over his sausages as if he had appetite, although only for eating. Jimmy wanted to put a hand on his shoulder.

But his shoulder was moist.

"What did you do before?" he asked Brian quietly, careful that no-one overheard.

"Before what?" said Brian, still chewing.

"This."

"O," said Brian, blank-faced: "nowt." The overalls clung to his pot-belly. His face was smooth and unlined.

Jimmy felt their eyes on him. The sausages glistened.

"You've been warned," Rocco told him: "it happens again, I'm fetching a gas mask."

A tall thin figure had arrived at the counter.

"Oh Jesus, the Skeleton..." someone moaned.

"*My dead mother*," they giggled.

Jimmy got up, and went. The thin man was somewhere close, at his back.

A black surveillance camera looked down on Jimmy from the rafters. He waved into it. Further on he came to the cabin, saw Malcolm in its window. The cabin was dark-planked, and roofed over with grey felt as if it should be in a forest.

Jimmy remembered what his friend had said about good football referees, the ones who disappear. Now he knew he'd disappear too, into his happy memories. He made a picture in his mind of Louise, thought of long grass and brown ankles...

In the time it took him to reach the supervisor's central position, he ran out of happy memories.

*

A crowd had pushed in around Brian. His overalls were splashed with water.

Jimmy pushed people away. "What's going on?" he demanded.

"Who threw this water?"

"Rocco," said Brian blankly.

"What for?"

"For stinking," said Brian.

Jimmy looked at him.

"He reckons I should get some of that stuff."

"What stuff?"

"Deodorant, it's called."

There was a strong taste in Jimmy's mouth, like onions.

"For the smell coming off me," said Brian.

*

They met inside Malcolm's cabin, where the machines faded to a muffled gush and Jimmy was able to hear a tiny clock, ticking.

Malcolm said, "You're spending too much time with Benny..."

"Brian."

"The idea's to keep things moving. Why the hell haven't you rotated Rocco?"

Jimmy shrugged.

Malcolm gripped his biro. Through the shack's window, a steel hammer fell slowly onto the cores of oranges. "Your eyes, Jimmy. I said to use your eyes."

"I've seen a few things," said Jimmy. "What about yours, though? Where are your eyes, Malc?"

"In the back of my head." Malcolm pushed back on his chair. "Listen, Jimmy – when I started here, I was no different from you. There was another bloke here then – a bloke like Benny, but tiny and thin. They called him The Runt, made his life hell. So, one day I decided I'd do it. I decided I'd smash the bully's face in."

"You?"

"Imagine it. Me. Dishing it out to the top bully. So I barge in... and catch The Runt red-handed, loading his pockets. Here, in this cabin. My bloody office. Pens. Juice. Fruit. You name it. Sneaked in here and helped himself, the little bastard."

"Natural enough."

247

"Sure. You get your own back. But he was a scrawny thief with a crap haircut, I realised I'd never cared about him. All I wanted was to get my own back, too."

"Own back on what?"

"On my own life," he said.

The steel hammer rose again.

Malcolm said, "I'll tell you what it is: they're going to push Benny so far that *you* can't take it any more."

"His name's not Benny, it's Brian."

Malcolm's heel screwed the floor. "Jimmy," he said – "were you this thick before you went to Uni? I honestly can't remember."

"A few years of thinking, it wears out your brain..."

Malcolm laughed, not enough to loosen any teeth. It turned into a sigh. "And one more thing: tomorrow I want you to sort out Margaret too."

"For looking like a horse? What do you want me to do about that?"

"I'd recommend you ban her from singing."

Jimmy looked at him.

"It's been getting worse. I said we'd sort it."

Jimmy looked out of the window of the cabin. Far down the central aisle, he saw a crowd gathering around Rocco. The unseen clock ticked. He couldn't tell whether the pounding in his ears came from his blood or from the machines.

"So I tell her she isn't allowed to sing anymore?"

Malcolm stabbed a pencil into his top pocket. "It's been putting people off their work," he said.

*

Rocco drew on Brian's back in felt-tip. He wrote WASH ME and ALSO AVAILABLE IN CREAM.

The juice boys pointed at the sewer. They said Brian was clumsy, and span him in circles to prove it. They chanted DEODORANT!

"I WISH MY BIRD WAS THAT DIRTY," they said to him in cloth-voices, pointing at his overalls, where sweat darkened along a line of grey stitches.

Rocco had on a gas mask – a brown one, from the war. Its straps dangled as he worked. The buckles were rusty. His eyes looked out through its brown glass.

"Health and safety," he said in a muffled voice to anyone who asked.

*

In the canteen, at afternoon break, the thin man got to his feet and cried: "Up yonder!"

Steam massed over the tea-urn.

"*My dead mother!*" the juice boys called. "*My dead mother!*"

"She is hovering above us," he declared, pointing to the ceiling. His watery eyes were trained on Jimmy. "I have made contact with a spiritualist in the Yorkshire Dales. I now have a direct channel to the Other Side."

High above the urn, droplets clung to blackened rafters.

"It is both a gift and a curse," said The Skeleton. "To those with second-sight, nothing is hidden."

Rocco lifted the gas-mask to slot in a forkful of beans. "Better than second-smell. Or that dirty bugger Benny'd poison you."

Behind them, Malcolm had approached quietly. "This is an official warning, Benny," he said: "no more defacing of your overalls."

Jimmy stared at signs. HATS ON. CLEAN HANDS. DO NOT. ALWAYS. NEVER. WARNING.

"He wasn't to blame, Malcolm."

The words spurted out of him like pips.

Beyond the despatch gate, light flared off office windows.

Jimmy felt their eyes on him, was aware of the camera staring down from the rafters, where steam floated with the dead.

*

He caught Malcolm on the other side, behind a crusher, close to the sump.

"Let go," said Malcolm.

"Not until he takes off the mask."

Malcolm wriggled. "Do you want them to know..."

"... that I'm your plant?"

"Say it louder..." said Malcolm. He lowered his head, muttered something under the roar.

"I'VE BEEN TO UNIVERSITY, I'M STEALING FULL-TIME JOBS," Jimmy shouted. "AND I'M NOT EVEN A PROPER SUPERVISOR."

The security camera looked down on them. Jimmy gave it another wave. Malcolm breathed deep.

"Look," said Jimmy – "Margaret's still singing. Shall we sack her?"

"That mask is the one honest thing in here," said Malcolm wearily. "The only thing not hiding anything. Don't you finally get it?"

"I finally get it. This company encourages bullying."

Malcolm nodded. "Unless it damages productivity."

Machines growled around them.

Suddenly Jimmy realised that the factory had freed him. He could scream or weep, or walk in a Completely Straight Line. He could howl, or put on a gas mask. Talk to the dead. Become steam.

Malcolm put his hands in his hair. "Welcome back to the real world, Jimmy."

Jimmy laughed bitterly. "This place? This place is about as real as the fucking stock exchange."

*

He stole the spanner from the folds of Rocco's uniform. Rocco was sweating in his mask; he didn't notice, it was easy.

He watched the juice boys. He walked around, watching them. And when Rocco sang the Benny Hill tune an inch from Brian's ear, that was the moment Jimmy chose to drive Rocco's spanner between the cogs of the line.

At first, he was going to take his clipboard to Malcolm's cabin and point at Rocco through the window, dream up some lie about industrial sabotage. Get him sacked, sent to prison. Better still: deported. Transported in irons to a semi-known continent.

Then he thought of Rocco's life – his grey hands forever in the shade, black boots never to walk in meadows. A third of his life lived here, under this gushing. The only relief found in leatherings and spite.

He went to Rocco and took his hand and shook it. It was a damp hand, and softer than he'd expected. It was a grey hand that had never lived.

"Thank you for wearing the mask," he said: "now everyone can see who you really are."

Rocco's eyes tracked him through the thick glass.

Jimmy took off his hat, watching boxes and bottles fall from the conveyor belt. He walked away. Distantly, Malcolm seemed to be calling his name, shouting, "Jimmy. Jimmy."

The line had stopped, but other machines grinded and gushed.

At the end of the factory he approached The Skeleton, who stared past Jimmy into the sump, where orange waste dripped from a pipe. Close up, there was a smell on The Skeleton's breath: potato and something stranger – offal, maybe liver.

"She is tending the machines," he said to Jimmy, in a strong, clear voice. "Do you see her yonder, bestowing holiness upon the nozzles?"

The Skeleton didn't blink. He had concentrated his gaze on his dead mother by the pipe. Jimmy walked away from him in a Completely Straight Line. The juice boys scattered before him.

Boxes were toppling into chaotic piles at the foot of the jammed belt. Jimmy skidded into some of them, stepped over the rest. He smashed into the gate and hit a fence. And then he was out, and there were roads to cross, and traffic to get through.

On a kerb at the edge of the bus station, he looked into the sky. It was featureless, vast, grey – the colour of steam.

Air whizzed over his face.

He tipped his head to the clouds and opened his mouth.

At first, under the weight of the drizzle, most of the town's hard-pressed shoppers were too busy lugging bags or changing buses to notice. It was only when Jimmy took hold of an old woman's umbrella that people began to stop and stare.

Then, as the old woman fought to regain her property, a small crowd gradually gathered to find out what the fuss was about, to see why the bloke in ill-fitting overalls was hopping in and out of the bus station's puddles.

It took a while, but eventually the old woman stopped fighting for her umbrella and joined in with him.

By then Jimmy was in his element. By then he had perfected all the steps, and was able to guide his partner through them.

"*Fly Me To The Moon*," he sang in a voice like a ratch, his shyness peeling away from him.

"*And let me live among the stars*," the old woman rejoined.

They splashed through the shallow pools in time with each other, kicking up diesel and oil, twirling each other around by the tips of their fingers.

At last, when they'd finished their routine, Jimmy bowed and kissed the old woman's hand, returning her umbrella with a lavish flourish while some of the wet onlookers scratched their heads and others applauded shyly.

For a time afterwards, the Technicolor puddles that they'd splashed through went on swaying slowly. Then buses trundled through them and broke their perfect mirrors.

But anyone able to sit on the kerb and look hard enough would have spotted a narrow slice of light – a small gift of the sky to the ground.

In The Country of Daft Pink Things

On the outskirts of town, where there had once been fields, thin green shoots were slowly appearing in the raked and flattened dirt. The naked houses waited for their lawns and hedges, blushing. They were built of smart redbrick, and smelled of painted wood. Their bow windows shone in the early summer sun.

But the shiniest windows of all were The Fancy Man's.

And a shiny new house is no place for dirty fingers.

"Look at the state of your hands!" Dennis's Mum gasped: "you look like you've been snouting around in the mud. Have you been down the river? What have we told you about rackin' about when you should be doing your homework? You're a boy, not a stray dog, Dennis."

Her Fancy Man looked on. "That river's out of bounds, lad."

Dennis studied his hand, where ink had rubbed off his comic, over the knuckle of his thumb. "Which river?"

"Never you mind which river," said his Mum.

The Silver Surfer's troubled eyes looked back at Dennis from the comic. He had been banished from his home planet, to roam the black ink. He gleamed like a car, lonely on a forecourt.

His Mum said, "I know things haven't been easy, lad. What with all the flitting and these... changes. But things are going to be different from now on, I promise you they are. We're going to get some direction in our lives. There won't be any need to rack about in rivers."

Clean light came through the windows. His Mum and her Fancy Man crinkled their eyes.

Dennis thought of wrapping paper on Christmas morning...

"... Oh, for goodness' sake, lad. The face on you. Like you've been hit with The Ugly Stick. Look: bringing dirt into the house might not have mattered in that pig-sty of your dad's – but while we're in Trevor's lovely new..."

Trevor interrupted quickly. "Your mum's just trying to warn you of the dangers on a new estate like this, where they've had to re-route water courses and so on, Dennis lad. I dread to think how that river's coping. It must be in full spate..."

Dennis tried to imagine how Trevor's smooth face would cope with an Ugly Stick. But he couldn't concentrate. One little mention of his dad – the first for weeks, and ace car salesman Trevor Fontaine wiping it away like grime.

The damp cloth that takes care of stains.

"What with the rain we've had," said his Mum.

Trevor said, "And that's just it, isn't it, pet? The point you're trying to make?" He ruffled Dennis's hair with a hand like a soaped sponge. "Up to now, things have been rough. Rough like a river. But now it's all under control. Calmer. The river's got solid banks. It isn't going to floo..."

Dennis tried to control his voice. It wobbled. It was going to break, like everything else. "What's the river got to do with it?" he said. "How come I get the blame for a *river*?"

The Fancy Man tutted quietly. He came across the stripped pine floor, and knelt before Dennis. "Dennis," he said in the serious, level voice that shifted cars at The Showroom You Can Trust: "let me make it clear: that river..."

"*It's ink!*" Dennis cried. "*It's ink off a bloody comic!*"

"Dennis!" his Mum cried.

The Fancy Man blinked, once. "No need to fret, pet." He took a mouthful of air.

"The language, though," she whispered.

But waited.

Trevor, after a pause, said, "We've heard worse. Isn't that right, mate?" He chuckled mirthlessly.

Dennis rolled his comic into a thin pipe and stood up.

"Sometimes," said Trevor, "on my forecourt... when the air turns blue..."

But Dennis cut in. "How can I go to a river if I don't know where the river is? If I've never heard of any river..." He was looking down on the kneeling Fancy Man from a great height.

The Fancy Man said, "Shall I tell him then, pet?"

"Tell him what, babe?"

"The truth," said Trevor, in the dreamier tone that sold the car to himself. *Sell it to yourself, you can sell it to anyone.*

Dennis's Mum sat upright.

"Dennis," said Trevor, eyes blue and clear as windows, hair buffed to a black shine, "I didn't want to scare you. But now I've no choice."

Trevor's cuff-links whizzed sunshine into the white corners of the room.

... He knew the women glanced sideways at him as they drove by:

– *Lovely teeth, that lad. Looks after his appearance. And his garage. You could eat your dinner off that forecourt.*

– *Ooo, I never heard it called that before, Barbara!*

Then the giggles...

Trevor looked out on Dennis as if from behind the blinds in his office. "On the banks of that river," he said, " there lives a witch..."

Dennis's Mum let out a puff of breath.

Trevor nodded slowly with narrow eyes, like an American President agreeing with himself. "That's right," he said. "A river witch..."

Dennis looked at him.

"With poisonous fingers," said Trevor, showing Dennis the backs of his hands. They swirled with hairs, like gas on Saturn. His cuff-links glittered. In that clean room, where stepfather kneeled before stepson, the sunlight seemed to have turned to water. It washed across the floor and swirled over the painted walls.

"And," said Trevor, "if Dennis touches those fingers..."

Dennis's mother sat stiff. It looked like she might speak.

255

But she didn't speak.

"... just one little touch..." said Trevor, "... and Dennis Will Be Dead." Trevor studied the white palms of his hands, as if to say, There. My final offer. Beyond that, I'm left looking at lifelines on my hand.

On the skin of my own hand.

Finally, Trevor smiled at Dennis. His smile was ten feet long and two millimetres wide.

Dennis thought: *Wipe that look off your face.* Take a cloth and rub it over the bonnet – rub it until rust shows through. Snap off wipers. Beat dents in panels.

Soundlessly, Trevor got to his feet, wiping a speck from his left knee. "As I said. No need to fret, pet. A short period of readjustment. Eh, Dennis?" He mussed Dennis's hair fondly. "In fact, I reckon this fellah and me will spend some time together later. Maybe play tennis. Ay, lad?"

"Yes." But Dennis scratched his chin, to show it was a lie.

"See?" said Trevor, proud of his salesmanship. "Tennis with Dennis."

Dennis looked at his Mum. She studied the pine floor.

Boards hacked from forests, light journeying from the sun. All the great distances everything has to cross.

"Tennis with Dennis the Menace," said Trevor.

*

Dennis stood on the Fancy Man's front step, looking into the sun. There were no pavements, just newly-sprouting lawns, and places for cars to turn and park. Through the bow window, he glimpsed the shiny Fontaine creeping to his Mother's chair.

A short period of readjustment.

He pulled twigs off the herbaceous borders. Across the avenue, his neighbours, a mother and her daughter, watched him in silence, the mother's face whitening almost to blue. The daughter, a thin, tanned girl about Dennis's age, sat cross-legged on the drive, sifting gravel between her fingers.

256

"Honestly," her Mum sighed.

"It's only grit..."

The mother had on bright pink plastic gloves. Her left hand gripped a black can by its wire handle. "Out from under the feet," she said.

The girl got up slowly, muttering. Dennis watched her tromp off down the avenue. Every now and again, she threw back slow, hard glances.

Her mother went on scouring the nicks and cracks.

*

Dennis fell into step with the girl. She had on a flowery dress that pulsed with little movements of the breeze. "I've heard about your type," she said over her shoulder. "I bet you'll keep following me now for ages, until I have to stab you." She seemed to yawn. "Stab you with office stationery," said the girl. "Because stalkers, right – they can't be persuaded by logic. Didn't you know that? Doesn't anybody read *papers*?"

"But I'm not a stalker."

The girl looked Dennis up and down, disappointed. "No," she said, tossing her hair, "I don't suppose you are." When she tossed her hair, everything smelled of coconuts. "Besides – this lot round here, they walk too slowly; you'd be stalking them for yonks. It'd get right *wearisome*."

She said *wearisome* like it was a bag of potatoes.

Dennis snorted a laugh. Breezes rippled the girl's dress. "Great. Pig noises," she said. Distantly, lawns fizzed. Dennis looked at the side of his neighbour's face, its features flat, as if they'd been slowly pressured backwards. "This place – listen," she said, "it's weird. It's in the future."

"Yes," said Dennis, shaking his head.

"It's in the Year 2037. And do you know why?"

Dennis kept his mouth shut.

The girl said, "Because the fossils, right – they huddle indoors behind their air-locks. That's why, thanks for asking. Huddle indoors, skenning at *monitors*. Because they're scared of skateboarders."

"Yes," said Dennis.

"Except, have you noticed, there *aren't* any skateboarders?"

"No."

"Does that mean, 'Yes, I have noticed,' or, 'No, I'm sorry I'm too thick and blind, and I haven't noticed'?"

Dennis looked at her.

"And maybe dumb too," said the girl, blowing upwards, into her fringe.

"There's no need to be tight," said Dennis, looking down.

The girl kicked a new lawn. "The year 2037," she said, to the dirt.

Her cheeks were smooth and clear, but her forehead was complicated, lined. She smoothed her dress. "They wince when they hear ice cream vans."

"Who do?"

"This lot. Do you know what their secret wish is?"

Dennis nodded. "No."

"Their secret wish is to be dead," said the girl. Her mouth tugged down at the corners. She pushed on to the bottom of the avenue, where the road split three ways into avenues that looked identical to their own. As they walked, Dennis thought about it, about the year 2037. It gave him a giggly feeling, low in his stomach. Clubs he'd go to, pints he'd drink. Clubs his dad went to, pints his dad drank.

But not as many, maybe.

Except he musn't dwell on the past. He had to think of the future. Except he *was* thinking of the future.

He should probably humour the girl.

"What's your name?" he said, reluctantly, at the avenues' three-way split.

"Citizen C3-89-28F," she said, without blinking.

*

They kept on walking, deeper into the new estate. "What I mean is," the girl was saying, "the only skateboarding they do is on their computers. Computer skateboard games. Because they're scared of going out. Because of paedophiles. So you end up with estates like this. Dead Zones. In 2037. Where there aren't even any pavements."

"Yes," said Dennis.

The girl turned to him. "The place I used to live, there were at least *fields*. You could go and lie in the grass. Maybe take a book. I mean, it were right flat, no hills. Because of this river, right. But at least you'd somewhere to *go*."

"There's a river here, too," said Dennis.

She didn't take him on. "I tell you: you don't want to get stuck in this place."

"I am stuck."

The girl's sudden laugh came out like a snort.

"Brilliant. *Two* pigs," she said.

*

On the corner of the fifth or sixth avenue – Dennis had lost track – they came upon a boy lounging against a sign. The boy wrinkled his nose. "You two stink," he said.

"Charming," Dennis replied.

"There's a stench coming off you," said the boy.

He had a tuft of blond hair that stood up on the top of his head, and black specks for eyes, like currants pushed into a sadcake.

"Shouldn't you be inside *downloading* stuff?" the girl taunted him. "Or are your eyes too small?"

The boy's eyes retreated still further into his face. He didn't speak. When Dennis looked back a few minutes later, he saw with a shock that the tufty-haired boy was still there, twenty yards further back, walking steadily in their tracks.

*

"Look," said Citizen C3-89-28F, pointing at two teenage girls in light cotton dresses, "the whole network must be down."

The two girls lolled on the unpaved kerb, sucking lollies. "Where y' going?" they chimed.

"To the river," said Dennis's neighbour.

Dennis flitted his eyes at her.

"We're Martha and Bess. We're right bored. It's so *boring* here. Int it, Bess?"

Bess nodded. "*Well* boring."

"So a river'd be smart, wouldn't it, Bess?"

"Double plus smart," said Bess.

Dennis started to speak, but found that no words would come out. The girls tripped along. "What are you two called?" they called.

"Dennis and..." He looked at his neighbour, scratched his head. The girls let it go. "So where's this river then?"

He flapped his hand vaguely.

"Right," said the girls, clacking lollies against their teeth.

*

On another avenue that looked like all the other avenues, Martha and Bess said, "Wait a minute, you two" and ran to knock on a door.

A lad of about 13 with the vague shadow of a moustache came out.

"Are you coming to the river?" they asked him.

"What river?"

"The river this lad's taking us to," said Bess, pointing across the new lawn.

The lad who almost had a moustache studied Dennis for a moment. "Wait while I get my shoes on," he said.

*

A buzz passed through the group.

"Will we be able to swim, do you think?"

Martha nodded. "Only – it's getting right hot."

Dennis fiddled with his collar, frowned. Twenty yards back, the boy with the small eyes was still following.

"I mean, I can't believe we've lived here two months, and we never even knew about the river. Eh, Bess?"

Bess nodded. "But how did *you* find out about it?" she asked

Dennis's neighbour, Citizen C3-89-28F.

"*He* told me about it," she said, pointing at Dennis.

The girls studied him. Dennis found himself nodding. Nodding like Trevor nodding like the U.S. President.

We're going to get some direction in our lives.

"Imagine that. An explorer," said Bess.

Dennis reddened.

"Like in a right good book," said Martha.

"I read this book about some explorers, and it were so cold, right, I mean you can't imagine how cold, because their teeth split," said Bess.

"Honestly?"

"Split in the cold," Bess nodded.

"What I heard, right," said Martha, "is if you go above a certain height, your fillings explode. Do you reckon that's true?"

With a start, Dennis realised they were asking him.

"It can't be true, can it?" they said.

Dennis nodded. "It certainly does sound a bit far-fetched," he said. "I mean..."

"Oi. You. Captain Oates," said the boy who nearly had a moustache. "How much further?"

Dennis smiled mysteriously. His heart was beating slightly too fast.

*

Still deeper into the estate, they were joined by a lanky boy in short trousers, whose knees stuck out like stale white cockle buns. "You lot don't half walk fast," he puffed.

Tendons pulled tight and yellow in the backs of his legs.

"We're that desperate for a swim," Bess called back.

"Swim?" said the lanky boy.

"Yes, in the river."

"Oh," said the boy, slowing to a crawl.

"What's wrong?"

"Nowt," he said. "Only I think I might be allergic to rivers."

The girls laughed. Bess nipped Dennis's side. "Imagine *you* were allergic to rivers, Dennis. You'd never have discovered it..." She turned to the lanky boy. "He's kind of an explorer, he is."

"Yes," the lanky boy gasped.

Bess looked at Martha. "I'll tell you what – he can sit on the bank, this long lad. Can't he, Martha?"

"If there int any dog shit in the grass," said Martha, her eyes gay and bright.

"No," Dennis heard himself saying, "there isn't any dog shit at this river."

The lanky boy smiled.

"In fact, there's a bench," Dennis told him.

"A bench!" said Bess.

"It's sort of a beauty spot," Dennis seemed to be saying.

Bess touched the lanky boy's shoulder. "You'll have to budge up, though."

The boy nodded.

"Because we like sitting on benches too," Martha told him.

"Sitting on benches next to rivers," said Bess. "In beauty spots."

"With massive picnics," added Martha dreamily.

"How much further, though?" asked the boy who nearly had a moustache.

"Yes, is it far? Because we're fagged-out, aren't we, Martha?"

Dennis flapped his hand again. It struck the arm of the boy close to his side.

Dennis had never seen the boy before. The boy had brooding eyebrows. He looked at his arm.

"Careful what you're doing with that hand," he said.

*

As they walked, Dennis glanced from time to time at his neighbour. She smiled thinly, a smile close to a frown.

"So much for your theories then," he told her.

"What theories?"

"Theories about paedophiles, and that."

He cast a glance at Bess. Bess smiled. Dennis crinkled his face.
"I mean – look at this lot, eh? We'll have tons of mates," he said.

His neighbour said nothing.

"Cat got your tongue, has it?"

"I'll tell you where the cat is," she said, lowering her voice.
"It's tied up in a bag. And do you want to know where the bag is?"

Dennis shook his head. "Yes," he said.

Behind him, another lad had tagged on to the group. He was
about 20 years old, sunglasses pushed up on his forehead. Dennis
noticed with a frown that the 20-year-old was carrying trunks
squashed inside a rolled-up towel.

"The bag," said Citizen C3-89-28F, "is in the river."

*

"Where the hell's he taking us?" asked someone at the back.

"Didn't you hear?" said Bess. "To the river! Int he, Martha?
Taking us to a lovely cool river. In a beauty spot!"

"Funny blummin place for a river. In the middle of an estate."

A cold feeling passed down Dennis's neck. All this time, he'd
been lost. But now he knew exactly where he'd led them – to the
centre of the new estate, an avenue he'd strayed down the previous
week, when his mind hadn't been straight.

It was because he thought he'd seen his dad.

"Dad!" he'd shouted.

And a stranger had turned to face him.

So this was as far in as you could go.

*

Dennis felt their eyes on him. He realised he was whistling. He stopped
whistling and knelt down to pick up a black stone. The stone felt
smooth in his hand, almost as if a river had washed over it. He weighed
the black stone in his hand.

"Fair jiggered, I am," said Bess. "How much further, Dennis?"

"My lungs are at full capacity," said the lanky boy with the

263

river allergy. "Are anyone else's? Are anyone else's lungs at full capacity?"

No-one spoke. Dennis noticed they'd put a gap between themselves and the lanky boy.

"I know this street," said the lad who nearly had a moustache. "This street is nowhere near any river."

Bess shook her head. "But you have to go down here to get to it. Don't you, Dennis? Probably go down this street to get to the river?"

Dennis looked at her.

The 20-year-old snorted. "Some explorer," he said, pushing the sunglasses over his eyes. He jabbed a finger lightly in Dennis's chest. "I went all the way back to my house to get a *towel* for this."

"And I were watching summat right good on telly," said the boy who nearly had a moustache. He looked sad. "I even put my shoes on specially."

"... just here," said the lanky boy who was allergic to rivers. "This bit of my chest here. Do any of you ever get that? Only..."

The stranger at Dennis's side interrupted. He glowered from beneath his eyebrows. "So you're the person we're supposedly following?"

Everyone nodded.

"The same kid who keeps banging his hand into me?"

Dennis tried to speak. The stranger with thick eyebrows said, "I'm not sure if I can trust someone who keeps banging his hand into me. What does everyone else think? About trusting a person with a tendency to jostle?"

Everyone looked at the stranger. He put his head down, a little self-conscious.

"Tendency?" said a voice at the back.

The 20-year-old wafted his towel. "Thought you'd impress the lasses, eh..." He walked away.

Martha and Bess watched him go. "Wait for us," they shouted.

"... maybe it's just a stitch," the allergic boy muttered, pressing his chest.

The dark-browed stranger pushed Dennis against a wall. "Loser," he growled.

"Put both my shoes on for nothing," said the boy who almost had a moustache.

They walked away.

"Sorry," said Dennis.

"Don't worry," coughed the lanky boy. "See, what with being allergic to rivers, I probably shouldn't come anyway. I'm on a low wheat diet, you see."

"Right."

"And, no offence, I can't risk it. My Mum would have my guts for garters."

"Okay."

"Bye, though," he said. "Have a good time at the river."

Dennis's neighbour gave a little snort.

"Go ahead: laugh. See if I care, Citizen sodding-89-shiting-28-F."

The girl's face settled. "My name's Mollie actually."

"Whatever your name is," said Dennis.

"And, for your information," she said, "I weren't laughing at you." She pointed down the avenue. Twenty yards further back, the boy with currant eyes was standing on the drive where Dennis had picked up the smooth black stone.

The boy watched them, wrinkling his nose.

For a moment, Dennis thought he might chuck the stone at the boy. Then the feeling passed, and he pushed the stone into his pocket.

Mollie walked on ahead. "Smell that," she said.

Dennis sniffed deep. A taste of bleach passed down his throat, into his lungs. He thought about the allergic boy putting a finger over his chest. Remembered the gap they'd made around him.

"This way," said Mollie, lengthening her stride.

Before he knew it, they were running. Running to the end of the avenue, and on – to the estate's far edge, a wasteland covered with concrete pipes, where the fence was plastered with warnings: BUILDERS' YARD. KEEP OUT.

Mollie took the fence in one jump, and, regaining her stride, darted past pallets and crusty buckets. At the other end of the yard, she vaulted another wall, and disappeared into a dark clough. Dennis followed. The trees closed around them.

Deeper into the clough, the land dropped away, and they found themselves in a shallow ravine filled with rubbish – bent window frames, stained mattresses, and a single, ancient car, its pale pink paint fading, the doors crushed.

Here and there, between gaps in the dump, a stream flashed. The stream was light grey, almost blue. It smelled of detergent.

Dennis stood on the bank, unsure.

"Come *on*," she said.

"I'm not supposed to."

"Not supposed to what?"

"Go in the river..."

"Blame me," she said.

He watched her unfasten his shoes as though it was happening far away, in another country. Then the shoes seemed to have been chucked into the rubble...

"Geronimo!" she called, and they were up to their shins in the stream, kicking dirty water, yelping.

"Silver Surfer!" he cried, balancing on a plank. Gazing up, he saw the evening's first few stars tread shyly through the sky.

*

Later, splashes still petalling her dress, Mollie led Dennis up the bank, to the pink car.

Click. Its smashed door opened first time.

Mollie moved into the driver's seat. Dennis took the passenger side. Smells of musty leather and coconut wafted around him. With a shock, he saw keys dangling.

"Where to, sir?" she said.

Through the open roof, trees rustled.

"Wigan," he said.

Mollie laughed. "But you could go anywhere!"

"I know. It's just, I want. Want to..."

"... see your dad."

He looked at her. Flat nose, broad eyes. She turned the key in the ignition.

Nothing happened.

"Give it a few minutes to warm up," she said. The key's fob trembled. Distantly, Dennis heard the bleep of reversing trucks. In the stream, a bag tied with blue tassels slowly swirled to the bank.

"When did you realise?" he said.

"Realise what?"

"You know..."

"About your dad? Oh," she said, "I don't know, you can just *tell* with lads."

He looked at the key fob. It was almost still. "You knew I was lost, too, didn't you..."

"No," she said, blowing her fringe. "Because you weren't. Because to be properly lost, you need some idea where you're going when you set off."

He snorted. "I've got a pig-laugh," he admitted.

She moved closer to him. "Can I rest my head?" Her hair moved over the nape of his neck. "I don't fancy you, though..." she said.

Dennis shook his head. His heart was loud in his chest. "No," he said.

"It's just I feel safe."

"Yes," he said.

She lay her head on his shoulder. He looked from the smashed car into the ravine, where water jumped half-bricks and trickled through slashed tyres. "Broken glass," he whispered.

But their feet had missed it.

Mollie placed a hand on his arm. Her fingers were grubby, and smelled of bleach. Dennis closed his eyes, feeling the car move on its busted springs – move almost as if on water, down the channel of the stream. He wondered: were rivers free? Or maybe trapped inside their banks? Trapped like Trevor Fontaine, doomed to his forecourt...or his dad, free to roam anywhere, hugging to pubs and bookies...

"Look there," said Mollie. On the other side of the ravine, a boy was squatting on his haunches under raggedy bushes.

"Currant Eyes. What's he skenning at?"

"Us," said Mollie.

The word made a new sound in Dennis's ears. *Us*, he thought. He pressed Mollie's fingers to his arm. Their tips left tiny black dabs on his skin. "How come he keeps following us?"

She shrugged. "Maybe he's not full-shilling. I mean – look at his eyes. And his face. Not to mention, his smooth face."

Dennis stared through the trees.

"Lads ought to have a bit of bristle," said Mollie.

Secretly, Dennis touched his face. "Maybe he's lonely," he said, studying the distant boy. "Maybe because he tells everybody they stink."

Mollie giggled. "Stink of what, though?"

"Coconut," said Dennis, putting his nose to her hair. She didn't move away, she let him. "Then again, why follow people who stink?" he said.

"They *all* followed us," she said. "Even *we* followed us..."

Dennis frowned. "You talk funny. Anyone ever tell you that? Like when you go on about the future. About the year 2037."

"What's so funny about that?"

He looked at her fingers on his arm. "And about us following ourselves..."

She spoke quietly into his shoulder. "Then how else did we get here?"

"How do you mean?"

"I mean – that stream. How does it get where it's going? It rushes along, down its own path... yet everywhere it goes is always new..."

Dennis pressed the car's horn.

Oink, it said, *Oink*.

"You'd make a brilliant pig, you would."

"Look who's talking," he grunted. "All that muck you splashed in..."

She sat up. "What we should do, right, is drive this thing down the bank. Through all that muck. *Then* you'd see splashes..."

"Drive this daft pink thing down there?"

She pushed her bare foot on the accelerator. "And keep going," she said.

"Into the stream..."

"*Down* it," she dreamed. "Down the stream, like a boat..."

"But where to?" he said. "Where would we go?"

She shrugged. "Go where the stream goes."

"Wherever that is," said Dennis.

She looked into his eyes for a long time. "To The Country Of Daft Pink Things," she said, at last.

He pressed the horn. *Oink*, said the horn. And more quietly: *Oink*.

"It's old, it's fading out," said Mollie.

"No way," Dennis told her. "It can go on for yonks, this horn."

"Want to bet?"

"Bet this," he nodded, pulling the black stone from his pocket.

"Okay, that diamond," she said.

And he pressed harder.

*

Across the valley, their watcher crouched in the bushes, wrinkling his nose.

Fading *oinks* wafted over the ravine. Trucks beeped through the trees. As night slowly fell, the boy with currant eyes shifted on his haunches, keening his ears into the ravine.

By then the horn had long since faded, and the only sound was the broken voice of the stream, pushing on through mud and rubble.

Pushing on, down its own path, to places it had never been.

High Tide

That day there was gunfire in the hills. We lay on San Sebastian's golden sand, and heard the pop-pop-pop of automatic weapons. Children played, waves broke. I lay back in sea the colour of TV after-shave and watched helicopters swoop over the beach.

We were tired, so we bought ice cream. It dripped down my chest as I carried it back from the promenade hut. The Spanish flag hung limp from the office of the Guardia Civil, where an armed policeman sweated in heavy fatigues. We looked at each other through layers of darkened glass.

The helicopters made wider arcs. Their blades glinted in the blue sky. Our eyes closed wearily.

Pop-pop-pop in the hills.

The Atlantic closed in on us. I fell onto my stomach and listened to the sounds. Children yelped as they jumped little waves and their castles broke and the beach shrank.

"Cuidado! Cuidado!" called the mothers to their kids.

We looked at the hills. We stared into the sky. The sea had turned the colour of steel. It rose like a wall from the sand. In the heat, mothers hid their babies while old men chewed bread, studying their shins. Beautiful girls with long black hair sat up straight, adjusted swimwear and lay down again. Their flattened bodies were piled around us. The sun bombed the beach with light.

We managed two throws of the Frisbee and then went to sleep.

270

A breeze woke us. The sea had drawn back, leaving a dark stain on the sand.

Silence in the hills. The helicopters swooped low over the beach.

The Privilege of Rain

I stopped him in mid flow.

"Don't say it again. Please," I said. "Please don't say *at the end of the day* again."

He picked a string of skin from his thumb.

"It's a cliché," I explained, confident in my role: I was the jail's new Writer In Residence. I had come here to help men like him with their self-expression.

Banged-up prisoners shouted from the opposite wing. Downstairs, canteen orderlies had started dishing soft-boiled potatoes onto tin plates. The air was wet with steam. Everything seemed to smell of laundry and oranges.

"And what would you know about the end of the day?" he said.

I looked at him and he seemed to smile, so I joined in, but it wasn't that kind of smile.

"At the end of the day," he said, "is when a stranger closes the door on you. When you hear this stranger take away the key on a chain, and the lights go out. When you start fretting whether your flask'll see you through till dawn. You're staring through the bars, trying to picture the kid you've not seen in three years, trying to remember what she looks like, her face, her eyes. Wanting to make up a nice place for her to live in, not just this dingy corner of your head. But you can't concentrate; you're on edge, waiting for something – some scream, or a bell, maybe just water in the pipes –

because the guy in the next peter is addicted to flushing his toilet. And you wonder how long *this* night's going to be. Worse still – Summer. Days stretching out, on and on. Hour after hour, standing at the bars – swearing at the sky, for it to go dark. Already dreading the *next* day and the one after that..."

I fingered the keys in my pocket – two keys for the eight gates that lay between the street and me.

"So I'll ask you again," the prisoner said softly: "what exactly is it that you know about the end of the day, mate?"

*

Advice came thick and fast when I was appointed to work at Nottingham Prison:

"Don't ask what they did"...

"Prepare for frustration"...

"Sit near the door"...

"Don't raise anyone's hopes"...

But nobody warned me about the smell.

Imagine a building which has housed 130 prisoners all day, every day, for the same number of years. Imagine a place with no female scents – which smells only of men, of their food, their hair, their glands: a place where smells are sentenced to life.

Add to the sourness of the air the shrieking of kitchen tins, keys chattering on chains, the grating of chairs, banged-up men roaring. Hem the sound with razor wire, bleach it with sodium light, clothe it in nylon.

There's nowhere more real than a prison. Naturally, therefore, jails are factories of fantasy, where the lathes spark with anecdotes, jokes, tall stories, lies, denial. Prisons are a good place to send a writer. But nobody except the writer wants to be there. And the things new to the writer – the body-tastes you smuggle out – are old hat to the inmate, who dreams only of ringing a door bell, walking in a straight line, sleeping with his door open.

*

The Last Days of Johnny North

On my first day, in December, under a sky as pale as the prison's faces, I set three inmates to write a description of a chair. I told them to try to evoke the unmentioned person who normally sat in it.

Two of the men wrote about chairs with massive rolls of padding and pillows, chairs as places to sprawl. The other man wrote about a chair with straps and dials, and a plug.

It was my first lesson.

*

A lifer told me his dream. He was digging with bare hands through dry red earth.

"All this dust sifting through my fingers. But I keep on digging and digging... until I start to realise – there are white bones in with it, in with the dust. Hundreds and hundreds of them, very white. Tiny white bones in these handfuls of red dust, all slipping through my fingers."

At his back, the winter moon was brilliant and low and yellow in the sky above the prison.

He stared at me. "This dream," he said. "What do you think it means?"

I coughed, covered my mouth. As I started to speak, he cut me off.

"I'll tell you what I think," he said, and he turned to point at the blazing sky. "I think it means I've been to Mars. Either I've travelled to Mars in this life, or I was once there in a past life."

I searched the side of his face for the joke, found nothing.

"The Red Planet," he said, still gazing upwards.

*

The sky – it was always the sky.

Jets hung their trails like bunting over the prison. Wandering aimlessly, I found a gardener staring upwards.

He pointed at the white trails of vapour. "Reminds me of the 'fridge in my old house," he said. "Exactly the same colour of white."

He gave me some fertiliser, grey and soft, like putty, in a thin plastic bag.

"Put it on the garden at home," he whispered, flitting his eyes.

I lived under a flight path in a big city.

That summer, blue cornflowers sprouted from the fertiliser.

Jets roared low over the garden.

*

Once, near Christmas, I escorted a prisoner between wings.

"It's years," he said, studying the stars, "since I was outside in night air."

Another time, a prisoner laughed at my umbrella. "Don't you know how lucky you are?" he asked.

He told me about the time it rained, when they tried to pull him in from the yard: "Screws to the left and right, tugging and pulling. But it was the first rain in a long time. Summer rain. The rain that smells of streets. So I stood my ground. I opened my mouth and tipped back my head. The raindrops tasted of soot and earth. I wanted to be wet. It was a long time since I'd had that."

*

A lot of the time, it was the usual stuff:

"Use your *own* words, not this 18th Century language"... Maybe try it without so many adjectives... Don't *think* about it – follow your pen..."

All year, I kept at it, preaching that the reader of the poem is the poet. It's in the reader's heart where the poem's action takes place. Don't crowd your reader. Don't poke her in the chest.

In the depths of winter, one of the men said, "I think I've got it. What you're saying is: the reader's free, don't lock the door on him."

*

Some prisoners simply wanted lessons in grammar, others help writing letters. Two or three were labouring over novels. A few sought advice with legal documents.

A man with scarred hands and a wide smile wanted me to write to his girlfriend for him. "Only it's embarrassing," he said.

"If you're in love, that's great."

"Okay," he said shyly. "Write this. Write, *Thank you for them knickers you sent.*"

*

I brought sonnets to my evening class, mentioned the way they bend two-thirds of the way through, into a changed feeling. The men listened, fairly intent. A few of them seemed to enjoy the idea of the *volte,* the change. One of them, soft-voiced, with boxer's fists, repeated the word quietly, as if it was a taste. Two mentioned Shakespeare, how they loved his words without understanding them. We discussed the role of sound in poetry, the power of music.

All the while, prisoners shouted from behind bars on the remand wing. Unlike lifers, they were banged up in the evening, so they stood at the windows and shouted, some to their friends, others at enemies. And some called to women standing in wait beyond the walls.

Each night, as it went dark, the shouting grew louder. Tonight, something seemed to be animating the shouters more than usual, but I was unable to understand. It was a general din, like Atlantic rollers.

The noise sometimes scared me – the way it kept on, its capacity for growing deeper and rawer, and deepening again.

That evening, our talk veered off, the way it often did. I don't remember the *volte.* All I remember is a mention of Byron mingling with the roar of the men in the remand wing, and that roar somehow coming inside, to the classroom.

Everyone in the room had started talking at the same time.

"The Bomb. Do you know what is planned for the fall of the Bomb?" one of the men asked me, wide-eyed. He ran his fingers backwards and forwards over the table, as if there was Braille inscribed there, a message I couldn't understand.

He said, "They will kill us. The first thing the screws will do, when the Bomb falls, is they will fire on all lifers."

His fingers halted on the table. He fixed me with brown eyes, not unkind, but wild. "There is a cupboard in this prison with an execution gun in it," he said. "You didn't know that, did you? They will put us to death rather than see us escape into the radiation and fall-out."

It was intentness I saw there on his face, as if he could smell and touch the events he foresaw. He was thinking like a writer, drawing on the senses.

"No-one will be spared," he said. "These are the facts. You ask your mate, the Governor. Maybe he will tell you the facts. That there are death squads waiting to put us to death."

It was quiet in the room again, but, across the yard, in the remand wing, the roar had kept up.

I took a breath, moved on. Talked about the connection between sonnets and romance. Talked about love.

In the tea break, no-one threw a kettle of boiling water, as I had read in bad books and heard in gossip. Nobody sliced anybody. Nobody buggered anybody. What happened is this: the men sat down and ate biscuits I'd fetched in, and drank coffee that tasted of acorns, and one man asked if I wouldn't bother with the Jammy Dodgers any more, on account of how they clogged up his fillings.

*

Change was coming to the prison. Two new wings were being added to the original Victorian structure. Drills shrieked and hammers clattered. Yellow-helmeted construction workers picked their way past JCBs, trucks, and piles of bricks.

Soon, remand prisoners were to be moved into the jail, and lifers allocated a separate wing.

I remembered advice I'd been given on my first day:

277

"Don't change anything too quickly. In jail, change is a threat. Go easy."

*

He had shot two people. In prison, they taught him to read and write, and he was angry at how the Newspapers were describing him. "They callin me a Gangsta," he said. "I's a pimp, but I ain't no Gangsta."

He wept when he told me his murders – two bystanders shot dead in a fight over drugs and girls. "I didn't mean for that to happen, man..."

I tried to get him to see Chekhov's law: a gun in the first act always goes off in the third. "If you hadn't taken a gun to town, it would never have happened."

He looked stumped.

He told me about his childhood in the Caribbean, going into the hills to hunt for land crabs. They were delicacies for tourists. But the hills were full of terrors: snakes in the prickly undergrowth, and dark nights, and the Rolling Calf, a feared ghost – half-man, half-beast – that made a noise like a rattling chain, coming close.

On one of these trips into the hills, a young friend burned himself to death on a makeshift lamp.

When I pressed the prisoner to tell me more about the incident, he shrugged. Next day, I took him a print-out of his hunting stories. He stared at the paper with wonder. He had small hands, and held a pen gently. He was well liked in the prison.

I found myself thinking about my Granddad. How he opened Christmas presents with a knife, and always folded up the wrapping paper to save for next year.

*

At Christmas, as I prepared to steal away, the jail became quieter.

I asked a lifer about this. I said I'd expected trouble.

"Think about it," he said. "You miss family, you've got no family, you feel jealous of blokes missing families – it's all the same: you just need time to think. In the end, you want what everybody wants: you want a quiet life."

Down at the end of the wing, two prisoners were carefully threading glittering gold and silver streamers through the suicide netting.

*

My writing career was going badly, I had little money. After New Year, I booked into a city centre boarding house, the cheapest I could find.

My room was painted mauve, with a red lampshade and a bright bulb. The television was tied by a chain to a metal shelf too high up the wall. The bed's mattress was sealed with a plastic sheet.

I woke up in the middle of the night, sweating. Next door, there were loud banging noises, then silence. Breakfast was a lump of colourless scrambled eggs, too hot, then suddenly cold.

I paid up fast and walked to the prison. It was Thursday. It rained every Thursday in Nottingham. My shoes leaked. At the bottom of the hill was a vast bakery. The street smelled of bread, and something fruity, maybe currants.

All the way up the hill, smelling this dough and yeast, watching vans go in and out, seeing flashes of white-capped workers, who reminded me of the orderlies in the prison kitchen, I worried about that smell.

Would you get tired of it? Was it possible in this world even to grow sickened by the smell of bread?

*

An ex-squaddie told me about the guy he'd killed while on active service abroad. "A maniac. He came at us, howling, swinging a blade. There was nothing else for it, the two of us stiffed him. I felt the blood on my hands, he was brown bread. He was brown bread, mate."

At the end of the man's bed, two joy-riders swapped bottles of hooch. One of the men farted. They giggled.

The ex-squaddie looked at his hands. He spoke very quietly. "Later, when I reported what we'd done, the officer was furious.

'You mean you've come here to tell me you stiffed a Chink?' he said. 'Ought to have tipped him in the briny,' he told us. It was the paperwork, see. The paperwork we'd put him to."

*

"*Who?*"

    "The Writer In Residence," I said, ashamed.

    "In where?"

    "Residence."

    "So you live here, do you?"

    "I just teach," I said. "I teach people to write."

    "Fiction? Fiction's a lie. Have you come in here to teach us how to lie?"

*

A man told me about his childhood in the big city. His Dad disappeared for days on end, no-one knew where. "Maybe pubs, maybe women. It was only years later I found out the truth. He went up in the attic. Only came down when the house was empty – for a few slices of bread, a cup of tea. The rest of the time, he'd listen. He'd press his ears to the floorboard and try to work out what the rest of the family was saying about him."

*

Inside the prison, there was an old swimming pool, overlooked by the squinting windows of the Segregation Unit. Officers had pinned a sign to the wall: "NO RUNNING OR ROUGH PLAY". At one end of the pool was a statue of Buddha.

    The pool was no longer in use. Men often stood at the bars of the Segregation Unit and stared at its dark water. Rumours said that the pool was kept on as a reservoir for putting out fires.

    In April, ducks flew in to rear their young. But it was a bad Spring. As I left the jail one night, I saw ducklings struggling on the tips of huge brown waves.

They didn't make it. Grown men with long criminal records wept. The mother duck wandered through the prison flowerbeds.

A few days later, RSPCA workers came in, and a group of prisoners helped them to fit a ramp to the pool. The ducks hatched another batch of young, which survived and then flew away again into the vast flat places of Eastern England.

One man told me he was looking forward to their return.

*

The prisoner said that he had spent most of his life seeking out cliff-tops, fields, bothies, the hems of trees. He described his love of storms and camp fires. I imagined his face lit up by the flames, and the darkness of the wilderness on his back.

"I remember the smoke off the peat," he said. "I used to breathe in big draughts of it. It smelt like whisky."

He told me about dancing to fiddles in an old hut, and he told me this as he picked boiled potatoes out of a slot in a tin plate, lights blazing in the yard.

*

The nights were shrinking, the world growing bigger again.

The joker stared out into the city. "I hate this time of the year," he said.

I looked at him.

He said, "You remember what's out there. You can't hide from it anymore, it's there facing you."

*

I was finding out about my freedom. I had the most liberty a job has ever afforded me: I talked (on landings, in libraries, a greenhouse, the gym) to men with chests twice the size of mine but legs far skinnier. I found a library book called *Great Walks* which hadn't been borrowed

281

for five years. It was like stalking a giant galleon that was forever cresting the hill, its decks laced with wire nets, sails never rigged, the crew within sight of a port which was always out of reach.

Staff talked about "going on the wing"; time was "bird". They named it "stir", and it never moved. Cells were "pads", as if they'd cushion a fall, or patch a wound, or launch them.

I had come "inside" and found the edge.

*

Burn was what everybody wanted.

"You go mad without 'baccy," a man explained. "Blokes in here'll smoke anything. 'S why bananas are banned. They used to dry the skins and smoke them. Mellow yellow. Tweet tweet tweet."

"What's the weirdest thing you ever smoked?"

"Hair."

"Did you feel anything?"

"Only the roots, when I pulled it out."

*

One day, three men told me their murders. Immediately afterwards, I tried to block out the stories. It was Spring, and I wanted to be on a mountain. I had a picture in my head of the staircase where one of the killings had taken place. The man broke in two when he told me the story. His sobs came in huge bunches, like fists.

I imagined a spindly banister and carpets the colour of old dogs.

Later, I went to the dirtiest café I could find, and ate a dead mound of fried food. The leather seats had been slashed, and joined together again with black masking tape. In the windows, trailing through damp sills like dying seaweed, were lace curtains, stained brown at the edges.

"This is what it's like," I thought. "This is almost what it's like."

*

In Robin Hood country, with the outlaws, my thoughts turned often to the prison's few trees, cut off from Sherwood by a wall, beyond which there was no longer a forest.

One of the trees, a weakly sapling, was close to the 'topping shed', where men had once been executed. I never found out what kind of tree it was. Some men said there were bodies at its base.

"Even after they'd been killed, they couldn't escape."

My favourite tree was the cherry blossom in the main yard. In spring, it burst into flower, dark branches sagging under the new weight.

"The last curvy thing in this whole place," sighed a colleague.

I told him the last lines of my favourite poem, 'A Blessing' by James Wright, in which the poet suddenly realises that if he breaks out of his body, he'll burst into blossom.

Later, they drove a giant metal pole into the earth beside the tree. Workers mounted a camera on the top of it.

"Rape," they called it.

*

Afterwards, nobody knew what had triggered it. Some said it was dust in the custard, others a change in the visits regime. In one way or another, everyone blamed the prison's re-building programme, which had transformed the routines that men despised, and relied upon.

Whatever the cause, plates went flying and punches were thrown. The Governor ordered everyone to their cells. All work and education was cancelled. The men went to their windows, and roared.

The cherry tree was in wild bloom. At a loose end, I stood in the yard and gossiped with my boss. Without anyone to sweep up, blossom had pooled in pink drifts against the inside of the wall. Nearby, workers were fiddling with the drains. I watched them work, thinking about that other world below, where men's hair and skin floated free, into the sewers, to the sea.

It brought to mind the yard cleaner who willingly picked up shit parcels thrown from cells, just so that he could feel the wind on his face.

"Look," said my boss, suddenly.

The workers had unrolled hoses.

"They're sorting out water cannons," he said.

It was a beautiful day, warm breeze, blue sky – the type of day you know the world will end.

We sloped back to the Education Block, and waited.

A long time later, word came down that one of the men wanted to talk to us about his A' level in English.

We went to the yard and stood in that incoming wave of shouts, trying to get the prisoner's attention.

"Thank God," he exclaimed when, finally, he saw us. "I've been trying to swot up, but it's bloody impossible with all this noise. I can't think straight."

The roar grew louder, some of it directed at us.

"But I was wondering – " he shouted, "I was wondering – the ghost in *Hamlet*, do you think he's an actual ghost? Not that I believe in ghosts, and that. But do you think Shakespeare meant him to be more than just a symbol of guilt?"

I don't remember what I said. I probably fumbled it. I just remember hearing someone call me a bastard, and two men begging for pens. And dark smudges behind the bars, asking questions I couldn't answer.

*

Somewhere under the roar, a desperate man was shouting, "Margaret!"

"What?"

His call came again: "Margaret!"

I stood in the dark prison yard, listening.

A Glaswegian voice called back from beyond the wall. "What, pet?"

"Margaret!"

"What?"

"Margaret!"

He must have been standing at the bars, the woman somewhere in the street. Like them, I could see nothing. All that remained of them was their grief.

"Margaret!"

"What?"

They were still calling to each other as I came out through eight gates, into the street.

"Margaret!"

"What?"

And as I climbed onto the bus back to my boarding house...

"Margaret!"

"What?"

"Margaret..."

*

Later, when things were calmer, I found one of the prisoners staring through the bars of the new wing, into the street beyond.

He was a small man with a quiet grin, and I felt he had been badly led in life. "Seen something you like?"

"My house."

I laughed. "Got your eye on a bit of property, eh?"

He nodded.

"Don't you think you should try to find a place somewhere further away?"

"Y' what?"

"When you get out," I said. "A clean break, sort of. Leave this place behind."

"Why would I want to do that?"

"Well, when you're free, you can live anywhere."

"You're not right bright for a Writer In Residence, are you? That one with the blue door. That's my house. I live there."

We stared through the bars.

"Your house," I said.

He looked at me like I was the world's most stupid man.

"I should have straightened the curtains," he said.

*

In the new lifers' wing, one of the men proudly showed me his view.

"I can see the whole of Nottingham," he beamed.

The Last Days of Johnny North

I didn't tell him what a forbidden map would show – that the city he'd lived in for years lay in the other direction, and his view was of drab outer suburbs.

Days later, he was still staring in wonder through the bars.

I wondered where his grey eyes had taken him – down which streets? Into whose arms? In which Nottingham?

*

On holiday, in Wales, a summer storm swept the clifftops. We took cover under an ancient stone and chewed sandwiches, watching a fox forage for seagull's eggs in the rocks.

Later, in a churchyard, we put our hands on a row of yew trees that bled red sap, and then walked down a valley where we heard the locals still observed the Julian Calendar.

Finally, tired out, we crested the shoulder of a wild moor and caught sight of our cottage in the safety of the valley, far from the sharp blue stones of the Preseli Mountains, stones which the ancients had quarried for their star-temple at Stonehenge.

Back in prison, I listened to where the rumours said I'd been. I wore my tan skin furtively, like something stolen. I was full of secrets: of ocean and stars, and ancient calendars, and the trembling red fur of a fox.

*

A disabled prisoner had punched a governor and been carted off to the Segregation Unit. The likelihood was that he'd be 'ghosted' – spirited away to another jail.

In the weeks before throwing his punch, the man had been writing vividly about dark periods in his life, but the circles were darkening under his eyes, and his smile had lost its spark. I went down to the Seg, full of foreboding.

His bare cell overlooked the prison swimming pool. He was stripped to the waist, with only a mattress and a cardboard chair. I noticed the delicacy of his shoulder blades, the whiteness of his thin arms.

A smile blared from his face. "I fucking socked him one," he said. His hands moved like wings as he told me the story. I'd never seen a man more joyous.

As I left the Segregation Unit, I was struck by its high ceilings, and tall windows, and the late summer light that flooded the building.

Grace, was the word in my head.

*

The man who was always at the bars, always watching the road, said to me, "See that truck? It comes in every day at the same time, and it goes out every day at the same time. It's full of junk, and I'm going to find a way to get on it."

"But you've only got a few months of your sentence left."

He pulled a face. "I am going out with the rubbish," he said.

*

On Guy Fawkes Night, the loop of the year almost complete, I dragged a bag of paper and pens from my evening class, and hurried away to the staff room.

The prison's *sterile area*, a zone of high security, where no-one was allowed to venture, winked with tiny fires – rockets and Catherine wheels burning out in the dark places beneath the wire fence.

The prison was quiet. For once, there was no-one at the bars, no-one yelling.

The only sounds came from the bonfire-builders on the other side of the wall. They were laughing and shouting, giddy with revenge.

All evening they went on with it, firing their rockets into the centre of our silence.

*

When I described the fox I'd seen on the cliff tops in Wales, I was told to open my eyes. "There's a fox comes *here*," the prisoner said. "Watch for him at dawn, you'll see him. He slips out from under the

The Last Days of Johnny North

Education Block."

Two other men verified the story: "They built this place across the line of his ancestors' paths. These bastards couldn't keep him out even if they tried. Not with the biggest fence in the world."

One man said he had seen the fox with a pigeon in its mouth. "Like it was grinning," he said.

That made them whoop.

Foxes and ducks. Wild, resourceful creatures living on their own terms, inside the walls.

*

The prisoner who was close to the end of his sentence had gate fever. Time had slowed down, he couldn't see any end to his sentence.

"I dreamed I got out, and the outside was just the same as the inside. Jesus Christ, I was hammering on the gates to get back in!"

His friend still had a year to go. He shook his head. "No," he said. "Get to them gates, and, me – I'm dust."

I told him that was a beautiful image. He only shrugged.

*

I arrived at HMP Nottingham shocked at how prison flattens the senses: the giant metal pole of a security camera disrupting a blossom tree's curves, the filling-in of the swimming pool with trash and a blameless tree. I had some heroic mission to use poetry to re-awaken the senses of men denied colour and flavour.

I left the jail on a bus, happy to hand silver coins to a stranger who bore me no malice. From a moving window, I saw the everyday miracle of a cat. Gutters glittered with rain. I had a key in my pocket.

It occurred to me, as I looked back one last time, that I was seeing inside from the outside – from the same place that prison had allowed me to view my own life.

This piece is non-fiction based on experiences gained as a writer in residence, funded by the Arts Council of England, at a British prison in the late 1990s.

The Scar

Beyond the garden, the burned French girl guides my hand to her scar.

It pours from neck to fingers – a scarlet flash, melted and frightening.

"*Ici,*" she whispers.

I watch, amazed, as my hand roves the burnt places.

"Velvet..."

We sway with the grass, watching breezes come down the fields.

You Know Who You Are

It's a decade since I started writing these stories, many of which had been brewing for years before that. So I apologise for becoming so old that I may have forgotten exactly who sheltered me from the drizzle and lent me pens. This list is an attempt to re-pay love, friendship, support, inspiration, wisdom, warnings, and a steady supply of biscuits, especially the chocolate ones.

Peace be upon them: Chris Aggs; Joe Alessi; Jan Ainsley; Allotment Tenders of Brighton (including John, Rachel, Rob, Bridget); Yousef Anani; Linda Anderson; Matt Argyle and his band (Pete, Jo & Carl); Steve Atridge; Richard Barlow; Pete Barnes (& Fiona, Jake, Joe & Ellie); Kerrith Bell; Ben & Jess; Peter Bennett; Kate & Dave Betts; Manuelito Biag; Chris Birdsall; Andrea Birkins; Tonya Blowers; Boz & Louise; Alan Burns; Charlotte Brunsdon; Antony & Elaine Butterfield; Sally Carr; Mary Catlow; Tamsin Carter; Lyn & Catherine at Lancaster University; Graham Caveney; Concetta A. Ceriello (Spitfire Press); Chairman John & his staff at the Bridport Prize; Greg Challis & Sue Taylor; Brendan Cleary; Dave & Pete Clee; Linda Cook (& all at *Holland Herald*); David Craig; Ian Crammond; Elaine Crinnion; Tony Crockford; Bill, Neville & Michael

Crossley; Joe Cushley; Muriel Dailloux; Andrew Davies; John Davies & all staff at The South; Don & Wendy; Eileen Duffy; Ian Duhig; Isla Duncan; Hugh Dunkerley; Richard Dyer; James Ebdon; Gillian Egan; Martin Elvins; Leighton Evans (& all at Chichester Fringe Festival); Various Steves & Ians at Wednesday night football; Paul Farley; Karin Fauria; Vicki Feaver; Simon Finch; Tom Flemons; Naomi Foyle; Paul Gateson; Ger, Evo (& St. Louis colleagues); Terry Gifford; David Gilliver; Sarah Gorbutt, Phil & Amanda Grabsky (& all at Seventh Art Productions); Bill Gray; Tanika Gupta & Dave Archer; Steve Halestone; Roz Hall & Dan Musty (film-makers of the future); Roy Hanney; Josie Harbutt; Steve Haywood; Dave Hesmondhalgh; Julie Hesmondalgh (& Ian Kershaw & Martha); Dave & Shelley Heys; Andrew Hook (& his wondrous Elastic Press); Geoff Hope; Clive Hopwood (& all at Prison Writers' Network); Ian Hornsby & Marisa Zanotti; Stuart Hounslow; Rachel Hughes; all the ISR staff who kept me afloat (especially Alicia, Emmanuelle, Yoli, Kim, Victoria, Barbara, Dee, Emma, Flora); Mick Jackson; Nick Jackson; Erwin James; Simon Jary; Chris Jones; Geoffrey Jones; Mervyn Kay (for my first break) and Phil Harris & Janet Woolley (& others on the *Accrington Observer* for teaching me how to type with at least 2 fingers); Jemma Kennedy, John Kennedy; Hannah Kodicek; Tanya Kirilova & Lora; Maureen Koeman; Cath Laing; Jeannette Laouadi; Jon Leahey; Stefano Luzzatto; Bernard MacDonagh; Daithidh MacEochaidh (Skrev Press); Poran Malani (& South London posse, including Kim, Hooni, & Co.); Zachary Malkinson; Tracey Mansell; Ian Marchant; Alison MacLeod; Jo Maher; Massimo & Valeria; Jessica de Mellow; Kai Merriott; Elina Milkova; Anke Mittelberg; Stephen Mollett; Sue Morgan; Jago Morrison; Julie Morton; Marc Munden; Bran Nicol; Helen Nelder; Stephanie Norgate; some lovely folk in Nottingham (including Txema, Ana, Rick, Angela, Pud, & Angeline) and all the anti-Voortuin people of Holland (but especially Rian & Tim, Lisa & Merel, Sam & Lasse); Christopher & Marissa North (Almaserra Vella Writing Centre, Alicante, Spain); Ben Noys; Saleel Nurbhai; Phil Oltermann (*Zembla* magazine); Aisling O'Gorman; Janet O'Neill; Kate Osborne; Natalia de la Ossa; Sarah Padmore; all the kind villagers of Loutro, Crete;

Victor Perkins; Bob Perris; Mario Petrucci; Keiren Phelan; John & Linda Phillips; Fiona Price; Malcolm Purdie; Frances Quirke & John Morgan; Michael Raine & Otelia; Johnny Rowley; Jack Rowley; Roger Rees; Mike Ribbans; Bethan Roberts; Walter Robinson (100 in 2004); Geoff, Shirley, Kim & Dawn Robinson; Jane Rogers; Susan Rukeyser; Jane & Dave Rusbridge; Deirdre Rusling; Lisa Marie Russo; Christophe Sainsot; Duncan Salkeld; Neil Sanderson; Nilly Sarkar; Graham Sherlock; Carolien Schoutsen; James Simpson & Cynara; John Saunders; Anthony & Mark Saulle; Maggie Sawkins; John Sayers & Megan Smith; Scott & Marein; Kay Sexton; Sue Shorter; Catherine Smith; Henry Shukman; Jan Willem Sligting; Chris Smethurst; all the staff at *Staple* (especially Ann Atkinson & Elizabeth Barrett); the Spencers of Water Street; Helen Steward (& Rosa & Joe); Karen Stevens (& Joe & Jamie); Neil Stoker (for the most necessary sandwich I've ever eaten); Joanne Swann; Steven Swann; Ella Swann; Georgina Taylor; Lorna Thorpe; Gordon Todd and his excellent colleagues in the library and education departments at HMP Nottingham; Pete Troutt; Tommy Turbyville; Mike Usiskin; Danny Verbeek; The Amazing & Gorgeous Sisters Vermond (Ellen, Karin, Mirjam, Angela); Tim Vickery; Mark Walker; Tim & Nadine Wall; Annie Wallace, Tim Ward; Tony Ward (& all at Littlewood Arc Books); Alyson Webb (& Milo & Louis); Joe Wells (& Maria & Kristian); Werner, Jan & all at Paradiso; Jackie Wills; Stewart Wills (& his *World Spirit Loutro Writers*); Carol Woodall; Robert & Pamela Woof; Ian Worden; *Words Allowed* (& Andrew Nada). Additionally, I would like to thank Morten's family in Silkeborg, Denmark, whose hospitality lives on in my memory, despite my shameful failure to send thanks afterwards. Also, the inmates and staff at HMP, Nottingham, for their kindness and interest. And whoever it was in Bulgaria who got me Johan Cruyff's signature. And all the drivers who ever gave me a lift, except one shifty fellow near Breda and that bloke wearing black driving gloves in the dark lane in rural Warwickshire.

Plus a few folk I'll never meet: Abba, Ivo Andric, Simon Armitage, Lynn Reid Banks, Ingmar Bergman, William Blake, Emily Bronte,

Noel Brotherston, Noam Chomsky, Steve Coogan, Johan Cruyff, Miles Davis, Claire Denis, Bob Dylan, Stanley Elkin, Andrew Flintoff, Janet Frame, Aretha Franklin, Jane Gardam, Marvin Gaye, Nicolai Gogol, Natalie Goldberg, Al Green, Werner Herzog, Michael Holding, Ted Hughes, Lewis Hyde, Denis Johnson, Salif Keita, James Kelman, Ryszard Kapuscinski, Nastassia Kinski, Halldor Laxness, Nelson Mandela, Harper Lee, Marx Brothers, Ian McMillan, Herman Melville, Edwin Morgan, Van Morrison, Morrissey of course, F.W. Murnau, Flann O'Brien, Flannery O'Connor, Clifford Odets, Will Oldham, Mark Olson, Steve Ovett, Tony Palmer, Ann Peebles, Christopher Priest, V.S. Pritchett, E. Annie Proulx, Monty Python, Paula Radcliffe, Jonathan Richman, Mary Robison, Kate Rusby, Antoine de Saint-Exupery, J.D. Salinger, Nitin Sawhney, George Saunders, Jerry Seinfeld, Sheeear-er!, Mary Shelley, Ken Smith, Stanley Spencer, Joe Strummer, The Silver Surfer, Stanley & Oliver, Andrei Tarkovski, Leon Trotsky, Francois Truffaut, Ivan Turgenev, Father Ted, Edward Thomas, Tinariwen, Studs Turkel, Mark Twain, Michael Vaughan, Vic & Bob, Tom Waits, Wim Wenders, Jeanette Winterson, Tobias Wolff, James Wright. Thank you.

A last word for the splendid Angela Vermond.

In memory of: Phyllis Crossley, Jacqui Clee, Steve Cresswell, Hugo Donnelly, Marcel van Hoof, Jim Osborne.